SKYFIRE

Aroon Raman is a Bengaluru-based serial entrepreneur and author. He ran his family companies for many years, winning critical acclaim for developing scientific talent at the grassroots. After successfully divesting both ventures, he now divides his time between consulting for corporates, non-profits, writing and travel. He is the author of the national bestsellers *The Shadow Throne* (2012) and *The Treasure of Kafur* (2013). He regularly contributes columns to *Outlook* magazine and other publications. He can be reached at www.aroonraman.com

Also by Aroon Raman

The Shadow Throne

The Treasure of Kafur

SKYFIRE

AROON RAMAN

PAN

First published 2016 by Pan
an imprint of Pan Macmillan India
a division of Macmillan Publishers India Private Limited
Pan Macmillan India, 707, Kailash Building
26, K. G. Marg, New Delhi – 110 001
www.panmacmillan.co.in

Pan Macmillan, 20 New Wharf Road, London N1 9RR
Basingstoke and Oxford
Associated companies throughout the world
www.panmacmillan.com

ISBN 978-93-82616-61-0

This is a work of fiction. All characters, locations and events are fictitious. Any resemblance to actual events or locales or persons, living or dead, is entirely coincidental.

3 5 7 9 8 6 4

Typeset by Manmohan Kumar
Printed and bound in India by
Replika Press Pvt. Ltd.

For Patti

In love and remembrance

And thus dissolution is this form: of earth in waters, of waters in fire, of fire in air, of air in ether, ether in the unmanifest – the end of all.

– The Vishnu Purana

Each State Party to this Convention undertakes not to engage in military or any other hostile use of environmental modification techniques having widespread, long-lasting or severe effects as the means of destruction, damage or injury to any other State Party.

– Article 1, Convention on the Prohibition of Military or Any Other Hostile Use of Environmental Modification Techniques (adopted by Resolution 31/72 of the United Nations General Assembly, 10th December 1976)

Season
day and hour
Went out of kilter
So did earth
water
the planets and the skies
fire
wind
the mountains and the stars:
O what a roaring meal
of chaos
our lord made
of the seven worlds!

– Nammalvar, *Hymns for the Drowning*, 7.4.4

PROLOGUE

The Karakoram Range, Western Himalaya. August 2010.

THE WIND SWEPT DOWN THE PASS AND THROUGH THE NARROW funnel between the great massifs. Gathering pace and power, it slammed into the flanks of the mountain, whipping the snowdrifts into a blizzard.

The peaks that hemmed the valley were titanic – grey rock and ice rearing 25,000 feet into the sky. And now, as the wind howled through the valley, they seemed to twist like giant corkscrews against its pull.

This was true wilderness, a remote mountain fastness set deep within the folds of the great Karakoram range in the Himalaya. No human had set foot on it till the early twentieth century, or come within a hundred miles of the great wall of ice that formed the northern wall of the valley.

But this evening, as dusk prepared to throw its mantle over the immense landscape, a beetle-like figure inched its way through the blizzard on the lower slopes of the mountain. It was a man, a lone trekker. One arm was flung over his eyes, the other outstretched as if to part the white blanket that swirled about him. He was clearly near the end of his strength. Now and then he emitted a soft moan, the sound of which was instantly snatched away by the wind.

He was one of a party of ten French mountaineers who had pitted themselves against the summit of Saltoro Kangri that summer. Their approach had been along the south-east ridge and the assault camp was set up at 18,000 feet. That was when a freak avalanche had struck and buried the camp, wiping out nine of them. Only he had managed to crawl out from beneath the icy crypt, barely alive.

Since then, he had been stumbling along, scarcely making progress in this no man's land that sat almost exactly on the Actual Ground Position Line between India to the east and Pakistan to the west. He rubbed his glove against the face of the digital watch on his wrist and pressed the light button. The compass function showed him bearing west as he intended, but then he saw the time and felt the onrush of despair. 4:30:42 p.m. The chronometer was accurate to 1/100th of a second, and he realized, even through his numb fatigue, that in precisely twenty-six minutes, night would fall abruptly and the darkness would be complete. He had already been without food for seventy-two hours; having eaten nothing but snow, swallowed painfully to keep the dehydration from claiming him even quicker. But the coming night would be his last. He was certain he would not survive it without food and shelter. He forced his gummed eyelids open yet again, peering at the murk through his fingers.

So certain was the climber that he was utterly alone, that he almost didn't notice it: a faint glow just over the ridge to his right. The snow was whipping around in eddies, and he rubbed it off his face to make sure. No mistake; the ridge line was touched with a faint luminescence. An inarticulate cry of joy and relief broke from his lips; he started forward, tripped and fell to his knees. He tried to get up, but the effort proved too great for his enfeebled legs. Gritting his teeth, he plunged his hands into the snow, dug his boots in and painfully heaved himself up the slope.

An aeon passed, and he seemed no closer to the ridge. He felt the blackness of despair. But the light was like a beacon – a call to life. And so he set his fading strength to it again. Imperceptibly, through the fog in his brain, he became aware of an odour, an acrid chemical smell, like burning sulphur, overlaid with a metallic tang. It stayed with him, growing stronger, till he could feel it burn his nostrils. By now he was at the lip of the ridge. He flopped down on the snow and lay there, giving himself time to recover his breath. Then he peered over.

It wasn't a light, but glowing, green smoke that seemed to hang over a bowl-like depression gouged out of the side of the mountain. Thick as a cloud, the vapour swirled about like a living thing, and deep within it, he thought he could glimpse the hazy outline of something – like a huge blotch of dark matter.

The green cloud waxed and waned, a pulsating haze against the deep darkness that blanketed the sky. Then it thinned at the centre and, before his stunned gaze, at the bottom of the bowl, stood a giant.

A giant was his first impression; then he saw that it was a massive robot-like structure. Even at this distance – a 100 metres away – it was enormous. It stood on four pillar-like legs, joined at the hip to a square box the size of a big car. From the box, two sinewy cable-like arms snaked out at an oblique angle. Held between the arms was a conical dish – a parabolic antenna. Even as the climber watched, stupefied, there was a faint hum and the giant arms twisted, raising and swivelling the dish. The snowfall ceased suddenly and the air became cold and clear. A waxing moon broke through the clouds and by its light the enormous mass of the Saltoro Kangri speared the Himalayan sky to the east like a needle at 25,400 feet.

The trekker acted reflexively. He pulled out his cell phone; his numbed hands encased in thick mittens could barely hold the instrument, which wobbled and vibrated while he tried to press the camera icon. The video mode turned on. Thunder boomed out again, confusing him. This time, it was a deep drumming sound that filled the heavens and caused the mountainside to tremor. The sulphur smell was heavy and choking. The green smoke had coalesced like a halo over the giant mechanical creature. To the watcher it bore an uncanny resemblance to one of those robotic monsters in the movies; except there was a raw, living power to this thing that held up the curved plate like a trophy.

With a blinding flash, an arc of light now appeared between the antenna and the heavens – a rope of incandescent light that writhed and twisted like a serpent. A *CRRACKKK* shook the earth. The watcher's eardrums burst, but he was barely conscious of it. The air, supercharged with electricity, blew out in a supersonic wave from the robot. He screamed in agony as it hit him. The hood of his parka flew off to reveal hair rising up straight from his skull as he writhed like a man in an electric chair. The thunder boomed again and the sky was rent apart. A hole formed where the arc touched it and around it, boiling clouds churned like water in a gigantic whirlpool. Down below, the livid arc lit up the great peaks of rock and ice that flashed in awful grandeur as if beneath a strobe.

And then, it was dark again.

The man would have no means of knowing that the whole phenomenon had lasted for less than ten seconds; for within moments he was unconscious, blood flooding from his nose, ears and mouth.

For long moments, nothing stirred. Then slowly, the tremors started. The snow began to slide off the mountain, and soon an avalanche of white matter was rolling down in a wave, gathering momentum. It smashed into the humanoid machine, blowing it to smithereens. By a peculiar dynamic of motion, as it hit the ridge and reared up, it tossed the limp body into the air like a doll and hurled it almost 500 metres away, into the valley below.

Within minutes, it was over. A deathly silence descended and the peaks resumed their eternal vigilance over the gorge. But 150 kilometres to the south in Leh, jet-black, pregnant clouds suddenly appeared over the northern horizon. Even as the startled inhabitants pointed them out excitedly to each other, the clouds expanded into gigantic balloons, swelling in size to fill the heavens. Bigger and bigger … till they burst, releasing a waterfall that spanned the horizon. Immediately, hundreds of fast-flowing rivulets were rushing down the hillsides. Coalescing rapidly at the head of the valley, they came roaring like a tsunami towards the settlement.

1

Madanpur Khadar, Delhi. May 2012.

THE NARROW ALLEY WAS DANK WITH THE ODOUR OF ROTTING garbage and burnt rubber rising from the heaps of trash thrown onto the street from the houses on either side. Gopal pushed the ancient moped along, keeping close to the open sewer that ran to one side, stepping softly so as to make no noise. He crept up till the end, leaned the two-wheeler against the wall and, ever so carefully, peeked around the corner. The Sarita Vihar Metro station was a distant glow to the west, but here, at the garbage dump on the fringes of the Madanpur Khadar slum, it was dark and deserted. The boy stared fixedly at the landfill for a full minute, but could see no movement. Then a shadow shifted near the edge of the refuse pile. It moved around some more, then emerged onto the pavement. By the faint diffused light, and from the bent posture and the way it shuffled, Gopal could make out that he – or she – was old. The figure squatted and began to chew at whatever it had pulled out from the garbage.

Gopal retreated into the shadows. His legs felt suddenly weak, and a shiver of anticipation rippled through him as he thought of how he would break it to Hassan saab: his first successful solo investigation of a major criminal gang on his own.

His mind flew back to when it had all started – three weeks ago – with a chance encounter. Actually, it hadn't been all chance, the man had somehow sought him out. He'd been standing with Chandra saab and Meenu madam in front of the school after evening classes when he'd seen the beggar squatting across the road. The man was clearly mad, hunched into himself, muttering and shaking his fists at the sky, but something stirred Gopal's memory, and when the others had dispersed he'd gone to take a closer look. The man wasn't immediately aware of someone approaching, but then went still and looked up slowly. Gopal started in astonishment. It was Pagal bhai. The beggar was terribly wasted – all skin and bones – but still recognizable as the vagrant who often frequented the Arab Sarai slum. Everyone called him Pagal – a homeless half-wit who was everywhere and nowhere at once, who hopped about giggling, his speech a meandering string of slurred words that made no sense. Except to Gopal. For the boy had discovered something extraordinary about Pagal: a piercing intelligence that flashed out, fleeting and brilliant, like a shooting star at night. And in those moments of lucidity, Pagal was a man transformed, capable of solving in an instant any of the cases of petty slum crime that Gopal took to him. It was as if the beggar observed everything, forgot nothing and could effortlessly hold in his mind the entire tapestry that formed the teeming life of the city, like a jigsaw master who miraculously perceives the final picture from the pieces heaped before him.

It was Meenu madam who had told him that such people existed, whose illness combined madness and genius like the warp and weft of the same cloth. And so Gopal had befriended this strange creature. But then Pagal had suddenly vanished and Gopal hadn't seen him for several weeks – till now. Finding him more skeleton than man, Gopal had cried out, 'Pagal bhai! What's happened to you?'

With an energy that stunned Gopal, Pagal bhai had leapt to his feet and looked about him fearfully. Then he had gesticulated at Gopal to follow and started to hobble away. Just around the corner was one of those empty DDA sites with a ramshackle hut set well back among the trees. It was to this that Pagal led Gopal. Understanding Pagal hadn't been easy at the best of times, but now it was as if his mind had completely gone. He gibbered, saliva drooling from his mouth as he jumped up and down, hands flinging about wildly, muttering 'Ompa, gid, gid … Ompa, gid, gid …' again and again, like a child reciting a doggerel. Gopal had been about to give up, when Pagal suddenly stopped and looked out of the door intently into the night. Then he had turned round to Gopal, his eyes flooded with total awareness.

They had started off together, cutting through south Delhi, weaving in and out of dark alleys and streets, till they were at Kusumpur Pahari, a basti that served the posh colony of Vasant Vihar. There, hidden in an alley rather like the one he was in now, he had witnessed the kidnapping.

That night he couldn't sleep. Even now, weeks later, Gopal felt the sweat pop all over his body each time that scene played out in his mind's eye. A little urchin playing on a heap of bricks at a construction site. A covered mini-truck driving by slowly and coming to a casual stop at the entrance, blocking the view. The door opening and two men dressed in the uniform and hard hats of construction workers jumping out, one of them holding a large sack.

It was over before he could fully register it. Within seconds, the men were back, but now the sack was bulging. They flung it into the truck, the engine gunned and the vehicle roared away. Gopal had stood there uncomprehending – till Pagal pointed. The brick heap was empty. The child was gone.

That had been almost three weeks ago. Weeks saturated with acute excitement and fear, once the twelve-year-old street urchin had decided that he would pursue the kidnappers and present the leads to the gang to his mentor and hero, Assistant Commissioner of Police, Syed Ali Hassan. And so he'd kept Pagal company. They stayed inside the hut during daytime, but at night they wandered the streets, from slum to slum, seemingly at random. Though Gopal couldn't see it, his instinct told him that there was a method to his companion's madness. As the nights blurred into days and back into nights, he waited impatiently for the madman's next moment of self-possession. What could Pagal see that he couldn't? How did he know about that first kidnapping? Apart from the now familiar mutterings and moans about 'Ompa gid, gid' and some vague references to mountains and rivers, Gopal could make nothing of it other than the fact that Pagal himself had been the gang's prisoner in recent months, had managed to escape and was tracking them ever since.

Gopal had also activated his street network. Of all the criminals, the child snatchers were the most cruel. If he was caught, death would be slow and excruciating. So he went forward carefully, working his contacts lightly, bringing to bear all the native cunning and caution of his years on the fringes of the underworld. As he did so, he became aware of whispers spoken in fear-filled undertones even among the most hardened street gangs. Of a new force that had risen. It was everywhere and nowhere at once. A poisonous snake that lay hidden during the day, but slithered around at night, choosing its victims carefully: the homeless and the fatherless, the orphans, the destitutes, the maimed and the crippled. And when it struck, it swallowed its prey whole – they vanished as if they had never been.

Once he realized just how large and powerful this enemy was, he grew afraid. He was half-tempted to disclose all that he had heard and seen to Meenu madam. In a way, she was the mother figure he'd never had. But she would instantly report everything to Hassan saab and forbid him to puruse the case on his own. More than anything else, Gopal wanted to impress Hassan saab, show him what he was capable of, so he'd said nothing – except to Pagal bhai. He'd taken him to the school, pointed out Meenu and Chandra to him from a distance and made it clear that if anything happened to him, he was to contact them.

Then yesterday, Pagal had regained his sanity briefly, taken him to this spot in broad daylight. The man had seemed uneasy, increasingly jumpy over the last few days, and he'd refused to accompany Gopal tonight. But with much gesticulation and guttural, misshapen words, Pagal had told him to be very careful.

The faint purring of an engine dragged Gopal back to the present. He dropped to the ground, making himself even more invisible. The sound grew to a growl and then appeared to the far right. It was a brand new covered truck – a big, heavy monster with eight wheels. It advanced slowly, the headlights switched off, the driver's cabin a black opaque rectangle. Closer and closer ... it came to a smooth stop, blocking Gopal's view of the beggar on the sidewalk. It paused there quietly for perhaps ten seconds, as if scoping the neighbourhood. Then the twin rear doors opened. Two men in hard hats and uniforms stepped down and vanished behind the vehicle.

A pause of perhaps half-a-minute and they were back, this time a limp body between them, legs trailing the ground. They pulled themselves in, the doors shut and the truck began to pull away.

Gopal felt the trembling in his limbs as he yanked the moped off the wall and mounted. He kicked the starter pedal and the ancient engine coughed to life. He waited till the truck was a good 50 metres away and then set off after it, carefully keeping dead centre and then accelerating closer so he wouldn't be visible on the side rear-view mirrors. At this range, he could see that the vehicle's number plates were masked.

The driver seemed in no great hurry, but kept at a steady pace westward. The traffic increased as they approached Mathura

Road and he had little trouble following unnoticed. His quarry swung north on the main highway towards Okhla. A good twenty minutes later, Gopal began to feel worried. The moped was a borrowed machine and he'd put in only as much fuel as he could afford from his meagre cash hoard, and the needle of the petrol gauge was well into the red band. He started to mutter a curse, when, almost on cue, the truck cut left onto the road that led into the Okhla Industrial Area. Sweat shops with their tube-lit sheds and night-shift labour crews flashed past in a continuous neon blur, as the truck arrowed deeper into the bowels of the vast estate and beyond towards Tughlaqabad. The moped engine had already coughed a couple of times in warning, when the truck braked to a stop. Gopal pulled back to allow distance, shut the engine, kicked down the stand and darted behind a tree by the roadside. The truck executed a U-turn and backed up against iron gates that fronted a large compound, judging by the height and length of the wall on either side. It stood there, its engine idling. The driver's door opened and a bulky figure stepped out. He went to the front fender and whipped the cover off the number plate, then went round to the rear. Gopal heard the rattle of a chain, the creak of gates and then the clang of the rear doors shutting. The driver came back, got in. The headlights came on, lighting up the road. The truck pulled away left, heading off in a different direction.

It was now or never. He darted out from under the cover of the tree and raced in a straight line towards the gates, then tacked right towards the truck's rear. Just in time to get a clear glimpse of the illuminated number plate. It was only then that he noticed he was standing almost directly in front of the gates. The wrought-iron pattern was overgrown with plants, but he could make out a heavy chain lock and some sort of an official-looking notice board hanging from one of the bars. Gopal didn't even think of going closer to explore. He was done for the night, with a triumphant sense of his mission being accomplished.

He was about to draw out his cell phone to punch in the vehicle number into the memory when a red wink caught the edge of his eye. It seemed to come from the top of the gatepost, behind the creeper's leaves. He went closer, craning to look. His blood turned to ice as he made out the snout of a video camera. The red light was blinking just below the glassy eye which was fixed on his face. The bile rose in Gopal's throat as nausea seized him. He fought it, taking a step forward, thinking to somehow climb up to the camera and rip it from the gate, when he saw the torches. They were bobbing up and down, coming at him from the blackness beyond the gate.

His heartbeat spurted in terror. He turned and ran as he had never before in his young life.

2

Nizamuddin, Delhi. 24 May 2012. 6 p.m.

THE DARGAH HAZRAT NIZAMUDDIN SITS AT THE VERY CENTRE OF Delhi, just a few kilometres south of India Gate. Arrayed around it, within almost walking distance, is the habitat of the city's elite: Golf Links with its verdant course, high-end residences, clubs – of which the India International Centre is the premier watering hole of the elite – and five-star hotels, hip restaurants and other happening places. In a metropolis obsessed with endless comparisons of money and power, the dargah is an oasis.

Here lie the mortal remains of the Sufi saint Nizamuddin Auliya who lived eight centuries ago. Such was the power of his teaching that it was said that the city itself began to give up material pursuits and turn to an inner life.

That seems impossible to imagine of today's Delhi with all its trappings of brash modernity and in-your-face consumerism. But as the qawwals' tempo reached its climax; as the singers and audience clapped and swayed to the beat of the tabla and the harmonium, it was possible to believe that there was something in the air of this medieval place that spoke directly to the soul, touching it with a special transcendence.

A few feet away, on the other side of the shrine, is the tombstone of Amir Khusrau – the great poet-disciple of Auliya – and his were the words that floated up in the high quaver of the qawwali:

O Khusrau, the river of love
runs in strange directions.
One who jumps into it drowns,
And one who drowns, gets across.

Immersed in the music, I should have been lost to the world, but all of a sudden my eyes opened of their own accord. The hair at the back of my neck prickled and I felt a strong sensation of being watched. The place was packed with the Thursday-evening throng; those who couldn't sit, stood at the edge of the courtyard, crowding beneath the shamiana to escape the light rain that had been coming down all day. The feeling grew in intensity and before I realized, I was on my feet, craning over the crowd, some instinct drawing my eyes to the far corner of the tomb.

A figure was huddled against one of the pillars, wrapped completely in a ragged cloak. The moment my eyes fell on it, it flinched, then seemed to shrink into itself, as if to avoid attention. It stayed immobile for some time, then slowly stirred and the head swivelled once more in my direction. The cloak shadowed the head, but just enough was visible to send a chill through me. It was less a face and more a skull – of a man. The skin was stretched tight, membrane-like, over the bone. His eyes were hollow sockets and for a moment I thought he was blind – till I saw the white of eyeballs. A wispy Ho-Chi-Minh beard added to the effect of extreme emaciation and suffering. We stared at each other across a distance of about thirty steps, and then he abruptly raised his hands and pointed skyward. Lightning flashed, a blinding burst that bathed the tomb in an intense glow. A boom shook the building. The crowds jerked up like so many puppets on a string, some clapping their hands to their ears. The thunder died with a deep rolling mutter, and a pall of silence lay over the shrine. The singers had stopped, uncertain, and some in the crowd got to their feet, blocking my vision. I quickly sidestepped them and pushed through the crush of bodies making for the far end, but he was gone.

I scanned the courtyard and then half-ran to the rear of the shrine. A few straggling worshippers, but no one resembling the figure. The rear entrance was padlocked with a chain. I spun around, crossed the forecourt and entered the narrow walkway that led to the main exit. The wind was starting to gust and the shops that lined either side were busy pulling down their shutters. Several twists and turns later, I was at the main road. It usually overflowed with chaotic traffic, but now it was eerily empty, except for a few autos lined up to my left, waiting for the worshippers to exit. The hawkers and vendors were gone, the ramshackle wooden stalls locked up for the night. A few pedestrians hurried along, sheltering their heads as best they could.

I stood there in the drizzle, undecided. It seemed impossible he could have vanished so completely in just seconds. I tried to recall his expression: the agony and pain that masked … I searched for the word … a *terror* beneath. Perhaps it was just some old beggar; they were all over the dargah precincts looking for alms. But I felt on edge. Had my imagination overheated, kindled by this unnatural lightning and thunder that magnified the mood?

The cell phone vibrated in my pocket and I snatched at it. It was Meenu.

'Chandra, can you come? Right now?' Her voice was taut, with a faint underlying tremor.

'Are you okay?'

'Just come quickly, Chandra. To the school.'

She hung up. All thought of getting back to the qawwali was gone. The wind was getting stronger, sweeping up the rubbish lying around and sending it spinning along the sidewalks. I walked over to the autos. The drivers could see the storm coming, and rates were adjusting themselves by the minute, but I was in no mood to argue with the 'meter pe double'.

As the auto sped north towards Lodi Road, the peace I had experienced at the dargah had vaporized, replaced instead by a nameless urgency that pressed down on me with each passing minute. I suppressed the impulse to reach for my cell phone to call Meenu; it was she who'd disconnected, clearly not wanting to speak further on the line.

Meenakshi Pirzada was born of a Kashmiri Muslim father and a Hindu Maharashtrian mother, which explained her rather unusual name. She had been my wife Yamini's closest friend and colleague at Delhi University where they had both taught history. When Yamini died of cancer in 2010, we had lost touch, till a bizarre turn of events had brought us together a year ago and propelled us headlong into a terrifying adventure. Meenu, Hassan and I had then started a school for street children, and what had begun as a feel-good project for us had now become a passion for her and she spent most evenings teaching there. But, now and then, I worried. These were children living at the very edge of survival and many had complex problems. From the start, Meenu's classes combined teaching and counselling, and the stress on her wasn't something that could be ignored, coming as it did on top of her full-time job at DU.

The auto swung into Golf Links and I directed it into a little lane at the south-west corner of the course. The school was housed in an eighteenth-century dilapidated haveli that had miraculously escaped Delhi's construction boom. Protracted litigation amongst the owners had helped, and thanks to our cop friend Hassan, the family had agreed to rent it to us while the case made its tortuous way through the courts. It suited our purposes perfectly: it had a quiet and dignified, if derelict, air that delighted the historian in Meenu, while serving as a haven for the kids.

The street lights had gone out and the alley was dark. The neon from the emergency lamps flared from inside the school on the ground floor. I paid the fare, walked through the door – and stopped dead.

Meenu was seated at the teacher's desk. Her face looked pasty and stressed against the blue wash of the back-up lamp. The kids were crowded around her, the smaller ones clinging to her fearfully. Seated across from Meenu was a cop, writing something in his notebook. Another stood next to him, feet apart in an aggressive stance, twirling a lathi.

She saw me and smiled weakly, the look of relief palpable. She rose from her chair. 'Chandra, thank heavens you're here. I'd like you to meet these constables.'

I nodded to them. 'What's happened, Meenu?' I said, disturbed by the fear-filled atmosphere of the room.

'The police are looking for Gopal.'

'Gopal?'

'Apparently, he's been involved in a major theft – working for a gang on Mathura Road.'

I shook my head immediately. 'Impossible.'

'That's what I told them, but they just won't listen.' Meenu's voice had risen in exasperation. 'I've even told them to check with Hassan's office – that the ACP knows the boy personally.'

I said to the cops in Hindi, 'Can I have your names, please?'

The man with the notebook looked up and said brusquely in English, 'Myself Constable Sukh Ram, and this is Constable Vikas Agrawal – both from the Tughlak Road police station.'

'Sukh Ram ji, we know the boy well. Yes, he was a thief at one time, but he's completely changed this last one year, and we can assure you that he cannot possibly be involved in a theft. There must be some mistake.'

The cop cut me off. 'Suboot hai, saab. We have full proof. This was a big job, and everyone on the street knows that this chokra is the best in the business.'

I knew straightaway what he meant. The major criminal gangs used children in every possible way: as courier boys, for solicitation, as eyes and ears against the cops and rivals. But most of all as entry specialists. Small-sized and agile, children were best for break-in robberies. And if things went wrong, they were expendable.

'Kya suboot hai? What is this robbery? How do you know Gopal was involved?' I said.

The other man said, 'None of your business. And if he's innocent, why hasn't he come to school for four days? It's exactly when the robbery happened.'

I stared at Meenu.

'What?'

Meenu said, 'Yes, he's been absent. But you know how it is … The children come and go as they please. There could be any number of reasons why he's not been attending.'

The street kids made their own rules and it was true that they came and went as they pleased; but thanks to Meenu, who was a born teacher, the school had become a second home to most of them. And Gopal was a boy transformed – the most regular of the students. No way would he miss four days without very good reason.

Sukh Ram said impatiently, 'We've been through all this, madam.' Then his voice hardened. 'I've already asked you once. Where does he live? Where's this new place you have found for him?'

Meenu said reluctantly, 'Arab Sarai. But I've checked there. No one has seen him for a week.'

Agrawal said triumphantly, 'I told you so.' He raised his lathi threateningly at the kids and shouted in Hindi, 'Kaun janta hai ki Gopal kahan gaya? *Kaun?* Bata do! Nahin toh …' *Who know where the boy's gone, tell me or else …*

The small ones shrank back, eyes rolling in fear, clutching at Meenu. The older ones – veterans of cop encounters – maintained a sullen, watchful silence.

Meenakshi said sharply, 'Stop that, Agrawal ji. This is no way to go about it. I'm sure you'll get more by showing some patience rather than scaring them. They're only children.'

Agrawal was bristling, his ego all up at this woman taking him on, but before he could respond, I said quietly, 'Why don't you have your superiors check with ACP Hassan? He'll guarantee that Gopal is not the …'

Sukh Ram rudely cut me off again. 'Yeh PC office ka mamla hai. Orders are direct from Police Commissioner office.' He pointed at the kids. 'The gandus know something. Look at them.'

I felt a flare of rage. He was calling them assholes to their faces. Right here in a classroom, a place of learning.

I took a step forward till I was directly up against the two of them. 'Get out. Or you'll have your names on the front page of every newspaper in Delhi. My name is Chandrasekhar. I'm a journalist, so run a check on me with the PC's office – or whoever sent you. Then we'll see whose gand is fucked.'

There was a long silence. The cops glared at me and I returned them stare for stare. Then, at last, their eyes fell, but not before I caught the uncertainty – and something else – creep into their expressions.

Sukh Ram said slowly, 'Saab, yeh bade logon ka mamla hai. This is a very big case. The boy is in serious trouble. If any of these gan … students … try and hide something from us, it will go very badly for them.'

He paused and then raised his voice deliberately. 'We will leave now but we will seek them out in the slums. We have our means of getting information.'

There must have been around twenty kids – girls and boys – in that room, from four- or five-year-olds to early teens; the thin, little bodies all crowded close about Meenu. A visible shudder rippled through the group when the constable finished.

I said nothing, keeping a tight check on my fury. It wouldn't serve any purpose to escalate the confrontation. And even through my anger, a thought niggled at me. These constables were low on the pecking order. The cop everywhere is a notoriously political animal. He smells power from a mile away. They tended to be arrogant with the poor and the powerless, but generally cautious with the educated class, never being wholly sure what 'pull' could be brought into play.

I had not just stood up to them but actually issued a threat. This was when they usually backed off. These two hadn't; instead they remained strangely truculent. But they were perspiring, sweat sheening their faces and spreading in pools of damp at the armpits. One of Agrawal's eyes blinked with a nervous tic. It struck me then that it wasn't just the children who were nervous; I'd missed it earlier, but these men were shit scared. And not of me. I could almost hear the barked order from above: *Find the fucking boy.* What sort of robbery could it have been that such pressure had piled up? I'd heard nothing in the news.

'Look, Sukh Ram ji,' I said as placatingly as I could. 'We would also like to locate the boy, to check why he's not come to school. Why don't you give us a couple of days and we will try and make enquiries? Let us talk to his neighbours at the Arab Sarai slum, some of the students … any other friends of his … That way we may get quicker results than these threats to the children.'

The cops traded glances. Then Sukh Ram nodded slowly. He took out a kerchief and wiped his face. 'Thik hai, saab. Please do. I am reporting our visit to ACP saab. Commissioner himself may call you.'

He shut his notebook with a snap and, without a further glance at Meenu, they both lumbered out of the room.

Meenu glowered after them. 'The goddamn morons. Threatening the children like that.'

Her arms spread wide, and though she could hold just a few of them, it seemed like the whole class was in her embrace. I sat down in one of the chairs the cops had vacated. The fear still lingered in their wake like a miasma as I struggled to rehash the strange events of the evening.

Meenu's anxious voice broke into my reverie. 'What do we do now, Chandra?'

I raised my eyes and took in her heart-shaped face, clouded with worry and, for the umpteenth time, felt a stab of guilt. Meenakshi Pirzada was small-made, inclined to plumpness, and to my admittedly biased eye, all woman. But what drew me most to her was the quality of her mind, with its finely-tuned emotional awareness overlaid by a razor-sharp intellect that ranged far and wide. Our relationship had deepened steadily to the point where she'd actually moved into my place. We were in love but just short of being lovers in the physical sense. Meenu was more than ready to give herself to me: had been for some time. Moreover, she had a traditional streak and was all for marriage. But even after more than a year into serious dating I wasn't yet ready to commit. Yamini's memory still lay over me like a veil, a shadow over my mind, and I seemed unable to break its hold, to give myself totally to Meenu in the way she deserved. We'd talked over my problem many times, but with no resolution in sight, the tension between us had grown like a tumour in recent months.

I brought my gaze around to the sea of pinched faces and said gently, 'Do any of you know where Gopal is?'

Silence. I waited. A few of the kids were tiny tots, but most of them were eight- to ten-year-olds and the eyes on me were knowing, old beyond their years, carrying the scars of Delhi's teeming slums; used, abused, often mutilated; ragpickers, forced beggars, petty thieves, slaves in deadly sweat-shops and apprentices to the criminal gangs of the Delhi underworld. Juveniles only in name, they had seen it all and more. In many ways they were more adult than all of us grown-ups put together.

Hassan had often expressed his anger to me, pushing me to write about them, to build more pressure on the state authorities. This was the national capital, the metropolis with the highest per capita income in the country. And it chose not just to tolerate, but to actually feed and fatten on the labour of the faceless, the unseen army of the poor and dispossessed – especially children.

Meenu and her school had shown that even the most hardened of them could be brought back from the brink. Within this refuge – the school was aptly named Sharana – new windows were being opened, and the hint of other possibilities to their lives. But with it, there was also a new vulnerability. The cops couldn't have come at a worse time.

I said quietly, 'Have you tried to get hold of Hassan?'

'No answer, but I left a message on his cell. He's been gone so long; it must be on one of his missions. Anyway, I think we should call it a day.'

I nodded agreement. Thunder rumbled in the distance and I could hear the rain starting to come down heavier. It was time to stop. Meenu rose to her feet. She swung up one of the smaller girls and kissed her.

'All right, off you go now. Don't forget to take your raincoats from the corner. You will all come to class as usual tomorrow, right? Remember, main intazaar karungi. I'll be waiting.'

There was a muted but definite murmur of assent and the children started filing out. Meenu watched them go, her expression pensive, conveying the unspoken question: *would they come back?*

I waited till the classroom had emptied and said, 'Shouldn't we have reassured them about the cops? The kids were petrified.'

'It wasn't the cops, Chandra. Cops they've seen all their lives; these kids, at least the older ones, know how to handle them. It's something else.'

'What do you mean?'

Meenu wiped her face with a kerchief, smudging her bindi in the process. She shook her head silently, *I don't know.* 'But something's scaring the children and it's not just the cops, who, by the way, are on hot coals. They admitted as much to me. They've been told to find Gopal or it's their jobs on the line.'

So my reading of the cops's behaviour was right. I felt a pang of unease, thinking back to my first encounter with Gopal. He'd picked my pocket clean in a single brush past. 'Do you really think Gopal could have gotten back into the game? Some big job he couldn't say no to?'

Meenu said no. She was sure he hadn't gone back to his old ways. But I thought about that twelve-year-old's blazing, restless intelligence. Hassan had told me more than once that Gopal was the smartest street kid he knew. The money to be made from the street for someone with his talents couldn't be discounted, and I said as much to Meenu. She shook her head, unconvinced.

'He loved school, you know that. Came in each day, regular as clockwork and stayed late. I had to almost push him out in the evenings. But a couple of weeks ago, he started skipping classes, and when he was here, he was fidgety, playing around with that old cell phone of his, looking this way and that – anywhere but at me.

'I tried speaking to him … He was evasive. Something was bugging him, but you know how it is with these kids … pressure them and they tighten up like clams. So I thought to give it time.

'Then, after a two-day absence, he was back on Monday, but not in class. I found him waiting for me at the back of the building.

'I should have seen it straightaway, Chandra. The boy was bathed in sweat, muttering to himself, swaying from side to side. My first thought was that he'd caught the viral fever that's doing the rounds, but he shook me off. "Bukhar nahin hain, madam. I have to speak to Hassan saab but I can't find him."

'He seemed beside himself – a strange mix of horror and excitement. He was about to say something to me, but then he looked beyond me, to the entrance, and his face changed. I turned, and just for a moment, I thought I saw a shadow flit across the doorway, but Gopal was white, like he'd seen a ghost.

'"Un logo ne mujhe dekh liya hai … they have seen me … !" That was all I got from him before he rushed out.'

Meenu's face was drawn, her lips clamped together in a thin line. 'That boy's as brave as they come, but there was something on his face … I should have held onto him … talked to you right away. Oh God, Chandra, I feel so responsible.'

I put my arms around her and drew her to me. The night was warm, but I could feel her shivering.

Over time, I had learnt to trust her instincts implicitly. Moreover, though she had a special bond with Gopal, she couldn't have held him down any more than one can hold down a cloud. The boy was a will-o'-the-wisp. Here now and gone a moment later. But he was the go-to kid for the others in class, their natural leader. And he was as tough as nails. Drugs, pimps, murderers and petty criminals: he'd seen it all and some. What could have spooked him?

Un logo ne mujhe dekh liya hai … Had the cops spotted him, trailed him back here?

I said as much.

Meenu pulled away from me and said frowning, 'I've been racking my head. Whoever it was he saw – or thought he saw – that night outside the classroom – couldn't have been a cop. He'd have known Hassan – or even we – could have protected him against one of them. The boy was out of his mind with fear.'

She shook her head, perplexed.

I said, 'Some of the gangs employ pathological types – crazies who get their high on drugs and violence. What if he was involved with some of these guys in a crime job? We read all the time about thefts going horribly wrong. The owner wakes up, surprises the culprits and there's a killing that wasn't intended. It would explain the cops' visit, his behaviour … all of it.'

Meenu shuddered at my words. 'That's what I thought too at first, Chandra. It's the obvious explanation. But if there's been a murder, the cops would have mentioned it. The thing is, I'm sure whatever it is that so frightened Gopal has also gotten to the kids. Maybe it's come from him.'

'You mean … something's scaring all of them?'

'I'm pretty sure of it. I've tried probing, to get to them to open up, but with Gopal gone, they have all clammed up. It's as if they've been warned to say nothing.'

'You've got to keep trying. Let's check with Hassan tomorrow. Rule out the crime possibility for sure. Also, it's time we informed him about Gopal's disappearance.'

Meenu nodded, but her discouraged expression spoke louder than words. A scraping knock sounded behind us and we both spun around at the same time. Peeping tentatively from one end of the doorway was a doll-like figure in a blouse and petticoat with a curiously malformed face. My breath caught in my throat before Meenu said, 'Shanti!' and I recognized the girl. A ten-year-old with a severe harelip whom the cops had rescued from a begging gang in north Delhi.

Shanti clutched at the door and stared at us with enormous eyes. Meenu knelt down and opened her arms wide. Shanti walked slowly towards us. She'd been drenched in the rain, hair loose and plastered about her shoulders. Meenu took her in gently and held her.

'Hello, beta. What is it, darling? Why are you still out in the rain?'

The girl was trying to say something. She kept opening her mouth to speak but in the manner of many hare-lipped children, the words took time to form. We waited. Meenu smoothed her hair with her fingers and caressed her face, all the while cradling her close.

Then the words came in a slow, slurred yet clear enough whisper, 'Kala Mill … Kala Mill.'

Thunder rumbled in the distance and without warning the emergency lamp gave out and we were plunged in utter darkness. Shanti cried out, pulled herself from Meenu's arms and bolted. We ran after her and out the entrance onto the street. 'Shanti … Shanti!' Meenu called out again and again. We cast about, but with the lights out and the now sheeting downpour, it was hopeless. Shanti was gone as if she never existed.

The rain felt warm on the skin, almost hot. I suppose I am an imaginative man – journalists and writers have to be by the very nature of their profession – but I also saw myself as a rationalist non-believer in whose make-up faith and superstition had no place. But in that darkened street I was all of a sudden assailed by a presentiment of doom so strong, that I staggered back a pace as if struck by a physical blow. I was struggling to get hold of myself when I heard Meenu call out.

'Chandra, let's go home and check out this Kala Mill place tomorrow.'

We ran towards her Maruti, careless of the puddles. She handed me the key, and just as I inserted it into the door, I looked up and my blood turned to ice. Lightning forked the sky, turning the raindrops into a hail of diamonds, and by its flicker I saw the man from the dargah. He stood balanced on a compound wall on the opposite side of the road. This time I saw him full, so thin and wasted that it was as if a skeleton had been dressed and propped up. The skull turned this way and that, then the sunken eyes of burning coal fixed on me. This time I didn't wait but started to run across the road. *'Ompaaa!'* The sound ripped from his throat in a high screech, then he swivelled and stepped off into space and fell from sight.

'No, wait … !' I shouted. I reached the high wall, jumped and pulled myself up to my chin. An expanse of garden with some wild, overgrown bushes and a lone tree met my eye. But the man was gone.

3

Chandni Chowk, Delhi. 25th May. 4 a.m.

THE PERSISTENT CLAMOUR OF THE MOBILE PHONE YANKED ME out of my slumber. I reached for it groggily.

'Hello?'

'Chandra, it's me, Hassan.'

I peered at the alarm clock on my bedside table. Four a.m. My sleep had been fitful at best, broken by chaotic dreams in which cars drove down the streets in heavy rain with screaming children hammering at the windows as I watched helplessly. The waking was to a palpable sense of relief.

'Hassan, it's four o'clock, man. Get a life, for God's sake.' It was one of my leg-pulling responses to a call typical among many over the years. For Syed Ali Hassan was a bundle of nervous, chain-smoking energy for whom night and day was a continuum, especially when he was on a mission. He lived a strange double life. In one of them, he was an Assistant Commissioner of Police, but this was a no more than a civilian cover for his true role as a full Colonel in the Defence Intelligence Agency's UB-2, the department of covert action and plans. Created to address the intelligence lapses that had led to the Kargil conflict, the DIA's remit was to act as the apex body of military intelligence covering the entire gamut of enemy communications, satellite weaponry and cyber warfare. The DIA coordinated closely with R&AW and the IB on internal security and external counter-terrorism, and I had good reason to believe that Hassan was one of its most effective operators – a fact that got him assigned to the most difficult and dangerous of missions.

Hassan's work took him away for long periods of time, and we did not sometimes see him for months. These long absences made me more anxious than I cared to admit even to myself, for we were as close as brothers. When one is chained to a wall, facing certain death – in Hassan's case, death by fiendishly devised torture – the true nature of a man is starkly revealed. In those desperate days and hours, my respect for him had soared to the highest plane.

This time Meenu and I hadn't clapped eyes on him for more than two weeks. 'Any new souvenirs?' I said. It was another joke between us. Where he went and what he did were, of course, national security secrets. He once showed me his passport and it had less than four stamps, where I had reason to suspect that he'd travelled practically to every country on the planet. But when he did come back it was sometimes with new injuries that added to the ever-growing tally of scars and tell-tale lesions all over on his body.

I could almost see him exhale the cigarette smoke with a hiss. 'Nope. Not this time. I've been in Delhi all the while.'

I sat up on the bed. Beside me, Meenu was also stirring, waking to the conversation. When Hassan was in Delhi, the three of us hung out together a lot – Thursday evenings, in particular, at the dargah followed by kebab at Ghalib's were an unwritten pact.

'In Delhi! What the … ?'

Hassan's voice cut in. 'Something's come up, Chandra. It's huge … unprecedented. It's been literally 24x7 here at the JIC. That's why I couldn't see you guys or even take Meenu's calls.'

He sounded exhausted and on edge at the same time.

'Anything we can do to help?' I said, concerned. 'I know it's all hush-hush, but if you and Pant feel we can be of any use, you know we're there.'

'I've already considered that. Pant and I even spoke about it yesterday. But this thing is … it looks to be beyond any of us at the moment.'

Beyond any of us. It was so unlike a Hassan statement that it threw me and for a moment I didn't know what to say. But he moved on quickly.

'What was that call from Meenu about?'

I rapidly sketched out the events of last night. Gopal was Hassan's protégé. In fact, we'd been first introduced to the boy through Hassan, who had employed him on some of his cases as a street spy. When he heard that Gopal was missing, he swore.

'If that kid's back to his old ways, he's in for a talking-to.'

'Meenu's sure that's not it. We think there's something more going on here.' I told him about the cops' visit and the children's sense of unease, almost bordering on panic.

He listened closely. 'You're saying that the cops seemed under pressure too?'

'Yes, they were over-aggressive and pissing in their pants at the same time. I think the pressure to find Gopal is huge.'

'Hmm … whatever it is, it must've ruffled some important feathers.'

'That's the other thing. Using your name seemed to have no effect. Apparently the word's coming from the PC's office. As you say, must be one hell of a robbery to have stirred up the top brass so much.'

Hassan paused for a beat, then he said, 'Hold for a moment while I check on the robbery thing. If it was that big, an APB would have been sent out to all stations.'

He disconnected. I was still relaying his words to Meenu when he called back. 'Chandra, there's been no word of any robbery.'

'What?'

'Nothing … in fact, it's been one of those unusually law-abiding weeks for Delhi. As a measure of caution, I checked across our NCR stations. Zip. Absolutely nothing on a scale that would have stirred up a hornet's nest at the PC's.'

I said nothing. Hassan too had gone quiet; no prizes for guessing the question going through his mind. *Why were the cops looking for Gopal?*

'So Meenu thinks it's the same thing that's bothering the kids and Gopal?'

'Yes. And from what you've just found, it's clear that it's not … can't be just a robbery. Something else is going on.'

'Did Gopal say anything when you met him last?' Hassan asked.

'Meenu says that before he ran away he mentioned he was trying to reach you and that someone had found him. The kid was apparently petrified. That's it. The other kids wouldn't talk … except for one girl.'

I told him about Shanti's scared whisper before she bolted away into the night. And then, finally, I described to Hassan about the sighting of that strange figure at the dargah and then again at the school. Recounting the events seemed to somehow accentuate the macabre drama-like quality of all that had happened the previous evening, an unfolding of events on a theatre stage criss-crossed by strange and unconnected shadows.

I could hear the click of Hassan's lighter, and then the hiss as he sucked in cigarette smoke. Then he said, 'Kala Mill. I don't like it … Dammit, I don't like it at all.'

He knew of the place. It was an old burnt-out factory between Okhla and Tughlaqabad village. Like the run-down textile mill compounds of Parel in Bombay before they morphed into swanky malls and residences, Kala Mill was a vast estate now caught up in lengthy litigation with creditors and banks.

'It's been in the news for all the wrong reasons. It's a notorious rendezvous point for the gangs, especially the drug mafia. There was pressure to crack down on the place a few years ago, and we had the usual raids. It went quiet for a bit, but I keep hearing stuff now and then. They say it's got heavy protection at the top.' Hassan paused as if considering something, then,

'Why don't we pay Kala Mill a visit? I'm tied up for the next few days, but can you meet me at my place, say 11 p.m., Monday, and we'll head out and take a look? Meanwhile, I'll try to poke around and find what got this robbery story on Gopal started.'

'I'll be there, Hassan. We were also thinking of scoping out Arab Sarai. We told the cops we'd make enquiries.'

'No, don't do that yet. Something doesn't smell right here. Let's wait a bit and see what the cops get up to next. You've already told them that Gopal's from Arab Sarai. If he's that important, a squad would be hitting the slum today.' He paused a beat and said, 'It takes something special for a boy that tough to get spooked. Whatever it is, it's not good.'

I disconnected and relayed the information to Meenakshi. She gripped my hand in agitation. *Kala Mill.* Even the name sounded ominous. I thought of the youngster with his cheeky smile, his cocky smart-aleck mien and his magical ability to be as invisible as a chameleon as he prowled the toxic streets of an unforgiving city. I hoped to God he hadn't gotten himself into something serious.

I hauled myself out of bed, into the kitchen and was putting the water to boil for the morning tea, when my cell phone rang again. It was the chief editor of one of the national dailies which regularly carried my op-ed pieces.

'I know it's really early, but I wanted to be the first to say congrats.'

'For what?'

'You mean you don't know yet?'

'Nope.'

'Well, then, I have the pleasure to be the first to inform the recipient that he's just received this year's Ramon Magsaysay Award for Journalism.'

'You're joking.'

'Far from it, pal. Your phone is going to start ringing soon enough, and so I'll let you go. I hope this doesn't mean you'll stop writing for us. Now that you're a big shot. Congrats again, Chandra. Drop by as soon as you can, we all want that treat.'

Sure enough, the phones started to ring – the landline and the mobile. I heard Meenu's also shrilling from the bedroom. The next half hour went spent dealing with a surprisingly large number of callers. I listened to their effusive tones with one ear, still trying to digest it. I was deeply uncomfortable about awards; at best they were an unnecessary distraction; at worst, baubles that drove all the wrong behaviour. Journalism was all about telling it like we saw it; and the only god worthy of worship was the truth. Too many times, I'd seen that the hunger for prizes did the opposite; the chase was after readership and popularity, the sort of stuff that drove up circulation and made celebs of the reporters.

After twenty or so calls, I switched the phone off and looked out. The sky was overcast again, and with a nip still in the air. If this was global warming, it had me foxed. Mid-May should have been an oven, but this year it felt more like a wet after-winter. The storms were another puzzling feature – short and sharp, filled with noise and light, clouds swirling about like soup being stirred by a giant ladle. It suddenly struck me that Hassan hadn't responded to my account of the sighting of that strange figure at the dargah. All these puzzles were piling up, as if the darkling heaven above had some deeper, sinister purpose for us on earth. The Magsaysay somehow had faded away to the background till I heard Meenu say behind me,

'Are you going to accept it?'

'No, I don't think so,' I said without turning. 'How did you know?'

'My phone's been ringing too. But I think you should take it. God knows we need more voices of sanity out there. And Hassan … you know what he'd say. If it means you can give stronger voice to those children, you should take the prize. I know you don't give a damn for accolades, but I'm going to say it anyway, this time the award committee got it right. I'm proud of you, sweetie, really proud. I just wish it had come at another time … when we could really have celebrated your turning down a Magsaysay.'

Hands circled me from behind. I poured the tea into the cups, and swivelled around. She smiled up at me, but looked tired. Her eyes were ringed with dark circles and I could see the sorrow that lay just beneath. Clearly, the previous evening lay heavily on her and sleep had brought no respite.

'I had these … really bad dreams, Chandra.'

'Yes, me too.'

I took her face in my hands and we kissed. Meenu pressed herself to me, and we stood there, like two people tethered upon a railway track hearing the first, faint sounds of an express train.

*

Nor were my fears of that morning fanciful. Had I but known, just a few kilometres away, an emergency meeting was in session.

The room contained all the key men representing the apex of Indian intelligence. At the head of the table was the player who had brought them all together: Nalini Ranjan Pant, Chairman, Joint Intelligence Committee. Three others in the room pulled senior rank: AK Davar, Head of IB and in charge of internal security, Shyam Malhotra, Director R&AW, the agency tasked with external counter-intelligence, and Lieutenant-General Parminder Singh, Head of the Defence Intelligence Agency. Also from the DIA was his deputy, Colonel Syed Ali Hassan. Only the sixth man did not have an intel or military background. His name was Pramod Das, and he was the Director General of the Indian Meteorological Department.

Pant, Hassan and the weather scientist were red-eyed; a fact not surprising considering that they had not slept for close to two days. The others in the room looked at them curiously, and with a sense of expectancy. The JIC Chairman had called for an emergency session of R&AW, IB and DIA together, and that usually meant trouble … serious trouble.

Pant dispensed with the pleasantries and came straight to the point. 'Gentlemen, I believe the country may be headed for a grave national security crisis. The stakes are getting higher as we speak. We're looking at another Kargil-type situation – this time with the possibility of escalation into a full-blown war.'

At this, the intelligence chiefs sat upright in their chairs. The Chairman of the JIC was a small-made man who wore thick soda-bottle glasses. Big eyes magnified by the spectacles gave him an owlish air, reinforced by the precise, almost pedantic manner of a professor. Passing by him on a street, it was easy to mistake Pant for an academic or perhaps even a dusty accountant; a mistake that many of his enemies had made to their eternal regret. For with the exception of the IMD man, all of them were aware of his extraordinary reputation. Within the national security apparatus, his role in unmasking a conspiracy to unleash a nuclear exchange between India and Pakistan a few years ago was already the stuff of legends.

'I have prepared a set of slides that outlines the latest situation. They are based on inputs from Dr Das at the IMD and General Parminder Singh's team at DIA-DIPAC – the people who alerted us to the situation in the first place.'

Pant hit a button on his laptop and began the PPT. 'All of you know that climate change and global warming have been dominating international affairs for most of this decade. Next to global terror, it is the biggest agenda at the United Nations, involving all the major powers. But, until now at least, we have assumed that this phenomenon is exactly that: global. And also gradual. But the events of the last few months have turned climate science theory – as we know it – on its head. The Himalayan region of the subcontinent is experiencing such freakish localized weather shifts, some of them so bizarre, that even international experts are at a loss for explanations.'

The next slide came up on the screen, showing a split satellite map of the Kashmir Himalaya, each quadrant separated by a month in time. Pant took up the laser pointer, but even without his highlighting them, the audience in the room could immediately make out the thick spirals of white nimbus clouds over large sections of the map.

Pant pinpointed them with his laser. 'Four storms in as many months. All intense, localized and exhibiting characteristics unknown in this part of the world. Dr Das?'

The meteorologist was a thin man with a prominent Adam's apple, a thin pencil moustache and a balding pate criss-crossed by wispy grey hair. He had the pre-occupied air of an absent-minded scientist, but his eyes were bright, sharp and expressive. For now, they mostly expressed the frustration and excitement of tangling with a momentous problem. When he spoke, it was in a high, squeaky staccato.

'In the high Himalaya, the sheer mass of the bigger peaks means that the mountains literally make their own weather. Snow storms and winds can occur suddenly and with little warning. But what we're seeing now is *impossible*!' He brought his fist down on the table with a thump and then pointed at the new set of photos that Pant had brought up.

The map that showed up split into two frames: BEFORE and DURING. The digital time signatures at the bottom explained what was agitating the Met department man.

'Less than five minutes apart ...,' Dr Das said. 'The satellite images are of the same spot five minutes before and then of the storm itself. *Five* minutes ... !'

The men stared at the screen in silence. The BEFORE images showed clear, even pristine weather conditions, but within a few minutes each spot was completely obscured by the storm spiral.

Davar from the IB said, 'You said impossible. How impossible – given the freak nature of weather patterns there?'

'Davar saab, you have to understand that even the fastest developing storms take time. To someone on the ground they appear to hit without warning, but to a satellite in the sky, the signs become visible well before – and at distances of even a 100 kilometres or more. The images you are seeing were captured by INSAT 3D from an altitude of approximately 36,000 kilometres over the earth, covering an area of 30 square kilometres. As you can see, there is *zero* sign of any disturbance in the area preceding the event in each case.'

Shyam Malhotra said in a harsh, smoker's voice, 'Mr … Dr Das, have you taken other expert opinion on what could be causing this?'

Being bureaucrats themselves, they half-expected the defensive reaction of a true babu: reluctance to concede that he didn't know all the answers. But Dr Das was clearly that rare type whose profession was his passion. The study of weather was his life and he had been vexed – and excited – as never before in these last months. He now jumped to his feet as if he had been waiting for this very question. He cracked his knuckles enthusiastically and began.

'Yes, Malhotra saab. I know exactly what you are asking. Have we in the Met department tried to get to the root of the phenomenon? Let me start with a history of weather prediction algorithms … I hope you don't mind some rudimentary exposure to linear programming and data analysis … ?'

'Yes. I do mind,' General Singh growled. 'I have another meeting at Staff Headquarters, Mr Das. All Shyam asked was a simple question: have you consulted other expert opinion?'

Das was far from abashed at this put-down. Instead, he seemed surprised. 'Consulted others? Of course, of course. Why would we not consult other leading practitioners of …' Then seeing the thunder gather on the army man's face, he interjected hastily,

'Yes, of course, General. I am the first to concede that we at the IMD have our limitations. And so I have personally reached out and spoken at length to my counterparts at the International Met Institute in Stockholm and the NOAA Earth System Research Lab's Global Monitoring Division in Hawaii, and Oxford's Climate Dynamics Group – which are among the top leaders on weather research at this time. We have exchanged a massive amount of imaging data from our surface, glacial and satellite observatories. At this time, they are as puzzled as we are. Nothing in their experience comes close to what we are seeing in the Himalaya. The analysis is still going on as we speak, but at this time there are no ready or dependable answers.'

Davar said, 'Okay, so we're having some crazy weather conditions there … what does it have to do with national security?'

The general said to Das, 'May I request you to wait outside for a bit. There are some confidential matters I need to discuss with my colleagues. But please don't go anywhere.'

Again, this dismissal seemed not to ruffle Das the least. 'Sure, sure. No problems. In fact, I am about to receive a new data stream from our Central Statistical Office. Maybe we will have some further clues …' His cell phone rang. 'Ah, it's them … Yes, Srini. Do you have the uplink? What is the temperature gradient across the … ?' With the mobile clapped to his ear, Das rapidly exited the room.

They sat in the silence left by his high, reedy voice. Then Singh chuckled. 'I like the chap. He took nothing amiss. Very unlike the usual government wallahs. Bit of a professor type too … seems to know his stuff … ?'

Pant said, 'You'd be surprised. I did the usual checks on the man. Came out tops. Among his international peers in the weather field, he is considered the best, with some pretty pioneering papers to his credit. Some people from the Brisbane institute he mentioned were actually here just last week. The senior guy on their team said as much to me, "If the mystery of these localized weather anomalies can be solved, Das is the man to do it."'

Hassan, who had been listening quietly, suddenly looked interested. 'I wonder how a guy like that with obviously no ability to play the power game made it to the top.'

Pant shrugged. 'Good things sometimes do happen – even in our system. But to come back to the point: what was it you wanted to say, General?'

'Just that we're heading towards disaster. Whatever it is, this weather thing is screwing up communication networks on the border big time. Each event seems to leave some sort of … electrical residue … that kills our radio for over three weeks each time. God forbid the other side decides to move one of their mountain brigades against us … we'd be completely exposed.'

Malhotra from R&AW sat up in his chair. 'You're saying the Paks are behind this? But how would they …'

Pant cut in. 'General Singh is only using it as a figure of speech, Shyam. If anything they seem even more affected. INSAT's showing a number of identical storms across their side of the Karakoram Himalaya. The few radio chatter intercepts we have tapped from Islamabad Military HQ and Rawalpindi show a level of panic we've not seen on their side for a long time. They suspect we're somehow behind this. General?'

Singh said nothing for a moment. Like many military men at the top whose requests for equipment had been stymied for years by the civilian bureaucracy, he was loath to cede a potential opportunity to pressure the government into some much-needed upgrades.

So he reluctantly nodded. 'Recently, two scout patrols blundered into each other and there was a shootout. As luck would have it, we managed to kill five of them before both sides pulled back. But it's raised their suspicions to fever pitch. We've asked for a flag meeting, but they've refused. Instead, they've mobilized two full-strength mountain divisions and are advancing east on the Saltoro Ridge. That's what we think, but with our satellites blinkered by heavy cloud formation, we have no means of verifying this. So we have taken blocking positions on the southwest at Siachen … with consequences that none of us can predict.'

Pant said in his gentle, reflective tone, 'In fact, gentlemen, it's getting to be quite dangerous at the moment. With communications down on both sides, it's becoming a case of two blind men armed to the teeth, each imagining the worst of the other.'

Malhotra said, 'Then we should escalate this to the political level, for God's sake! Way beyond a flag meeting. And what about the Chinese side of the border?'

The military man replied, 'Calm. Nothing to report – nothing beyond the usual incursions and beating of the chest by both sides.'

The R&AW chief sighed with relief. 'Thank God for that. But what now?'

Before Pant could reply, the door burst open and Dr Das came flying into the room. He held the phone in front of him and shook it at them. His voice was even higher than usual.

'MOB … Met Office Bhopal … just called. Hurricane-speed winds hit Indore half an hour ago. In less than ten minutes, highly localized heavy cloud formations were sighted. They moved over the city at a speed of twenty knots, carrying what seems to be a form of acid rain … severe enough to cause skin burns in a large mass of the population.'

Das stopped, his mouth working convulsively. Everyone in the room had gotten to their feet.

Hassan said, 'What are you saying, Dr Das?'

'It means … whatever it is … it's now come into the central landmass of India.'

4

GLOBAL WARMING'S DEADLY NEW PHASE?

Times of India, 28 May 2012

THE STORM THAT DEVASTATED INDORE CITY ON FRIDAY lasted less than fifteen minutes. Yet forty-eight hours after, the damage is still being assessed. All that we know is that it has wreaked havoc on a scale nothing short of horrendous; and that the city's inhabitants are living through a nightmare whose after-effects are likely to be painful and prolonged.

The most obviously visible sign of distress is the number of people afflicted with skin burns of varying severity caused by the acid rain over western parts of the city. Infants and children have been most affected, presumably due to their more sensitive skin. More than 1,50,000 cases of second degree burns have been reported and these appear to represent only a fraction of the actual numbers. Public health is potentially at acute risk with possible contamination of potable water sources – both at Yashwant Sagar Reservoir and ground-water wells which feed much of the city's needs. Fatalities have been few thus far. The first ominous signs have appeared of nausea followed by death in some cases.

The government's municipal and state health authorities are expectedly overwhelmed. Poor training, pathetic condition of government hospitals, acute shortage of doctors have been the bane of the government's health departments all over the country for decades now, and in this crisis we see once again the consequences of criminal neglect of the system by successive governments. The few private hospitals are filled to overflowing, threatening to overwhelm the staff and with it, the police. In other words, law and order is on the verge of a breakdown and the army has already been called in.

The acid rain was preceded by a hurricane with wind speeds of over 80 kilometres per hour and has left much of Indore's physical infrastructure in shambles. The National Centre for Medium Range Weather Forecasting in Noida has come round to the inference that the extreme heat carried by these winds were caused by a heat burst, a rare atmospheric phenomenon characterized by a down draft of hot and dusty air from high up in the atmosphere. But other Indian and international experts are not convinced. 'This does not square with a simple heat burst explanation,' said a statement issued by Centre for Global Weather Monitoring in Hawaii, which has been collaborating closely with Indian authorities.

Mobile networks are down and the telecom operators are predicting that it will be another week at the minimum to get the system up even partially. A spokesman for the main networks said, 'The towers were simply not designed for winds of this type. We do a typical wind history assessment for each area and Indore showed up historically as a calm zone, being so far inland.' Whatever be the case, the collapse of infrastructure has made relief work far more challenging.

As an anxious nation awaits further news from Indore, one light shines bright throughout the city: Dharma Foundation. As they have done so many times in the past, most notably during the Leh floods in August 2010, the NGO's thousands of volunteers, each equipped with short range radio sets, have fanned out into the city, assisting the authorities and, in many cases, taking over their role. A spokesman for the Foundation said, 'We have pressed more than 600 trucks into service, carrying medicines for burn and water-borne diseases. We have set up treatment camps manned by our own paramedics. Our disaster management experts are working closely with IWSSB to assess groundwater contamination and to discuss counter-measures.'

From Kashmir to Kanyakumari, the Dharma Foundation has been in the forefront of relief efforts and reconstruction after every major disaster. So effective has it been during cyclones, floods and earthquakes; so quick in bringing relief to millions that the popular phrase 'Leave India to Dharma' acquires added meaning each time it swings into action. Even as the Prime Minster, joined by the MP Chief Minister, has expressed his deepest gratitude, the Chairman of the Dharma Foundation remains typically in the background. When this newspaper reached him after much difficulty, all we got was a terse comment, 'Please don't give DF too much credit. All we're doing is backing up the heroic work done by the locals and the government officials themselves.'

Harshvardhan Dharma has time and again refused the highest honours the government has offered to bestow upon him. The time has come for a grateful nation to overrule his wishes in the matter.

*

Kala Mill, Delhi. 28th May. Midnight

The drizzle had continued unabated for the past two days. The newspapers were full of Indore's acid rain, and this rain had spooked people, pushing them off the streets. Delhi tonight was a ghost city.

We crept alongside the wall, Hassan leading carefully. He stopped and pointed and I instantly saw why he was being so cautious. The video camera was well hidden behind the vines, and I would have missed it but for the winking red light.

Just ahead to our left loomed the massive wrought iron gates of Kala Mill. Centred in the elaborate grille was a rusted colonial crest with a coat of arms and Latin letters which spoke of better days under British masters. I could easily imagine that in its heyday, the visitor's first view of the place would have been an impressive one. But all that was long gone. The high walls on either side were broken everywhere, the cracked brick showing through an overgrowth of creepers, as if the mill had been in a siege and taken heavy cannon fire.

A yellow board painted over with red letters was fixed below the coat of arms: ENTRY FOR AUTHORIZED PERSONS ONLY. BY ORDER, DELHI POLICE.

This was a dilapidated ruin, but Kala Mill did not feel dead. The impenetrable blackness beyond the gate seemed to suck the light from the torch and swallow it whole as if it was somehow alive.

I glanced at Hassan, and that was enough to calm me instantly. He was squatting on the ground, rooting around in his backpack with quick, economical movements. He was wearing a waterproof jacket with a hood that partially covered his face. Over the years, it was a face that I'd gotten to know well; the thinning hair neatly brushed back over a high forehead, accentuating the lean features. It was also a face I had grown to love and trust utterly. Not long ago, I had been with Syed Ali Hassan when he faced torture and death. I knew the measure of this leather-tough, chain-smoking, supremely competent professional, with a suppressed nervous energy that gave him the edgy look of a man perennially on the prowl.

Still, I felt a wash of relief that it was just the two of us. Meenu had initially been insistent on coming along, but then her aged aunt had taken ill and she'd been forced to drop out in order to spend the night at the hospital.

Hassan produced his service weapon – a Walther PPK 0.38 calibre pistol – and and began to screw on a silencer. Then he raised it, aimed and fired. The gun coughed once and the camera shattered with a dull *thunk.* Hassan shoved the pistol into his belt at the back, zipped the bag, slung the straps over both shoulders so as to leave his arms completely free. He stood up, and we resumed our forward creep. I noticed he was being careful to stay out of frontal line of sight in case there were other video devices.

The gates were lashed together with the padlocked chain, but oddly enough, there was enough play to force the gates apart just enough for us to slide through. Hassan pulled out a small tube and screwed it to his eye. Some sort of a night scope. We stood still while he did a wide, slow sweep. But my eyes were getting used to the dark and I could make out straggly islands of bushes everywhere, mainly congress weed with pale, anaemic buds in a sea of ankle-high grass. In the distance, perhaps 150 metres to the right, I thought I saw the outlines of a long, sloped roof.

Hassan tapped me on the shoulder. He pointed two fingers to his eyes, pointed his thumb to his chest and wiggled the fingers commando style to mimic walking. *Look sharp, stay with me.* I nodded. I knew it wasn't just human presence he was warning me about; a place like this had to have its fair share of reptilian inhabitants.

He moved forward quickly. The grass rustled unpleasantly against my shoes, and in no time the canvas was wet through, the damp seeping in through my socks. We weaved through the bushes like it was an obstacle course, striking a diagonal path towards the shed. It loomed larger as we neared, a big rectangular structure, the farther end so far out it looked positively tiny. I could see now that it was just red brick, coated by the night with a grey pallor. Ventilation holes the size of windows ran the length of the wall near the roof. Hassan turned a sharp right, from where a truck ramp led up into a yawning entrance. A rolling shutter listed fan-like from the top, the ratchet mechanism stripped long ago by vandals. The smell of pigeon droppings hung heavy in the air. Hassan stood still, studying the building. He looked about him carefully, then started up the ramp.

There were bird droppings everywhere. Within the cavernous space, it shimmered in the torchlight, a luminescent carpet of white stretching out before us. The floor was coated so thick that I felt I was walking on a layer of foam. The smell mixed with the damp was overpowering. Hassan turned the flashlight towards the roof. I half expected to see a legion of birds, but the roofing struts were bare, the sheets punched with irregular holes through which the rain fell.

We walked into the shed. Hassan seemed to be paying particularly close attention to the corners – where the walls and floor met. But it soon became clear that it was just one giant enclosed space, filled with pigeon crap and pretty much nothing else. Hassan paused for a moment, listening. I tried to do the same, but all sound was dead. I couldn't hear a thing. Our eyes met and I raised an eyebrow in query. This place was just one part of a large mill compound. Shouldn't we be moving on? He said nothing, but I sensed tension. What was he looking for?

Suddenly he moved off along the periphery, this time pointing the torch at the roof. The beam played on a crane hook that hung from one of the cross rafters, long rusted into immobility. He brought the light down onto the floor directly below and then I saw it. The carpet of droppings had a different quality … as if the stuff had been scraped away and then carefully replaced on the floor. Hassan started to push the stuff away with his shoes and slowly a sheet of modern ply-board came into view, set into the floor on a hinge. Hassan stooped and tugged at the clasp and the board came up noiselessly. Steps led away into the dark depths below.

I thought I heard the scurrying of feet and an odd hissing, slithering sound. I stepped back a pace involuntarily and Hassan swiftly drew his gun. We waited in absolute silence. He gestured for me to step behind him and started down the stairs.

We may have descended perhaps 15 … 20 … or even 40 feet. With my mounting claustrophobia it was impossible to know, but we seemed to be descending forever. I suddenly bumped into Hassan. We were on level ground again and he'd come to a stop. The light showed a rectangular room filled with pipelines. At one end, six massive cylindrical brick vats took up the entire wall.

Hassan put his lips close to my ear and breathed, 'Textile dye storage.'

And then it fell into place, all these vats and pipes. This was the underground utility which fed the textile dyes to the main factory floor upstairs. It all looked old and rusted out, in contrast to the brand-new plywood sheet above us. Clearly, someone had put it there recently.

Hassan started to move towards the vats. Iron bar ladders set into the brickwork went up along the sides of the tanks. For the first time, we saw the signs of recent human presence: scuffed footprints in the dust. Hassan shoved the gun back into his waistband and started up the ladder. He reached the top and I saw him peer over, and go still. He stood there for a long time, his rigid outline faintly backlit by the beam as he shone it around the interior.

He climbed down carefully, and I felt a chill when I saw his face. All the familiar signs were there: the slightly flared nostrils, the lips compressed in a thin line. He handed me the torch without a word. My pulse raced as I started up the ladder.

I shone the flashlight inside. White tile reflected the light, throwing it back as harsh neon. The vat had been used as a prison. Handcuffs screwed into the walls hung like ghoulish torture instruments all along the circumference, about 3 feet from the floor. Dark crimson stains splattered the tiles. Frayed pieces of rope, syringes and wads of cotton lay scattered around. My light caught a flash of black on my side of the wall, where the surface curved away, just beneath me. I craned over to get a better view, holding the torch away and pointing backwards. It was a crude drawing in black showing up sharp against the white backdrop. Several short match-stick figures stood one behind the other in a queue. A bigger one stood at the head wielding what appeared to be a sword. It was clear what he was doing: cutting off their heads. Headless bodies lay sprawled all over, their arms and legs flung out. The chopped heads had been neatly stacked into a mound, each face with bug-like eyes and mouth open in a soundless scream.

5

Chandni Chowk, Delhi. 29th May. 8 a.m.

I JOLTED AWAKE. I WAS LYING ON MY BED. MY HEAD FELT CRUSHED by a vice, the bedsheets damp and twisted like rope around me. I became aware that it was morning; my little flat off Chandni Chowk was bathed in a pale wash of light. From the street below, honks of autos and the sound of shutters being rolled up presaged a new day. I usually woke up feeling energetic, but now I pulled the pillow over my head and curled up into myself.

The muted buzz of an insect sounded loudly from the dresser. I stuffed the pillow harder around my head – till I realized it was my mobile. I'd set it on silent when we had entered Kala Mill last night. I leapt off the bed, ran to the dresser and snatched up the phone. Several missed calls from numbers I didn't recognize which I put down to other congratulating callers. But one was from Meenu and two from Hassan.

I punched Hassan's number and he picked up on the first ring. He cut in before I could speak. There was a hard edge to his voice.

'We've been screwed over, Chandra. I should've never left the place.'

'What … ?'

'The vats have been wiped clean. No manacles, no evidence … nothing.'

'What thc hcll … ?'

'I think we were watched from the start. I don't know how … but they … whoever … knew instantly the moment we entered the compound and got to work. *Shit* … !'

Hassan and I had left Kala Mill at 3 a.m. The light being what it was, Hassan had planned to get back to the station, put together a proper back-up team with forensics and hit the place in full force in two hours – by 5 a.m. latest. With his usual efficiency, he had got back to the compound by four-forty-five.

Which meant that in an hour or a little over after our departure, the place had been sanitized.

'Whoever it is, they're well organized, Chandra.' The frustration and anger at himself was still there, but I could sense the cop taking over. 'The forensic team is giving it a thorough once over. They would have been in a hurry and it's always possible they've left some trace behind. I have another team scoping the rest of the compound. We're going to rip the place apart. I'll call you when I have something to report. Meenu's been calling me, but I can't take more calls just yet.'

'I'll speak to her right away. Can I tell her … ?'

'You decide, but I think it's better to leave the details out. Knowing Meenakshi, she'll freak out.'

'I don't want her to get it from the papers.'

'We're playing it close to our chest; we don't need the press on our tail just yet. There's something else that I want you to keep to yourself for the moment. The Indore storm has set off serious law and order alarms within the national security establishment. Pant's working overtime, and I might be tied down for a couple of days. So if you have to do some poking around Arab Sarai, do it. We need to two-track this thing. But … be careful. The people behind this don't play games, Chandra. They're utterly ruthless and I'll bet they have more than a few cops in their pocket. But I have a contact for you. There's a guy in the slum who's been helpful to me in providing a place for Gopal. His name's Abu, they call him Abu kaka. Seems to be the slum elder to whom everyone goes for advice. Take care and report back as soon as you have something.'

He clicked off. *We'd been observed all along.* What in God's name was I to tell Meenu? The terrible things we had seen in the mill, inside the vats … dredged up by some dark, utterly perverted imagination? It would freak her out. But I was a poor liar and she would instantly know if I was trying to hide something.

As I was wrestling with the problem, the phone buzzed again. It was Meenakshi, sounding both anxious and irritated. 'You were supposed to call me, Chandra. Immediately after. I stayed awake most of the night at the hospital, you know.'

'Sorry, Meenu. Really, I got home and was so bushed that …'

'Never mind that. What did you guys see at Kala Mill?'

I paused just a fraction, then said with as much conviction as I could muster. 'Nothing. It was an absolute wash out. One big shed with nothing in it.'

'Damn.' Meenu cursed under her breath. 'I guess you couldn't get to see the whole place?'

'Not a chance. It's huge. But Hassan and his posse have been there the whole morning. He said he'll give us an update mid-day.'

She sighed. 'I'm worried, Chandra. Still no Gopal in yesterday's class. Only some kids are coming in, the class is half-empty and they're very clingy. I get the feeling the class is not a class … but a refuge. Whatever it is, it's very much on their minds and I can tell you it's not science or math.'

I said, 'Have you tried asking Shanti again? The one who put us on to Kala Mill.'

'That's the other thing I can't get out of my mind. She hasn't been back to class either.'

I said nothing. Hassan's words came back to me. *Whoever it is, they don't play games.*

'Chandra … ? Are you still there?'

I cleared my throat and said carefully, 'When do we meet?'

She seemed to brighten at that. 'This morning, if you can make it. I have a donor visit today. You remember Yuvam Foundation, the guys who visited us last month? They got back last evening to say they really liked our ideas for the future: solid academics with vocational trade mixed in for kids at all levels. They say they can help with post-school placements. I don't want to get our hopes up yet, but it's a real chance of some serious funding at last. We've even talked of four schools to start with.'

'That's fabulous, Meenu,' I said, knowing how hard she was looking for money to expand.

'And they're moving fast. I've been asked to their offices for a meeting at eleven. I know you must be exhausted … but, want to come?'

'Yeah, I want to come. It's been a whole night since I saw you last.'

'Maybe I should stay away more. It'll probably do us some good.'

She was half-joking, but only half, and her tone was tart. I said nothing.

She sighed. 'Ignore that. I'll text you the Yuvam address. See you there at eleven.'

*

It appeared that the donor, Yuvam International, operated from a rented house in Patparganj. The place was a modern two-storey residence, with a slightly overdone exterior typical of up-and-coming families who were slowly taking over in this part of the city.

Behind the reception desk, a girl wearing a bright yellow pin with white letters *Yuvam – for Young India* looked up with a cheerful smile as we walked in at 11 a.m. When we introduced ourselves, she nodded at once.

'Of course, our CGO is expecting you. Please follow me.'

She took us through the door and into what was surely the dining area, but was set up as an office with partitions. At least fifteen sat around working on desktops. A closed door of one of the bedrooms had a board outside that said 'Pawan Hansraj – Chief Grants Officer (CGO)'. She knocked once, opened the door and waved us in.

The CGO of Yuvam was a white-haired man of around sixty with a ruddy complexion. Snowy hair and a pair of Gandhi specs perched on a little snub of a nose gave him the air of a kindly Santa Claus.

He half-rose up in his chair and clasped my hand, gave it a quick shake and did a namaste to Meenu.

'Welcome, madam, welcome. Hope no problem finding us?'

'None at all,' Meenu said. 'This is my colleague, Chandrasekhar. Mr Sajid and Ms Lotika were very clear in their directions. So we're on time as you can see.'

Mr Hansraj chuckled. 'Unlike most of the people that we support. Sab log Indian Standard Time se chalte hain, madam. Especially NGOs. Me, I'm from the corporate sector. Focus on efficiency, modern management methods … I'm always saying: "Care for others, but do it efficiently." Much better that way, no?'

Meenu nodded. 'I have to agree, Mr Hansraj. I just wish Delhi University would take that same advice.'

Hansraj shook his head mournfully. 'These sarkari outfits … I'm sure your history department is still in the Mughal Era in these matters.'

Meenakshi said surprised. 'You know where I work?'

The CGO nodded. 'Of course. I think you mentioned to my team yesterday that you taught at Delhi University. That was enough to look you up on the Internet. We even have some printouts.' He tapped a folder on his desk.

I shifted in my seat. My face must have reflected something, for he said, 'I hope that was okay? We need to do a scan of our donees. Sab theek-thak hona chahiye. We have to give a full report to our trustees. But I can tell you right away, this is only a formality. Sajid and Lotika's report was most appreciative of your project.' He stopped as if that explained it all.

'Anyway, let me not take up too much of your time. The first problem, madam, is that you need to form an NGO – with a no lien account. We don't give money to individuals ... But we can help you with the trust deed and other paperwork.'

The discussion got into technicalities, forms which needed filling and so on. This was stuff where Meenu was far more competent than me; I was a zero when it came to legal or money matters. What little savings I had were mostly inherited from Yamini and I had entrusted them completely to Meenu. And so I tuned out and started to idly scan the room. It bothered me that the man had done an Internet search on Meenu. She had a heavy presence on the Net as she was widely published both in Indian and international journals. Of course, I was being irrational; checking someone out on the Net was pretty routine and people did it all the time. There was very little on her that could be construed as personal, but still ... it niggled at me.

Hansraj certainly seemed well organized; everything was visually put up on a notice board to my right. Colour printed charts showed grants sanctioned, utilization rates and progress on various projects running – almost all of them in Corporation schools in the city. The exception was a white marker board to the left carrying a big heading – Indore Emergency Relief – and below it a series of listed points. *Emergency medical kits – Intr. Vir. Vaccines Infants – Quinine tabs 50/100 mg – Vol mob. 400 from Dharma Indore for distribution.*

There was a lull in the conversation with Meenu studying some of documents. I said, 'How is the relief work in Indore going, Mr Hansraj? Must be tough, if the newspapers and TV have it even half-right.'

Hansraj let his breath out with an explosive sound, riffling the papers on his desk. He removed his specs and ran his fingers through his hair. For the first time, I noticed his eyes were red-rimmed with fatigue.

'Sir, for once, the media is not exaggerating. It's terrible … just terrible. Central government has asked many of us NGOs to assist in infant relief. Medicine is pouring in from all over, but what people don't realize is that in natural disasters, the problem's not the quantity of relief, but how to get it to the people. The hospitals are simply overwhelmed and with networks down we have to go house-to-house.'

He pointed to the white board. 'We needed 1,400 volunteers to manage the door-to-door distribution. We would be nowhere but for Dharma. Beg, borrow, steal … I don't know they did it, but they managed to get us college volunteers from all over Madhya Pradesh. And believe it or not, this is peak exam time! Amazing people, I tell you, simply amazing.'

One country, I thought to myself, but we might as well be multiple planets spinning in separate orbits. Just a few kilometres from here, I had just seen human nature at its most depraved, and here in this office, was evidence of exactly the opposite: people working selflessly to save thousands of lives – of infants and children. The resentment about his Internet search faded away; people like Hansraj, organizations like Yuvam, Dharma – these were what kept the country ticking. They deserved the best support that we as a society could give.

Meenu looked up and said, 'I am fine with this, Mr Hansraj. But if you don't mind, let me discuss everything with my accountant and get back to you soon.'

'Of course, no problem. Please take your time. We look forward to a long association, madam.'

Meenu looked more than pleased. Just as she tucked the envelope into her bag, Hansraj said, 'Oh, by the way, I almost forgot. Yuvam is organizing a fundraiser this evening. All our major donors will be there. It's an event for us also to introduce some of our new partner NGOs to them. If you both can come, that would be very nice.'

He opened his drawer and produced a card. I took a quick look at the venue. The Hyatt Regency. A five-star fundraiser. Years since I'd been to one. Back when I was an eager young reporter on the beat, I'd been assigned to cover a few of them, and found the Delhi versions to be self-serving bashes by the rich for the rich. High-society page three pissing contests.

Meenu beat me to it. Even as I started to decline, I felt just the faintest pressure of her arm on mine as she said smoothly, 'Thanks. We'll be happy to come.'

6

Chandni Chowk, Delhi. 29th May. 2 p.m.

HALF-AN-HOUR'S METRO RIDE AND WE WERE HOME, THE IDEA being that we'd have a quick lunch and head out to Gopal's slum. We had both been quiet on the way. When I unlocked the door and let us in, Meenu turned and put her arms around me. She raised her face up to mine and we kissed. I held her close, feeling her heart beat strong and steady against mine. For some reason, that I guess only psychologists know the answer to, tension fuels sexual passion and we'd both been in the grip of unrelenting anxiety the last two days. Desire now flamed up, and we strained against each other. This was where I'd usually freeze; some or the other vision of Yamini would pop up and bring with it a wash of guilt and self-reproach. But, instead, I brought my hands up and cupped her breasts.

Meenu paused as if in disbelief, then moaned and crushed her mouth against mine, moving her hips urgently. We propelled each other towards the bedroom, but just as we entered the doorway, it slid into my brain before I could stop it: the tank, the handcuffs and that crude drawing, all part of some obscene shadow that rose up like smoke and darkened my spirit. I felt a sudden weight, as if someone had thrown a heavy iron chain around my neck.

Meenu sensed it right away. She broke contact and I saw the familiar vexation gathering on her face.

I said quickly, 'It's not her … not Yamini.'

She must have caught something in my tone, for her expression changed and she looked at me searchingly; reached up and combed back my shaggy locks with her fingers, and then cupped my cheeks in her palms.

'What's wrong, sweetie? You've not been yourself all morning.'

I wanted to deny it – I didn't think I could relive last night. But it was no use. This close, Meenakshi Pirzada could read me like an open book, and her next words proved it.

She said quietly, 'Hassan and you saw something last night.'

I described what we had seen: the mill, the underground chamber and the vats. Meenu grew pale as I spoke. Try as I might, I could not bring myself to talk of the picture on the tiles, but she had heard enough.

*

If my account of Kala Mill had shaken Meenu, she also recovered quickly. She was now a woman possessed. We bolted down a quick lunch and took off. Within minutes, we were weaving in and out of the dense traffic at the south end of Chandni Chowk in her Maruti 800. She flicked her wheel left and right, expertly weaving through the traffic with just inches to spare. As we zipped alongside the throngs milling around the Jain Mandir, I knew deep down that we were now committed to finding Gopal, no matter where it took us. My mind went back to another ride I had taken in an autorickshaw not so long ago through these very lanes – headlong into a hair-raising adventure. And here we were, entering the rabbit hole once more, hurtling into the unknown. The echoes of the earlier premonition would not leave me no matter how much I tried. I glanced across at Meenu and, for an instant, a ghostly vapour seemed to hover over her head. I blinked and it was gone. Sweat pricked my face and I turned away from her, cursing myself for being a hyper-imaginative fool.

In a country that is already one of the most unequal on the planet, the jhuggis of Delhi give a whole new meaning to the notion of inequality. The Arab Sarai slum was a little tenement that had sprouted up during the Commonwealth Games building frenzy and now sat sandwiched between the manicured fairways of the Delhi Golf Club and the Mughal gardens of Humayun's Tomb to the east. Hassan had chosen it for Gopal to get him closer to the school, and as slums went, Arab Sarai was much better than the vast cesspools of Bhalswa and Madanpur. Still, in this pocket of densely packed shanties lived more than 1,500 people – part of Delhi's vast sea of the unknown and unseen; a menial class on which this city depended for its essential survival but would barely acknowledge.

There was no way that even Meenu's little 800 would fit into the slum's alleys, and so we parked it in a gully off Zakir Hussain Marg which ran along the settlement's western periphery. A small statue of Ambedkar in his suit pointing to the horizon greeted us at the beginning of a path that wound into the jhuggi. Little mud and brick structures with tin roofs ran on either side. The smell from the open sewers hung over the place like a fog.

Meenu led the way and I followed her, looking about for someone to ask for Abu kaka's butchery. It was about three in the afternoon. I'd expected the slum to be mostly empty as the inhabitants would be out on work. But not all the women worked, and on the other occasions we'd been here, we had seen several of them sitting out on the step, gossiping with each other. But today it was empty. The doors were shuttered and the lane devoid of any life.

Another 200 metres and we were in a cramped square at the centre of the jhuggi. Little gullies branched out in multiple directions, heading into other parts of the settlement. Still nothing. Meenu looked at me and shook her head as if to say, *something's not right.* I went up to one of the houses, checked that it wasn't locked on the outside and rapped on the door. There was a flurry of sound inside and what I took to be whispering. And then silence. I knocked again with no result.

I was about to go to the next house and try again when a man emerged from one of the lanes. He was lean and stringy, wearing a dirty banyan and jeans. And in his hands he held a sickle – one with the long, curved blade used to cut grass. Doors creaked open and closed behind us. I turned around and saw three more men, two with short axes and another with what appeared to be a lathi. Others emerged cat-like from the shadows, and before we could even process it, there were at least a dozen of them in the square, surrounding us.

It was deathly quiet. No sound of the traffic penetrated, though the main road was less than a 100 metres away. Acting on reflex, I pulled Meenu towards me and raised my arm placatingly. But before I could say anything, a shriek rang out, piercing the air like a knife. Meenu blanched at the sound. The men facing us were pushed aside to reveal three women. Two of them held the third between them. The woman's feet trailed the ground and her head jerked about, her mouth working. Again a moan and then a bubbling shriek.

She pointed at us and hissed, 'Where is my baba? Mera baba kahan hai … *kahan?* What have you done with my baby?' Then she spat on the ground. 'Maro madarchod ko … dhire se! Kill the motherfuckers, slowly.'

I shouted desperately, 'She's Gopal's teacher. We're from the school. We are here to help.'

I might as well have been speaking to an empty space. The faces were alight with anticipation as they advanced, intent now only on one thing. Meenu swivelled around so we stood back to back, facing the circle that was closing in. I felt rather than saw her spring forward. There was a hissing sound followed by a howl.

I risked a quick look over my shoulder. One of the attackers was reeling back, pawing at his face, shouting. Meenu had hit him with a burst of pepper spray. I'd completely forgotten that she always carried a can in a special belt pouch for self-protection.

The guys on her side fell back a pace, momentarily shocked by this counter-attack. Meenu was already following through. She spun around once again, the spray can held ready to tackle the frontal threat, but it was too late. One of the men swung hard with his lathi and slammed me on the hip. The hot, burning pain took the strength out of my legs and dropping me to my knees. Even as I fell forward, I caught a glimpse of Meenu, mouth open like a wound in her bloodless face. The spray hissed out again, but one of them had already gripped her arm and twisted it so that the can pointed away. And then she was also falling. The lathi landed once again on my back. Through the mists of searing agony, I thought I heard a shout coming from a great distance. Then a foot lashed out against my stomach and it all went black.

*

I came to in a fit of coughing. My mouth was being forced open and a warm liquid gushed down my throat. I twisted in panic, but found my arms pinned down. A deep voice said, 'Dhire se, dhire se. Give it to him slowly, buddhu … !'

My first reaction to this water-boarding was fading; it wasn't water that I tasted but a bitter concoction that didn't quite make sense and the hands holding me down were powerful but surprisingly gentle. I opened my eyes to see an old, bearded face peering down at me, and in those light grey eyes there seemed to be more than a touch of anxiety.

Meenu … I swallowed the vile stuff, gagged and struggled against whoever was holding me down.

'Meenu … Meenakshi …' I croaked out and to my astonishment it was her voice that answered. The old man drew back and it was her leaning over me. I flung my arms up to wrap her close, when she disengaged gently but firmly. That was when I became aware of the occupants in the room.

They were seated on the floor along the walls. I recognized some of them, faces that not long ago were twisted with violent hate but now bore an anxious yet hopeful expression. The room was quiet, waiting for me to recover.

'Our apologies, Chandra saab, maafe karo,' the old man said. 'Our community is not given to violence, but the loss of our children is more than any one can be asked to bear. Death from God's hand we understand, but not from the hand of man. Then we fight back.'

It turned out that he was Abu kaka – the butcher – and something of a pillar of the Arab Sarai jhuggi. As I sat up and accepted a cup of hot milky tea, he explained what had happened. It turned out that Hassan had taken the precaution of calling Abu kaka to expect us. Abu had been away on an errand, and had caught the call just in time. Expecting the worst he had rushed back to Arab Sarai – just in the nick of time. There was no doubt that, given a few more minutes, Meenu and I would have been injured perhaps fatally; but as it was, apart from a severe soreness around my back and hip, I seemed fine. Meenu, even more luckily, had been barely touched.

'You see, Chandra saab, it all started with some people: well-to-do people, dressed like you. They came here three months back. They said they were doing a slum survey … something about a project to start a school for the children right here. They seemed particularly interested in orphans. Naturally, we were happy and everyone cooperated. These people never came back … and the disappearances started.'

Abu kaka spoke in Hindi and as he went on the tension in the room grew almost palpable. At first a couple of the orphans went missing. No one noticed for a while, for they were the older boys. Theft … drug courier work … menial jobs for the gangs, or just the plain need to drop out of sight of the cops; these were lives lived at the margins, and they often went missing for weeks a time.

But then some of the smaller ones – four- and five-year-old boys and girls – started to vanish. In this slum, we learned, no young child was totally an orphan. Despite the desperate poverty, neighbours took turns to clothe and feed them, and many eyes looked out for these waifs. Food was shared out and bare necessities provided.

'So when the young ones started to disappear, fear set in. We tried to keep them close, but it is hard. Everyone here works long hours in houses or construction sites, and no one will allow children there. Today is a holiday weekend, and that's why you found most of the men folk home.'

Meenu interrupted. 'How many children, kaka? And over what time?'

'Six of them – in less than three weeks. We went to the Nizamuddin police thana,' Abu kaka continued. 'But the law is stupid … no insaniyat, no humanity. Who were we to complain, the police wanted to know. It seems only parents and appointed guardians could even complain! But, we said, the very word "orphan" means they have none. Are they any less for that reason? But who is to teach the guardians of the law?

'Then, Kamala's own child went missing last month. This time we had a mother. We went again to the police station.

Of course, they took down long notes … "When? Did you see anything unusual? Any strangers hanging around?" On and on. And then – nothing. We go every day to the thana, but it's the same story: *we're looking into it, we need time.* Of course, we know nothing will come out of this. When you're poor, Chandra saab, you know that your fate has to be grasped by you and you alone. There is really no one else.'

Abu kaka's face was lined and grim; in its leathery seams I could see his unending struggle against odds that I could only dimly guess at. But his eyes were calm and reflective. And the manner of his statement allowed for only one response and I took it.

'Abu kaka, that need not always be so. If you allow us, we will help.'

I looked at Meenu as I said this, and she touched me gently and then nodded vigorously in agreement. And then – Meenu being Meenu – was suddenly in overdrive.

Looking around the room, she said, 'But we too cannot do this without you. We will call on each and every one of you for help from time to time. Mothers, fathers … old and young. Together we will find who is doing this to you. Do I have your commitment?'

The cries of hope that followed her question left us in no doubt. They crowded about us, apologizing again and again for the blows … how they'd mistaken us for the ones before … But beneath it all lay the terrible burden of expectation, that we would protect their young from the predators that stalked them.

Meenu said, 'Abu kaka, the children in the school were not just from Arab Sarai, and they were all frightened. So the first question we need answered is this: are the children going missing only in here in Arab Sarai or in other jhuggis too? The answer will be important to our search.'

Abu kaka's response was to turn and rap out some orders. Instantly some of the men got to their feet and took off.

'I told them to check with Tilak Nagar, Mayapuri and with the new bustees coming up along the GT Karnal Road. We'll know something by evening.'

Meenu said, 'Thanks, Abu kaka. Now, did you meet Gopal or speak to him before he went missing?'

The old man's expression became sharp, filled with speculation. 'The police were here, asking me the same thing,' he said softly. 'They made the usual threats, but I think they were also afraid. I wonder why they would want the boy so badly? But I told them nothing.' He spat on the dust. 'I will tell those bastards nothing.' Then his expression softened. 'But the ACP, Hassan saab … Gopal has told me so much about him, I thought to speak to him myself when his call came asking me to meet you at once.'

I said quickly, 'You know he was studying in our school and …'

Abu kaka held up his hand. 'You do not have to explain yourself, Chandra saab. I know all about Sharana. It meant everything to that boy to attend that school.' He turned to Meenu. 'Do you know he wanted to be a policeman when he grew up? Constantly trying to solve this or that theft here and quite successful he was too. The older ones used to make fun of him, called him "Inspector Gopal", but he never cared.'

The butcher chuckled. 'Yes, the chokra even had his clients; people who would come to him for help with some minor crime or the other, or get him to follow someone they suspected. About a week ago just before he vanished, he said he was working on a "bada case" – a big case, and that it was about the missing children.

'I immediately pressed him about it. But he would say very little, except that he thought he had found a source of information. His exact words were "Woh vapas aa gaya hai. Usko sab pata hai." Then he ran off and that was the last I saw of him.'

He has come back. He knows everything. What did the boy mean? I asked Abu kaka who shook his head mournfully. 'I wish I had pressed him then. But I'll tell you this: he changed the last few days. Earlier he came and went as he pleased, and was happy to greet and chat with everyone. But now he was quiet and withdrawn. More than once, I caught him looking over his shoulder, as if someone was after him. I asked him if anything was wrong, but he wouldn't say. More and more, he had started to keep to himself.'

'Did Gopal have a room here?' I asked.

Abu hesitated. 'It's one of Gopal's secrets. One that he shared only with me. Hassan saab said I could trust you both completely, so I will tell you. Gopal slept outdoors most nights, but sometimes when it rained he slept in my store. A small place he called his own: just a little storage at the back. I'll take you there, if you wish.'

It was a small lean-to behind the butchery, about 3 feet high and 3 long. The tin door was flimsy and the latch held down by a bolt. The hasp held a lock. Abu kaka forced it with a twist and it snapped. The old man seemed frail, till I remembered the strength of those arms that had held me down – the arms of a butcher.

Meenu and I put our heads into the chamber together. A thin blanket and pillow were placed neatly in one corner. Next to it, a plastic mug with a toothbrush and a tube of Colgate. A lump of red Lifebuoy soap into which a soda bottle cap has been pressed and attached to a small magnet on the rear of the shack. A nail had been hammered into the wooden slat on one side, and hanging there, in a cheap metal frame was a picture of Syed Ali Hassan, looking smart and dapper as he always did in his police uniform. And that was it. I scanned the space again carefully. I reached out and turned over the blanket, pressed the pillow all over thoroughly. Nothing. Then Meenu pointed at the roof where the sheet was simply placed on two struts. I reached up and worked it loose, and all of a sudden, it came sliding out – a small, battered aluminium box.

I flicked up the clasp. Abu kaka, Meenu and I peered at the contents. Right on top of the heap was another photo: of Meenu, Hassan, and I at the Qutb Minar, with Gopal standing proudly in front. I remembered it from a picnic more than a year ago, and now seeing it suddenly hit me hard. Meenu was also silent, then she reached into her bag and began to dab at her eyes with a tissue.

Abu kaka said hoarsely, 'He really worshipped all of you, Hassan saab most of all. I think that's why he wanted … wants to be a policeman. Wherever he is, I hope he – and other little ones – are under Allah's protection. And whoever does them harm – may they burn in eternal hellfire.'

I rummaged through the box. A few marbles, a roll of twine, a rusted penknife, a discarded Nokia mobile with a cracked screen. I picked up the cell and turned it over in my hands. It was one of those ancient push-button models. Several keys were missing. The rear casing had been completely shorn away to reveal the inner PCB – blackened and half-melted. That was it. The whole of a child's life in this little box of odds and ends.

We did a last sweep of the little hut. I pulled the door to and was about to step away, when I saw a glint of white in the far corner – wedged between the plywood and the floor. I crawled in and gently eased it loose. It was a piece of torn envelope and on it written in childish scrawl with a pencil:

Meenu squinted at it closely and said, 'Ompa 610. Or the last three could also be the letters, G-I-D. The boy was just about getting familiar with his A-Z; spelling of basic words would have been the next step. Wonder what this means?'

Ompa. It was gibberish yet somehow familiar ... as if I'd heard it before. I mouthed the word silently, wrestling with it, to see if it would trigger some memory, when Meenu said, 'The mobile. Give me the mobile.'

I reached back and took out the Nokia from the box and gave it to her. Meenu turned it over in her hands, examining it closely, pursing her lips in concentration. Then she said to Abu:

'Do you have a charger for this phone?'

The old man led us to the store front and pulled out the charger from a drawer. Meenu pushed the connector into the socket, plugged it in. She waited for a full half minute, and then pressed the ON button.

To my amazement, it buzzed to life. We hunched around the instrument. I could see enough through the cracked glass, to make out that there were none of usual icons: no signal, no battery life, nothing – just a blank screen. Meenu pressed the call button to check the call register. Again nothing. The system seemed damaged beyond repair. Then she pressed the Menu button, and the screen came to life. One single Picture Gallery icon with a jumble of alphanumeric characters with a jpg subscript. She pressed it and a photo appeared on the screen. I squinted at the mish-mash of colour through the veins of cracked glass. It appeared to be that of a man. Bearded. Young – about thirty or so. He seemed to be grinning, but it was hard to say.

I stared at the gaunt, bony face and a faint memory stabbed at me. It seemed familiar, but even though I cudgelled my brain, I could not say from where.

Abu kaka spoke up, surprise in his voice. 'Why, that's Kannu ... we call him Pagal bhai ... the mad one.'

Meenu and I said simultaneously, 'Pagal bhai?'

'He lives everywhere and nowhere. One of those homeless who're not quite right in the head. He used to wander into Arab Sarai often, but I've not seen him for weeks. Gopal used to wander all over with Pagal. They made a strange pair.'

Pagal bhai. The mad one. Meenu and I took another look at the face and then it hit me. It was the man in the dargah and then again near the school. Perhaps it was unconnected ... a long shot, but I didn't think so. Meenu's eyes met mine and she nodded slowly. Gopal – and my beloved history professor – had together just handed us our next clue. Two clues possibly; for I now remembered where I'd heard the word *Ompa* that Gopal had scribbled on the paper before. Pagal bhai had screamed it out before we lost sight of him.

If Abu kaka hadn't been present, I knew I would have given her one of my bear hugs.

'Okay, Ms Holmes, educate us lesser mortals.'

Her eyes sparkled and she flushed faintly at both my and Abu kaka's open admiration.

The old man made no secret of it. 'Beti, aap ek jadugarni ho – you are a magic worker,' he declared. 'How did you know?'

She held up the phone to the light. 'See this. The phone is almost totally gone, but see these parts of the outer casing? They're new, untouched, no scratches. And the battery is still in it – a bit unusual unless he intended to power the phone. In class that boy was constantly fiddling with electronic throwaways like radios – and most recently a mobile phone. He seemed unusually pre-occupied with it and when I saw it in the box, I had a hunch he'd kept it for a reason.'

I took the phone from her, giving her hand a quick squeeze in the process. 'You and your hunches. Thank God for them.'

'Careful, Chandra. Better we take it to Hassan – get the experts to work on it,' Meenu said quickly. 'There may be more stuff in there. That's one smart kid, and I wouldn't put it past him.'

'But why does he have a photo of Pagal bhai?'

All three of us went quiet. Then Abu kaka recited slowly, '"Woh vapas aa gaya hai. Usko sab pata hai." Gopal was after the mad man.'

I wrapped the phone carefully in my kerchief and put it into my pocket. I told her about Pagal's scream. *Ompa.* But she couldn't make any more sense of it.

'But at least we know where he disappeared. Time to pay Pagal bhai a visit.'

7

NALINI RANJAN PANT LEANED BACK IN HIS SWIVEL CHAIR AND closed his eyes. Slowly, he slumped over, chin on his chest. His soda-bottle specs sat precisely aligned amidst stacks of files, in equally precise arrays covering the entire surface of his desk. The sideboard carried the phones – including a hands-free with a bulbous scrambler attachment. The wall by the door was entirely taken up by a massive satellite map of the subcontinent decorated like a dart-board with pins and Post-its of various colours.

A stranger looking in would have assumed the chief of the Joint Intelligence Committee was enjoying a power nap at his desk, but that impression could not be more mistaken. Ever since his elevation as Chairman JIC from relative obscurity in 2011, Pant's legend had only grown. The events of that year – when a greatly outmanned and outgunned Pant had taken on a powerful rogue group within Indian intelligence that had planned nuclear Armageddon in the subcontinent – had sealed his reputation as an intelligence professional of the first rank. A string of other coups had followed, including the break-up of a Chinese hacker group operating within India.

Along the way, his odd habits had also become a byword. One of them was his famous nap. 'Boss so rahe hain' was a phrase made famous by his subordinates, and by now everyone understood that it meant that the boss was in one of his thinking sessions, and was not to be disturbed.

As a seasoned intel professional, Pant knew that success in his profession was as much as matter of chance as ability. In some respects, the luck factor was even more vital. In the affair of the Shadow Throne, he and his little group of allies had won –

but only just. Other challenges, thankfully less serious, kept popping up over the months and to each he had brought his deep, instinctive feel for the problem, trying to steer his political masters in the right direction. From a national security viewpoint, the country was chaotic at the best of times, and the labyrinthine establishment was ill-suited to handle even basic challenges. Paradoxically, this had its advantages – at least with state actors. Even its bitter enemies were careful not to destabilize it beyond a point: no one could predict the consequences. But that didn't apply to extremist and jihadi groups; and it certainly didn't apply to this latest enemy: an impersonal, elemental force that was starting to hit at the country at will. First Indore, then the Kerala coast. And just yesterday, a cloud formation had swept by the Orissa capital of Bhubaneswar at high speed. Like a bomber missing its target, it had dumped the pH4 acid shower just outside the city, still managing to leave a wake of skin burn and cholera. Looting and violence had broken out and brought under control with only the greatest difficulty. It seemed ominous to Pant that each report came from a new cardinal direction: west-central, then south, now east. It was as if the country was being encircled.

And it wasn't even an intelligence problem, rather it seemed entirely a scientific one – with extremely serious national security implications. The paramilitary forces were already stretched. That left the army. Troops had repeatedly been called in to carry out R&R – Relief & Reconstruction – but the army too had its limits and the military leadership had started to complain that defence preparedness was beginning to get seriously affected.

Pant tried to think of a worst case scenario playing out on this one and found his imagination balking. Multiple Indore-like events … each one a hammer-blow bringing the population to the edge of panic. No government could maintain control under the circumstances. *Chaos … total societal breakdown …* that ultimate nightmare.

So he sat slumped in his chair, trying once more to empty his mind of its crushing worry in order to allow the computer inside to range far and wide, steadily sifting the data from the ground and satellite reports and meshing them with the military and Met briefings – seeking out patterns, connections … anything that could give him a sense of this latest foe.

What foxed him – and the scientists – was, *Why only the Indian subcontinent?* The Americas, Europe, the African continent, Russia, China and the rest of the Asian land mass were unaffected. Earthquakes, hurricanes, tornados, yes … but nothing untypical or unexplained. And certainly no instances of highly localized bursts of toxic rain. He had made enquiries independent of Dr Das. He had spoken to leading weather experts around the world and no one had a clue. In fact, a new scientific term had already been coined for the Indian phenomenon. LAW – Localized Anomalous Weather, and it was fast becoming the rage in weather science circles.

He parked the question in one part of his brain and turned to the Army reports from the Karakorams. He had been pressing for a political level engagement to assure the Pakistanis that they were in it together, but the government was moving at its usual glacial pace. The LOC was one of the world's most volatile flashpoints. The porous and wild, mountainous terrain meant it was vital to maintain a high state of SIGINT (Signals Intel) preparedness. But now, Indian Army intercepts of Pak radio communications from their signal HQ in Rawalpindi showed a level of panic that was dangerous.

Pant possessed a photographic memory. He remembered every detail of every report that had ever crossed his desk, and they ran into hundreds every day. He now let his subconscious take over, feel its way through the mass of the SIGINT intercepts over the last year. Many of them had to do with the severe electrical storms along the outer Himalayan chain – very similar to that reported by General Parminder Singh. None had any eyewitnesses: the storms had happened in impossibly remote sectors, devoid of all military – indeed all human – presence.

It was then that Pant felt a faint prick in his memory. It was down, way down, and it took him some minutes of intense concentration to tease it out from the recesses of his mind. And then he had it.

In August 2010, buried among a number of routine general intel briefings from the office of the Indian DGMO, the Director General of Military Operations, was a terrestrial communications intercept. The sender was the Pakistani Mountain Division on the Saltoro Ridge. At that time it seemed a routine report: a recent trekking rescue in the Karakoram Himalaya by the Pakistani army and air force. A French group of mountaineers attempting to scale Saltoro Kangri had been caught in a blizzard halfway up the mountain. In response to a radio SOS from the climbers, the PMD had been despatched on a rescue mission, but before they could get there, a severe electrical storm had triggered an avalanche, killing the entire party.

No bodies had been found on the mountain. But 2 kilometres to the west, one of the expedition members had been found lying dead right on the frozen-up Skardu River. A mobile had been recovered. The report had a brief mention of some video footage on the phone. End of report.

Pant thought about that for some time. He couldn't recollect more – for the simple reason that he had simply glanced at that report very cursorily before putting it aside as unimportant. Now he stood up and walked up to the satellite map. The body had been found almost exactly at the point marked with a blue pin. So maybe there had been an eyewitness. An eyewitness who was dead. But he had left something behind, and that something was on the other side of the border. He pondered over it, figuring the angles, wondering how he was going to reach out across the border one more time.

*

Pant could not have had even the remotest inkling that even as he stood looking at his map, a similar satellite image – this one in real time and of a much greater magnification – was on display less than 2 kilometres from his office. About halfway along Barakhamba Road and a stone's throw from the bustling shopping district of Connaught Place, the Zenith Plaza building rose to a modest height of eight stories. The builder had originally planned for a grand 40-story upmarket development, but ran out of money in the bust of 2009. The result was a seedy-looking, badly painted eyesore, now caught up in the tangled web of the Indian courts as creditors pressed for their share from the long-bankrupt owner. Meanwhile, small, equally shady businesses – chit funds, blade investment companies, import-export agencies and the like – occupied six of the eight floors and effectively kept the municipal inspectors at bay with a steady flow of bribes.

The top two floors alone seemed slightly respectable, with one-way glass panelling, and software types who came and went in the pan-stained lifts. The tenant here was listed as DataZone Smart Analytics, to all intents and purposes just another of the mushrooming small ITES players.

DataZone was indeed a data analytics company. But not even the most sophisticated searches would reveal who the owners of this company were. Cut-outs by way of cross-holding entities, many of them overseas registered, created a maze that defied all penetration of the true ownership of DataZone. Extremely sophisticated and high tech security systems, well beyond the budget of all but very large trans-national companies, blocked entry into the 7th and 8th floors. Biometric and laser sensors controlled ingress and exits, and hi-res video surveillance covered every inch of the area. On the roof, an antenna, supposedly for DataZone's data streaming needs, was in reality an MEKP 2,400 transponder system, capable of military scale satellite-linked transmissions.

Six people – four men and two women – were assembled around a conference table in a secure room on the top floor. A 10' x 10' ultra-hi-res image of the Indian subcontinent filled the wall-to-wall screen. A tall man leaned forward and tapped a key on the console in front of him. Instantly, the projection of the subcontinent began to shrink, homing in. A two-way microphone on the table came live and a hum filled the room.

The tall man said, 'Mission Control, are we ready to go live for the demo?'

The answering voice came through clear as a bell, 'Ready, HQ. Demo site coming up.'

The 3D projection panned to what seemed to be a remote mountain valley – a lush meadow surrounded on all sides by heavily wooded mountains. Snow-covered peaks lined the far horizon like little jagged teeth. A few buffaloes and several shaggy yaks grazed in the meadow under the summer sun.

The beautiful pastoral scene made no impact on the audience: they waited, rigid with anticipation, as the calm voice on the mike began the countdown. *Ten … nine … eight …* A black cloud appeared at the head of the valley, sudden as a conjurer's trick. It spread over the valley like a spreading ink stain, darkening the sky to a steel grey as it blotted out the sun. The bodies around the table jumped as a *CRACK* exploded shockingly loud in the room. An arc of electricity now lit up the screen with cold fire. An incandescent, twisting rope of light shot out from the valley floor and speared the dark heavens. It lasted no more than a few seconds, but the cloud swirled and suddenly it was sheeting with rain. The heavy shower saturated the valley, drenching it as if from a giant high pressure water hose, and then as sudden as it came, it quickly faded away.

The audience sat rigid in their chairs, eyes staring, gripping the armrests painfully – scarcely believing what they had just witnessed. The sun was out again now, the valley as it had been before. It was as if nothing had occurred. With this difference: the grazing animals were all sprawled lifeless across the meadow, and the grass, so green just moments ago, had turned a mottled yellow.

The calm voice was back over the intercom, 'Precipitation controlled to 2 inches per minute. Transit time: 4 minutes at cloud speed of 26 knots. Wind temperature at 86°C. Mortality is at 100 per cent.'

The conference room was deathly quiet, then a collective sigh, a release of pent-up tension. The tall man reached out and touched the transmit button on the two-way mike. 'Acknowledged, Mission Control. Congratulations. I will inform Central. Be ready for a direct briefing at 1430 hours tomorrow. Team Leader 3 over and out.'

He cut the connection and swivelled his chair to face the others. 'Well, Dr Seema?'

Three of them wore lab coats – including a woman, who said softly, 'The main challenges thus far have been the targeting accuracy and control distances. I think the demonstrator shows these have been conclusively overcome. I think we're good to go, sir.'

'And the pathogens?'

'We are scale-ready. Precise calibration for degree of fatality has been established for both epidermal and ingestible pathogens. We need to do verification checks on the animal carcasses as soon as we get the biopsy samples. But I'm confident we are on track to deliver the cloud seeding quantities. Are we still planning on a thirty coordinates delivery, sir?'

Team Leader 3 tapped another button on his keyboard and the satellite panned away from the valley back to a projection of the subcontinent. A series of pulsing dots appeared all over India.

'We will strike in series over thirty cities. The number has been chosen with care and after repeat scenario mapping on our computers. The chaos must be absolute, but we cannot have a complete system collapse as that would defeat the whole purpose of Pralaya. Our bursts will coincide with the onset of the south-west and then the north-east monsoons and will have additive and disruptive effects simultaneously on existing atmospherics. The rain will carry pathogens A456 and C449.'

He addressed an overweight, bald man to the left. 'How are we placed for the ground interventions?'

The man looked down at his notepad and said, 'Geared and ready: mobile vans, vaccines and emergency supplies will be in position by 25th June. Spatial localized reach will be 10 square kilometres radius for each city. I presume the earlier estimates of affected population hold?'

Dr Seema said, 'Yes. Computer simulations have reconfirmed 42.3 million human impacts. The distribution of symptoms will follow a statistical normal across diarrhoea, dysentery, skin burn and the other pre-designed viral forms. Elevated wind temperatures will serve to compound the impact.'

The team leader said with a dry smile, 'Believe me, there's going to be a lot of shit around.'

They all tittered. The leader continued. 'I'd like everyone to remember this: pathogen design and our ground interventions have been designed to ensure that Pralaya will sow chaos, but fatalities are to be limited to less than 200,000. The objective is to bring the country to its knees, not make it ungovernable.'

When they had all left, the tall man sat alone, making some notes. Then he pulled out an odd-looking handset with a scrambler device attached to it. He punched a number. Without even being aware of it, he had risen to his feet and was standing almost at attention. The phone rang four times and was answered by a single, husky, 'Yes' on the other side.

'Demo 100 per cent successful, sir. We are moving now to Pralaya Strike 1.'

8

Chandni Chowk, Delhi. 29th May. 5 p.m.

Yuvam's invite for the fundraiser said 7:30 p.m. onwards. I was inclined to show up as late as possible – and leave as early as we could. The Delhi rich were predictable in one thing at least. They always came late for parties. But Meenu – ever practical and goal-oriented – firmly overruled my strategy.

'Chandra, none of your left-wing nakhras. It's just one evening. We should get there by eight, see if we're able to catch some of the big fish before it gets too crowded. What's more, I want you to mingle with the high and mighty, and melt them with the Chandrasekhar effect.'

I grimaced. 'Yeah. Last I knew, the Chandra effect is all about black holes. Let me loose and maybe I'll gobble up everyone we meet – then we'll have the place to ourselves.'

Meenu still looked peaked with stress, but that managed to raise a little laugh. She took my hand, kissed it and placed it against her cheek.

'My suave hero.' Then she said seriously, 'I mean it, darling. Remember, it's the schools and the children that count. The Chandra effect is even deadlier than you think: see what it's done to me. And Hassan says you're a closet Bond.'

I grinned. 'Yeah, yeah. Talking of which, let's see if he has anything for us.'

He picked up at the first ring.

'Hey Chandra. I was just about to call you myself.'

'And ... ?'

'All six vats had identical manacles and chains. Blood in some. A couple had variations of the drawing. Even more disgusting stuff, and in bright colours – orange and green. From the varying heights at which the handcuffs were set, we're thinking kids of all ages … total capacity of at least thirty to a tank. We combed through the rest of the compound thoroughly. Apart from the factory shed, lots of smaller buildings, offices and the like. The mill's seen some pretty heavy action over the years. We found an old hooch distillery, and enough used drug ampoules to put a herd of elephants out of action. But nothing that directly ties in with what we saw inside the tanks.'

His voice was level, but I could hear the suppressed rage. Like Meenu, Hassan was fond of children and Gopal was a favourite. Before he'd joined Meenu's school, the boy had been a part of Hassan's extensive intelligence network in the old city and one of his best eyes and ears on the street. I tried to imagine it. *Thirty children handcuffed to the wall, deep inside a well of stone and tile. A weak light perhaps … just enough for them to see the drawing on the wall.* I clenched my jaw to stop a stream of invective.

Meenu fidgeted, not being able to hear the conversation. I forced my face to relax and shook my head at her to say … nothing special, and then Hassan was continuing.

'… it's going to be a slog. I don't think we're going to get anything out of the main force – they're after Gopal, not the gang behind this racket. To make any progress, I have to go solo and the timing's not good right now; things are heating up at JIC and Pant urgently wants me back. Apparently some new development.'

I cursed under my breath. With the cops ranged against us, Hassan would have to get personally involved if there was to be any progress, and his primary role was within the national security and counter-terrorism apparatus.

'Well, we have some news for you as well.' I gave him an account of our visit to Arab Sarai. He whistled softly when I told him how we'd been attacked and then saved by Abu kaka in the nick of time. I described Meenu's inspired breakthrough with the cell phone.

'That girl of yours is quite something. Any time she wants to work for Indian intelligence, the job's hers for the asking. This madman … Pagal bhai … are you positive he's the guy you saw at the dargah and then at the school?'

'I'm pretty sure, though both times the sighting was not the best; he looked sort of crazy: bug eyes … didn't seem quite all there. And he was beyond thin … never seen anyone so emaciated … just skin stretched over a skeleton. I think he was shadowing me. No other explanation of how he showed up the second time. Anyway, he's the best lead we have right now. We are going nuts, Meenu especially, imagining the worst for those kids. Arab Sarai is seething, but we've made some strong allies there. They've fanned out to check if kids are vanishing from other slums as well. Hassan, this is top priority for us: we're ready to drop everything and get to it.'

The line was silent.

'Hello … Hassan … are you there?'

Hassan cleared his throat. 'I don't like it, Chandra. I'm worried you guys may be getting into something way over your heads. And I can smell the danger here. The two of you can disappear in a flash and none of us will be any wiser. These people are ruthless.'

'Well, we can't sit idle and do nothing. That's definite.'

Hassan said nothing for bit, then he sighed. 'Look Chandra, you may as well be prepared. I did a little reading, talked to a couple of colleagues who are familiar with the juvenile scene. Child abduction in this country takes place for three main reasons: child labour, forced beggary and prostitution. None of this stuff is good. But the drawings on the tiles were at a whole new level.

They had a cruelty to them that is unusual. They handcuffed the kids to the wall and then deliberately used the drawings to terrify them out of their wits. The forensic psychologist says there's a lot of thought that's gone into the drawings ... the crudity carefully designed to arouse the worst fears in the child.

'But it's not all bad news. The techs did a terrific job on the drawings. The science is becoming better by the day. A SEM scan of the ink scrapings allowed us to identify the marker pen. It was a top-end indelible marker of a brand called Copic.'

'Copic?'

'Yes, C-O-P-I-C. This stuff is a cut above your Staedtler or Faber or other markers that can be found everywhere. It's actually a pretty expensive piece of equipment ... it's the instrument of choice for top artists. It's imported into India, and used to be sold in the high-end art supplies stores in Delhi, but now you can get it off Amazon and Flipkart.'

I said, 'What in the hell's going on, Hassan?'

'Exactly what I'm asking myself. Well-heeled artists ... the level of organization and speed of the enemy ... nothing makes obvious sense. Whoever these guys are, they're way above the usual gangs. We're facing a rabbit hole.'

I thought about that. A rabbit hole. I too was beginning to feel it in my bones, an undercurrent of a far-reaching, labyrinthine evil working deep beneath the surface.

'What do you want us to do?'

'Have a word with Meenu. We could use some of Ms Pirzada's brainpower right now. You can play Dr Watson as usual.' Despite his words, Hassan was completely serious.

'Will do.'

'Start looking for Pagal bhai, but I repeat: proceed with caution on this one. Talk to you soon.'

I disconnected and got straight to the point with Meenu.

'Kala Mill was not a total blank, but if anything, it looks even more confusing.'

I gave her the gist of my conversation. 'Hassan's tied up in some national security thing. Some sort of crisis, or else he would never have slackened on this. He thinks you're our best bet, and I have to agree.'

Meenu chewed on her bottom lip, deep in thought. 'I'll have to organize some slack time, fix it with my department so they can manage without me for a few days at least.'

Then she said slowly, 'Gopal's not the only child missing. These children may be the forgotten ones, but they're not *that* forgotten. And if it's happening in some of the other jhuggis, the enemy may have left other clues. Why don't you pursue the Copic thing while I visit the hospital and we'll meet back here in say a couple of hours? Call some of the stores. I know it's a very long shot, but if any of them have been selling these markers in bulk, they would have a record. And don't forget to call Abu kaka to see if he has anything for us.'

'Shouldn't I go look for Pagal bhai?'

Meenu shook her head decisively. 'No, Chandra. There'll be too many eyes in the daytime. It's quite possible that after your visit to Kala Mill and then the Arab Sarai we're already under surveillance. Pagal is our best chance and we should keep him that way. Let's attend the Yuvam fundraiser and then go after him at night.'

*

Seven-thirty that evening saw Meenu and me speeding along the Ring Road towards the Hyatt Regency at Bhikaji Cama Place. The AIIMS hospital complex, brightly lit by mercury lamps, came up on our left. The service road was choc-a-block as usual, the crowds spilling out on to the pavements. The hawkers' carts did brisk business, doling out chole bhatures, roasted peanuts and sweet milky chai to the patients and their kin.

The day had been long and both of us were exhausted. The Copic clue had predictably been a complete dead-end. I had googled high-end art supply stores, and called several of them without success. None of them stocked Copic markers, and none knew any others who did. Flipkart and Amazon had them, but any enquiries there would have to be pursued through the police. My body ached in a dozen places – a delayed reaction to the assault at Arab Sarai that reminded me even more potently of just how close we'd been to disaster. I tried Hassan a few times to update him, but got the switched off message. Clearly whatever it was that was tying him up had become an overriding priority.

Meenu was wrung-out too, except that she was in a state of fevered excitement, caught up in a chase that would give us no rest till the end. But that was not all; she sensed that my barriers were crumbling at last, that Yamini's ghost was being finally laid to rest. She reached for me and I held her hand tight as the opulent edifice of the Hyatt pulled into view.

As I'd expected, the ball room of the hotel was as empty as a tomb when we entered. Just a lone waiter doing the final arrangements. I raised a mocking eyebrow at Meenu, but she was having none of it. The tables had been set 'ball-room style' with eight ornate chairs each. She steered me to one close to the stage.

'I'll bet you some big shots will come early. And we might as well get comfortable while we're waiting.'

The hotel guy in his waiter's uniform came up to us. I could see him making one of those rapid assessments – trying to place us in the pecking order. He frowned slightly, no doubt concluding correctly that we were not VIPs. None of them ever came early.

'Excuse me, sir. You're invited to the function?'

I held up the invite to let him know we were not gate crashers. 'The invitation says 7:30 p.m.'

He looked nonplussed, then delivered a universal truth. 'But the function will start only when everyone comes.'

'That's okay,' I said. 'We're quite used to waiting.' He hung around, but I offered no other explanation. Then his five-star training took over. He coughed and said, 'Can I get you anything to drink, sir … madam?'

We both asked for a glass of water, and I said, 'Since I have an hour to kill, do you know if there's a TV anywhere I can catch cricket?'

The waiter shook his head curtly. 'Sorry, sir, nothing here. But you can try the sports bar.'

'Sorry, I can't afford the drinks,' I said blandly. This admission really threw him. Then unexpectedly, he grinned.

'Same here, sir.'

I stuck out my hand. 'I'm Chandra.'

And after that, of course, things sorted themselves out with magical ease. He couldn't afford the sports bar at his own hotel, but typically Delhi-style, he did have a smartphone with 3G streaming. He brought up the TV channel and handed it to me before taking off to get us the water.

At around 9 p.m. – full one-and-a-half hours after the time on the card – the guests started trickling in. By now the tables and the bars had been set up and the hotel serving staff had gathered in full force. Men in Ray Bans and safari suits lined the hall. Our new-found waiter friend told us that these were specially hired private security specialists – given that the who's who of the Delhi circuit was expected for the party.

The room started to fill up quickly. By the amount of laughter, back-slapping and hugging everywhere, everyone clearly knew – or pretended to know – each other. The men, especially the younger ones, were sharply dressed and many had pomaded hair. The women outdid them by a fair margin in their low-cut couture dresses and gowns, matched with the shoes and clutches.

Many of them were easily recognizable; politicos in and out of power, film stars and businessmen. I saw Kamesh Malhotra, the steel magnate, in deep conversation with Siddharth Maheswari who was supposed to own most of coal blocks east of the Vindhyas. No guesses as to what they were discussing. In one end of the room, a pack crowded around the CM of Delhi. He was without a security escort, which said something for the people at this event. There were also the usual media people in the room: young rookie reporters out for the Page 3 story.

I guess I should have tried to follow Meenu's instruction – which was to mix and mingle, but truth be told, I kept thinking of the boy's entire possessions in that little tin box. Suddenly, the opulence in this room was almost too much to bear. I had put on my best kurta, but it was a still a well-worn Khadi Bhawan job and I stuck out like a sore sartorial thumb. People looked my way, sized me up, then their eyes slid away dismissively. At the other end of the room, Meenu was in animated conversation with a society lady. She too was in a starched Bengali cotton sari and without jewellery or make-up, but it didn't seem to discomfit her in the least. Yamini, I recognized wryly, had possessed this exact same quality of being totally comfortable with herself.

And so I stood amidst the clink of glasses and the buzz of conversation, not quite able to make the first move. I was interested in no one and no one was interested in me. I'd been standing all this while, feeling the fatigue creep up. I retreated to a corner and pulled out the phone and did a quick check on the score. Reckoned by the scoreboard, India was going great guns, but I thought the batting too brittle for the run-rate to sustain.

A voice said softly, 'I'll take a bet we'll cross 300.'

I looked at the man before me blankly, my thoughts still on the game. And then the shock hit. The face before mine was one of the most famous in the country, made even more prominent by the fact of the owner's refusal to give interviews of any kind. Harshvardhan Dharma. Himself. Standing right in front of me.

I became conscious that I was gaping. I recovered and said in what I hoped was a normal voice, 'You'll lose. We are going to be skittled out for less than 250.'

Dharma smiled delightedly. The few photo clips of him in circulation showed him to be youthful-looking despite supposedly being in his early forties. But up close, the man appeared impossibly young: no more than thirty. Of medium height, Dharma had regular, almost classical features: a straight nose and a wide forehead crowned with jet-black hair parted at the centre, falling in loose curls to his shoulders. The smile showed even, perfect teeth.

The crowd was beginning to gravitate towards us. A buzz of excited whispers travelled around the room, eyes swivelled in our direction as if drawn by a magnet. In no time, the rest of the hall was sucked empty and packed in a circle around us. I saw some of the reporters on the society beat cast frantically about for gaps in the crush of tycoons and society high-ups. Cameras had been banned at the party, but no one had said anything about smartphones and people were jostling about, manoeuvring for selfies without making it seem obvious. Others were recording Dharma's every move.

Dharma turned around and said pleasantly, 'My friend here predicts that we won't go beyond 250 runs. We are already at 160 for 2 and the batsmen are going strong. Who will bet against him? All wins go to Yuvam.'

'And the losses,' I said.

'Of course, those too,' he replied promptly. 'Yuvam wins either way, even if India doesn't.'

There were several laughs and people started to place their bets, everyone eager to please, clearly competing for his attention. One film star set it off with what I thought was an outrageously high amount, and others quickly followed. Dharma didn't even have to request it, but the organizers were already wheeling a giant TV screen on to the stage.

For the next hour or so, Dharma sat absorbed in the cricket match, while some of the most powerful men and women in the city hung around for a chance to speak with him. He insisted on seating me next to him, giving me the chance to observe him surreptitiously. There was about the man a sort of glow that set him apart from the crowd. His clothes were simple to the point of being plain and he appeared to wear his power lightly. He thanked the attendants who served him and had none of the stand-offish air I saw in almost all of the high and mighty. I had always fancied myself as an observer of people, and I thought I saw in Dharma a sort of diffidence in the presence of adulation that said a lot.

The Indian score was 240 all out at close of play, and Yuvam emerged richer by a staggering sum in excess of one crore rupees. The programme finally got underway with the officials from Yuvam – Mr Hansraj included – going up to the mike and making a series of speeches; thanking people, laying out new projects and new schools. People barely listened; they were itching to get close to Dharma, but it appeared – much to my embarrassment – that he was interested only in talking to me.

I discovered that the Chairman of Dharma Enterprises possessed a multi-faceted mind. He straightaway wanted to know how I had got my score prediction right. I had majored in math and statistics at college and had specialized in probability theory. Dharma grasped the calculations behind my thinking in less than a minute. He then veered the conversation away. I was astonished to discover that he was familiar with several of my despatches and feature pieces over the years.

He saw my reaction and said, 'You seem surprised, Mr Chandrasekhar. But you really shouldn't be. There are very few like you left: journalists capable of forcing us to hold up a mirror to ourselves. Do you know you are mandated reading for my senior management?'

'I'd hardly think my stuff would interest corporate types …'

'On the contrary. You constantly remind us of our limits. I couldn't agree more with your recent pieces on the creeping corporatization of public services in India. But have you wondered why there's such a divide between writers, civil society and so-called capitalists? I must say I have serious differences with many of you in your inability to engage with the very forces you rail against.'

'Now, just a minute, Mr Dharma. If you're saying that …'

'Harsh … please.'

'What … ?'

'Just call me Harsh. And may I call you Chandra? And why don't you come home for dinner sometime – so we can really have a chat?'

I couldn't believe he'd said that. To cover my confusion, I looked about the room. Many curious eyes were on us, and I could sense the naked speculation about the kurta-type who was hogging time with Dharma. I caught the waiter's eye. He was looking at me with undisguised awe – and a touch of apprehension. Had he been too familiar with me earlier in the evening? I smiled weakly and held up his smartphone. There was a sudden stirring in the hall, followed by a hush and his gaze slid past me.

Dharma was also looking past my shoulder, smiling. I twisted in my chair to look over my shoulder – and had to use all my self-control to stop myself from crying out.

A woman has entered the hall. Tall and dusky, raven hair falling in a wave to the waist, she is dressed in a silk sari that clings to her perfectly moulded figure. She walks towards us and the onlookers part for her like courtiers for a queen. Dharma stands up and she kisses him on cheek. I am aware of a subtle aroma of jasmine mingled with sandalwood. Dharma puts his arm around her. He turns to me and says something. But I can make no sense of his words. They are distorted, as if passing through water. I am suspended in space and time, possessed by a force so intense it has stopped my heart entirely.

Before me stands my wife Yamini.

9

THE ADRENALIN THAT HITS THE BLOODSTREAM IN MOMENTS OF crisis is the pure physical reaction of a biological organism driven by one purpose alone: survival. Textbooks call it 'flight or fight'. But overlaid on top of this is a kind of sixth sense, an instantaneous awareness of the nature of the threat. And when it knows that neither flight nor fight is possible, it trips the body and mind into default mode: paralysis.

Dharma said again, 'Chandra, this is my sister, Vaishali. Vaish, this is Mr Chandrasekhar, a cricket wizard on whom I must now rely for my match bets. He made Yuvam a fortune today. By the way he is also …'

'Mandated reading for Dharma Enterprises,' Vaishali finished.

Dharma laughed. 'Have I repeated myself so often?'

Vaishali did not answer. I was dimly aware of a pair of brilliant, jet black eyes studying me frankly. Then she extended her hand.

'Hello, Mr Chandrasekhar. Congratulations on the Magsaysay by the way.'

Dharma shook his head ruefully. 'And here I was in conversation with the man and missed it completely. Congratulations, Mr Chandrasekhar. Long overdue, if I may say so.'

I barely heard him; instead I took her hand mechanically. Trying but unable to speak a word, I was aware of staring fixedly at her face. The moment stretched awkwardly. Then the swish of a sari and suddenly Meenu was there beside me.

'Hi Chandra, it's pretty late. Shouldn't we be going?' she said brightly.

I realized I was still holding on to Vaishali's hand. I released it and stepped back, feeling the sweat on my face.

'Meenu, I'd like you to meet Harsh and Vaishali Dharma,' I said in a thick voice I barely recognized as my own. Then turning to them, 'This is Meenakshi Pirzada.'

Meenu had approached from behind the Dharmas. They turned to say their hellos. Even through my own lock-down, I felt the shock coming off Meenu in waves. Dharma and Vaishali seemed to notice nothing amiss, and greeted Meenu warmly.

'Vaish, what do you say we have Chandra and Ms Pirzada home for dinner one day?'

Vaishali nodded. 'Of course, Harsh. That'd be nice.'

They looked at me, waiting for a reply. I nodded, still not trusting myself to speak.

In any situation it was not the politest of responses and then Meenu said formally, 'Thank you very much. We look forward to that.'

'Excellent, someone from my office will be in touch and get a date that suits all of us.'

Meenu took my arm in hers and we started towards the exit. A waiter came up to me halfway. It took me a while to understand that this was the guy whose cell phone I still had with me. I murmured my apologies and handed it to him, aware now that a couple of the media types were moving purposefully towards us. We ignored them and made rapidly for the exit.

Meenu drove silently, her face drawn and somehow shrunken. I had recovered enough by now to acknowledge that my first impression of Vaishali Dharma had not allowed for the differences. The woman I'd just met had somewhat fuller features and was taller than Yamini. Still, there was more than enough of my wife about her to have left me shaking inside. It wasn't just my imagining; Meenu's reaction confirmed mine. Yamini had been gone three years; Meenu had entered my life, and just this morning, I thought I'd finally laid Yamini to rest. Until now.

I sat slumped in the seat. The two of us were no longer alone. A ghost that I had put into a bottle and corked up only with the greatest difficulty had somehow worked its way out and now sat with us in the car – a tactile, living thing.

Meenu braked and brought the car to a halt. We sat in silence, neither of us wanting to be the first to speak. I looked out of the window and realized that we were by the wall where Pagal bhai had jumped off and vanished. With a huge effort, I took hold of myself, opened the door and stepped out.

It was now almost midnight. The night sky over Delhi was mottled ink, patches of black cloud against grey. The street lamps cast a copper glow over the pavement. The six-foot wall ran for a length of about a 100 feet, unbroken by any gate or entrance.

We walked along the sidewalk and turned right. A little ahead was a single wicket entrance – a small fabricated iron rotating gate with a padlock. The lock, listed to one side, was open. The catch looked forced. Pagal bhai? Or had someone been here before us? I drew the pencil torch from my pocket, but did not click it on. Meenu reached behind her belt and pulled out her can of pepper spray. I gripped the turnstile. It creaked and resisted. No point in advertising our presence. I pocketed the torch, climbed onto the bottom member and pulled myself awkwardly over the gate. Then I helped Meenu over.

I felt the déjà vu hit me instantly. Kala Mill all over again. Thickets of wild bush, interspersed with trees. The undergrowth was heavy like at the Mill, but this was a much smaller plot, perhaps an acre, with the boundary wall visible on all sides. A caretaker's hut fifty yards to the left gave the place the feel of a DDA civic amenity site – perhaps a park – waiting to be developed.

A mud track led towards the hut and we started forward cautiously. We'd only gone a fifteen or twenty yards when Meenu clutched at my arm.

'Smell,' she breathed in my ear.

It hung in the air: the odour of rotting flesh. I switched on the torch and we crept forward in single file with me leading and Meenu just behind. It got stronger as we approached the hut. I put a hand out and pushed the door. Darkness. The odour now so thick and miasmic we could hardly draw breath. I shone the beam inside – and Meenu screamed.

In medieval times, in Europe, drawing and quartering a condemned man was a common practice. It literally meant carving up the body into four parts. That was what had been done to Pagal bhai. He lay on the floor of the hut in four carefully arranged parts. The hacking had been done with a blunt instrument for the severed body ends were horribly mangled – flesh, veins, organs all hanging out in a thick pulpy mess. Maggots crawled in and out of the gaping wounds in a thick, twisting, curling mass. Flies crawled around between the maggots, but the skull-face was relatively clear of them: enough to see the expression of extreme terror and pain. If Pagal bhai had been mad before, this was the face of a man driven insane a second time.

Meenu ran out of the hut. Retching and heaving sounds followed. I could feel my own gorge rising. I clamped a hand to my nose and mouth and played the torch about. A gleam of white showed up briefly on the torso. I took the kerchief off my mouth, bent down and waved it about. The flies buzzed and took off in a thick cloud, brushing close by my face. It was a piece of paper – pinned by a nail to the man's chest. On it were two words in Hindi. *Agley Tum. You next.*

10

The Ridge, Delhi. 30th May. 5 a.m.

HASSAN TAPPED OUT ANOTHER CIGARETTE FROM THE BENSON & Hedges pack and lit up. He drew the smoke deep into his lungs before expelling it through his nostrils. He automatically scanned the sky as he tended to do each day now, but nothing was untoward this morning – just night giving way to the silver of dawn. From his seat on the balcony the trees lining the Delhi Ridge were dark serrations against the breaking light. Clouds of parakeets rose and settled among the leafy canopies and their screeches punctuated with the cawing of waking crows marked another day. He turned another page of the Urdu poetry book in his hands and read Faiz's nazm, lips moving silently.

Last night I recovered a lost memory of you,
As if a desolate place had suddenly bloomed
As if a moist breeze had washed over a parched desert
As if a man, suffering, had a sudden peace assumed.

Hassan glanced at his watch. Five a.m. Faiz really read best early in the morning. He leaned back in his chair and rubbed his eyes tiredly. Two hours to go before Chandra and Meenu were expected. They'd finally got through to him last night and the news was extremely disturbing. The discovery of Pagal's body and the naked threat by the killers made it now intensely personal. First Gopal, and now his closest friends. Hassan was an old hand at handling emotion. His initial rage now transmuted into a laser-like focus as he considered all the angles carefully in his own mind. But the conclusion tasted like bile on his tongue. There was nothing he could do to help his friends at the moment.

These two were the closest to him – more like family – and normally he would have taken to the field with them instantly – put everything aside to go after whoever was behind it. But these were anything but normal times.

LAW – Localized Anomalous Weather – incidents were piling up. None had yet caused civilian distress on the scale of Indore, except for Salem in Tamil Nadu. There it was winds; so hot that parts of the city had caught fire. The rain that followed was more alkaline than acidic; but, if anything, infinitely more ominous, saturated with pathogens that had set off a cholera and typhoid epidemic that the local administration was struggling to contain.

The pins dotting Pant's map grew relentlessly, spreading like a cancer across the entire country. Yesterday a new pin appeared in hitherto empty Bhutan. Bhutanese state security had sent in a report to say that a local herd of livestock had been completely wiped out in a remote valley. Tissue samples sent by the Bhutanese to the Indian IVDS showed no sign of any known toxin or virus. Cowherds close by had reported a sharp localized shower at the time of these deaths – an ominous similarity to Indore and Salem. As with all the other reports, he had sent this straight on to Dr Das.

The media was having a field day, producing weather experts out of thin air who spouted climate change theories and generally castigated the government for inaction. Social media frenzy added to the confusion and doomsday sites were springing up like mushrooms. The mood in the country was getting darker by the day, with full-blown panic being not very far away. The Cabinet Committee on Security was due for an emergency meeting that morning. The CCS had another – thus far top secret – item on its agenda: the rapid military build-up on the LOC. Absent satellite eyes in the sky, they were down to HUMINT ground intel reports that pointed to a massive military mobilization on the Pakistani side over the last forty-eight hours. Six Pak mountain divisions were massed below the Siachen heights. The Indians were bracing for an attack that seemed imminent.

Hassan breathed deep, tamping down on a deep atavistic anxiety: an emotion he couldn't ever remember experiencing – even in the worst spots of a long and dangerous career. He had faced and dealt with terrible enemies before, but this one was formless, a primordial force against which the human race seemed puny and helpless. The country was teetering on the brink of a precipice that he – a seasoned intelligence professional – couldn't even begin to comprehend, let alone the man on the street, or for that matter the Indian government. All hope now was concentrated on one man – Dr Pramod Das. Hassan grimaced. The meteorologist hadn't slept for days and looked like a grey ghost, but the man just wouldn't give up, moving his living quarters to the office and poring over his computer banks day and night. But as of now – nothing.

*

Chandni Chowk, Delhi. 30th May. 5 a.m.

I awoke with a start. As if lying in wait, images started to rip through my brain, like a fast-forward video film, but a hundred times more vivid and magnified. I took several deep breaths to calm myself and pressed the light button of the bedside clock. Five a.m. I'd been asleep for less than three hours.

We'd dialled 100 and reported finding Pagal bhai to the police emergency room. The cops wanted us to come to the station right away to record our statement, but we'd managed to get through to Hassan and he had had them push it to later today. It had arguably been one of the longest and most stressful days of my life. One in which I had woken up to Hassan's update on Kala Mill, had been attacked and barely escaped with my life at Arab Sarai, had been all but overwhelmed at seeing my wife reborn in another woman, then stumbled upon a horribly dismembered body.

And if I was beyond exhaustion, what about Meenu with her sensitive nature – for whom each event would have been pulverizing in its power? We had both dropped into bed more dead than alive, yet for all that, my dream that night – for the first time in more than a year – was of Yamini. When she died, I had hardly slept for months, most nights filled with haunting memories and a yearning that gave me no rest. Meenu coming into my life had started to fill the void, though it was not until yesterday that I was sure that I had finally come to terms with my loss and was ready to move on.

But last night Yamini was back – and in full force. We were alone on a beach. She waited for me near the waves, her sari made transparent by the moonlight, and I knew we were about to make love upon the sand. I reached for her … she turned … and it was Vaishali.

Beside me, Meenu lay unnaturally still and I realized that she too was awake. The instant she had laid eyes on Vaishali, she had known. I was a loner and shy when it came to women, but when I fell, I fell hard. The intimacy that had started between us had been forged in the fires of danger and death and in Meenu I had found my soul mate, my rock. I knew it. Yamini was gone.

I knew that too. But Vaishali's coming was a thunderbolt that had arrowed deep into my soul and set it aflame with a lost desire. What defence did I have against something like this?

*

Meenu and I rang Hassan's doorbell at seven o'clock. He let us in, took one look at us and said, 'Sorry, guys, but you both look like hell. Why don't you get in to the guest room? Have some rest and we'll catch up in a bit?'

We shook our heads in unison. The last twelve hours had been a roller-coaster ride that had left us raw and drained. The adrenaline was still coursing its way through my body and sleep was the last thing on my mind. Meenu and I had hardly spoken, but I knew the turmoil she too was going through.

I said, 'Hassan, you're not looking much better. What's been happening, man? All we know is that you're in some kind of emergency.'

Hassan's face too was lined with fatigue, with dark pouches under his eyes.

'Emergency is right. We're in the midst of a looming national crisis.'

I said, 'The weather patterns … and the rainstorms. The media is saturated with it.'

'Yes. LAWs are erupting like boils all over the country. It doesn't take a rocket scientist to guess that we're staring at a potential catastrophe. The social media activists and the press have taken the paranoia to a whole new level. The climate-changers are in a full-blown "I told you so" mode. Government's all but overwhelmed and but for the Dharma Foundation's outreach, I think we would have had a full scale breakdown on our hands. DF's been phenomenal, but even they have their limits.

The Cabinet's meeting again this afternoon, but they've been blindsided by this thing as much as everyone else. So yes, we're in a fucking crisis, unless someone waves a magic wand and makes it all go away – which somehow doesn't seem likely.'

Meenu said slowly, 'So missing people don't really come into anyone's priorities, does it?'

'*People*. I thought this was about Gopal?'

'We heard from Abu kaka yesterday. Multiple disappearances in other slums. Women and children, young and old – and especially the disabled. Apparently all homeless. Gopal's just one of a whole bunch who've vanished.'

Hassan sat down and paused to light a cigarette. The he said, 'All unreported, I presume? Anyone filed a missing persons report at the station?'

'No. No one to report them.'

He nodded at that. 'I thought so. Guys, let's get real here. Law enforcement's been on maximum stretch for weeks now and the stress on these guys is off the charts. There's no way the disappearance of some of the city's homeless is going to get anyone worked up right now.'

I took a sip of the scalding hot tea and said deliberately, 'But what about you, Hassan? Gopal's got to mean more to you than a statistic. The boy hero-worshipped you.'

Hassan's face tightened. He stood up and began pacing about the room restlessly. 'You're right, I love that boy. But since you mention statistics, do you even know the numbers, Chandra? I did some checking. The NCB crime database lists that 60,000 children have gone missing last year alone. Many states haven't even sent in their reports, and the numbers are probably close to double that. That's over 100,000 children missing each year. And the solve rate is less than 60 per cent. That's for kids with parents or close relatives who file the FIRs. The orphans … the homeless – who even reports them? They're gone, Chandra, they're gone. The kidnap gangs are stronger than ever now and the local cops couldn't care less.

'Do you think I don't want to look for him? But Pant will absolutely refuse to spare me right now. And he's right. It's the entire country on one side and a single boy on the other. The calculus is cruel, but there you have it.' He spread his arms helplessly and then let them drop to his side.

Meenu said quietly, 'We understand, Hassan. You're wanted desperately by the government and it isn't fair on our part to pull you into this. But after last night, we have to do something with or without your help. And now's the only time we have with you face to face. What we need is some advice.'

Hassan said nothing for a bit. Then he sighed and said,

'The logical thing would be to wait this out. Frankly, I'm worried for the two of you – after what happened with Pagal bhai. I'd like to place you both under police protection till we can tackle this together.'

Meenu said sarcastically, 'You mean have the cops who came to the school protect us now?'

Hassan smiled mirthlessly. 'Point taken, Meenu. But despite what you might think, not all cops are bent or incompetent. They're people like us, reacting to impossible pressures the same as any of us. But I agree it's at best a temporary solution. No protection is capable of stopping bastards as obviously powerful and organized as this.'

I said quickly, 'So you've given us the answer, Hassan. We can't be protected forever. You've always said attack is the best form of defence. We have to move on our own – and fast. When I think of Kala Mill … God knows what that kid is going through right now – if he's still alive. Time's running out for all of us.'

Hassan nodded. Unexpectedly, he took our hands in both of his.

'It's what I expected you guys would say, and I can't say I disapprove. And after what you achieved with the Shadow Throne case … who knows … ?'

Dropping our hands, he became business-like.

'Okay, let's review the evidence that we have and then take it from there. Let me make a call to check if the investigators have found anything at the site.'

He made the call, spoke briefly and disconnected.

'As we expected, the site's clean as a whistle. Just the corpse. We've moved the corpse for autopsy. But our first impression is that the killing was done elsewhere and corpse placed here. The note pinned on the body was meant as a warning – to whoever these guys expected to trace the victim to his hideout. Might be Gopal if he's still on the loose, or even the two of you.'

Meenu's hand clutched at mine. I tried to return the pressure, knowing her stress was peaking, but to my shame, all I could think of was another hand in mine just hours ago at the Hyatt. I avoided her gaze, trying to focus on Hassan, who had again stood up and was pacing the room – as he always tended to do when thinking aloud.

'Let's ignore the fact that adults too are missing. Maybe it's some slave labour thing; but child trafficking is far more profitable so let's stay with the kids for the moment. The first thing that strikes me about this case is the level of sophistication about it. This is not one of those amateurish gangs that kidnap children and sell them at the earliest possible opportunity. We've cracked many of these operators in the past and even the bigger mafias are little more than peddlers to the begging groups and to the flesh trade. But this looks … smells … different. The tanks, the drawings, choice of pen markers, the killing – all add up to a whole different level of organization.

'And if it's a large, organized set-up … that means overheads … costs. They've got to get after enough kids to make it worthwhile. Which explains why all the kids in your class were petrified … and why you were attacked in the slum. The scale of the operation was enough to spread fear right across communities. So I wouldn't rule out a big, multi-city operation.'

Meenu nodded. 'That makes good sense to us so far, but how does that help?'

'I doesn't right away, but it's important to get a sense of the enemy. Next, how did Pagal bhai appear at the dargah and then again at the school? It's almost as if he knew you, Chandra.'

I thought about that. 'No idea, really. Maybe he saw me with Gopal at the school and somehow connected us. Maybe Gopal told him about me … to get hold of me if anything were to happen to him.'

'You mentioned that Gopal had the murdered man's photo in his phone. Can you show it to me?'

I pulled the broken gadget from my pocket, and the slip of paper we'd found with it. 'I was waiting to meet you to hand it over. Maybe there's more on it. You could get your guys to check. As usual, it was Meenu who discovered what was on it.'

Hassan nodded appreciatively at Meenu and pressed the power button. He peered at the dead man's photo, asked us to recount our visit to Arab Sarai.

I said, 'Gopal was definitely on to something, Hassan. I'm sure of it. He said as much to Abu kaka – that Pagal bhai had returned.'

Hassan held the paper up to the light. '*Ompa. 610.*'

'Or *Ompa-GID*,' Meenu said.

'Could be,' Hassan said thoughtfully. 'Wonder if it's a vehicle number … a string of letters ending with numbers. Doesn't look like a vehicle number, but could be it ends with a 610.'

I told him that 'Ompa' sounded similar to Pagal's scream – but I really couldn't be sure.

Hassan pocketed the phone and the slip. 'Okay, I'll send it to the techs to see if they can come up with anything else on the phone. We'll also run a check with the RTO and list all Delhi vehicle registrations that end with 610. Now about your next …'

Meenu interrupted him. 'Wait … Hassan can you give me the phone again?'

She took the phone from him and brought up the photo again. She held the phone out for us to see.

'There's just this single photo in the gallery, right?'

I nodded.

'So what did we miss?'

We both stared at the smiling face, distorted by the splintered screen. The Pagal in the photo was almost clean shaven, where the man I had seen had a wispy beard. But even with the beard missing it was definitely Pagal. I looked carefully, but could see nothing else.

Then Hassan breathed softly, 'The file name.'

Meenu nodded. 'Exactly. Each picture is usually a jpeg file and will have a dot jpeg file name. Look at it.'

I looked at the photo's file name. DH0482133.jpg. The sequence had a familiar feel, jogged by what Hassan had just said. Then I had it: it was a vehicle number. The three of us stared at each other. Hassan's nostrils were slightly flared. He pulled out his cell and placed a call to police HQ and started to speak urgently. The voice on the other side said something and Hassan replied,

'Okay, I'm waiting. Call me as soon as you have it.'

He cut the call and said, 'They need a few minutes to put out the trace through the RTO database.'

We waited in breathless silence. Hassan lit another cigarette, eyes on Meenu. He shook his head in mute admiration and tapped his forehead, smiling. 'It's not the first time I'm saying it; I wish we had more people like you in counter-intelligence. We'd make mincemeat of our rivals.'

The detective in Meenu loved nothing more than being able to spot clues and produce them before us with the air of a magician pulling a rabbit out of a hat. This obvious salute from a seasoned investigator like Hassan would normally have had her perk up like a teen. But not this time. She seemed withdrawn, and for the first time in all the time that I'd come to know her, filled with grief. Hassan took in her downcast mien, and his brow contracted into a frown of concern. His jet eyes flicked to me but before he could say more, his phone was shrilling. He put it to his ear and listened for a full minute, writing on a pad. Then he thanked the caller and disconnected.

'The vehicle is a goods truck belonging to an outfit called Sarvabharat Transport. It appears they have a large fleet – around 500 vehicles of various makes registered with the RTO in Delhi alone.'

'Sarvabharat Transport. Can't say I have heard of them,' I said. 'Not that I would have anyway. There must be hundreds of transport companies that operate all over the country. Any idea who owns the company?'

'It gets interesting. My guys checked with the registrar of companies. There's no record of them with the ROC. Which means they're either a partnership or a sole proprietorship – typically more opaque and harder to locate the owners.'

I said, 'So it's a dead end?'

'Not necessarily. We still have the NIA and IB databases. The CMS is maintained by all our main domestic and external intelligence agencies. Let's see what we can find.'

He made another call and this time the revert was quicker and the conversation longer.

Hassan said, 'Again no record of Sarvabharat's ownership, but the transporter does a lot of ferrying of stuff into Bhutan. Since that's a cross border activity, our reports caught it and cross-referenced it with customs. The trucks carry mainly engineering supplies for a single client – the Trans-Himalaya Power Company.'

I sat up. 'Them I've heard of. Aren't they the guys setting up those power projects in Bhutan?'

Hassan nodded. 'They're being touted as the answer to India's coal energy dependence. More than 20,000 MW of power is to flow from their stations into north India in a few years.'

'So who owns them?'

Hassan drummed his fingers on the handle of his chair. 'A faceless consortium based out of Mauritius and the Cayman Islands.'

'Another cut-out,' Meenu breathed. There was silence as we struggled with it.

'Guys,' I said finally, 'I think the power company has nothing to do with this. They're just the customer, and it's surely not the first company to be registered in a tax haven. Anyway what would a giant energy major have anything to do with criminal gangs? Let's focus on Sarvabharat. A 500-truck company can cart off a lot of children. At least we know that one of their trucks was recorded by Pagal or Gopal.'

Hassan replied soberly, 'I agree, Chandra. But it's not going to be easy. You're going to need help – and big time. How are you going to investigate the trucker? I know you've done your fair share of scoops – better than most – but it'll all take time and that's the one luxury we don't have – time. The police are tied up, the nat-sec apparatus is snowed under with the weather crisis and Pant is breathing down my neck. We need a godfather outside of the government who has the clout to put together an investigation. And I'm frankly out of ideas.'

I shifted in my chair. 'Well, there's one man who can do it for us – if we can get him to agree. But it's a very big if.'

Hassan's eyebrows lifted in surprise. 'And that is … ?'

'Harshvardhan Dharma.'

11

THE TALL, THIN MAN WHO WENT BY THE CODE NAME OF VARUNA sat in the conference room in his office on the top floor of the Zenith Plaza building, writing on his legal pad. Varuna was the god of rain; everyone in Project Pralaya had a code name that approximated their role. It was simple and effective – a hallmark of the shadowy genius that had put together Project Pralaya.

Varuna controlled the thirty-city weather-strike plan. From time to time, he glanced at his laptop. Connected to a high-speed modem with a direct satlink, the screen pulsed with real-time images of the skies over the Indian subcontinent. Twenty-eight dots blinked red across the map. Only Indore at the centre and Salem down south blinked orange – the sites of limited demonstration strikes. A twelve digit number kept shifting on the top right hand corner of the screen. Pulling in data from global weather satellites as well as the INSAT systems, the super-computer buried deep within the Zenith's basement funnelled trillions of bits of information into a complex self-correcting algorithm built for one purpose: to predict the exact moment at which the southwest monsoon would breach the Indian coast over Kerala.

Varuna sat up and stretched his stiff back. It was 8 a.m., but then it didn't matter – day or night was all the same when you worked for HIM. In exactly one hour, he would make his mandated daily report. He thought of that husky voice hollowed out by the scrambler echo and involuntarily shivered. Thankfully, everything was going as planned and today would be a routine all-systems-go report.

The landline suddenly buzzed, startling him. He snatched up the receiver.

'Yes?'

'Sir, this is Sarkar reporting in.'

Varuna stiffened. Sarkar was the code name of the man tasked with liaising with the state and government actors vital to Pralaya's success.

'IB se report abhi aaya. Our contact says a search was ordered on Sarvabharat Transport and the Trans-Himalaya Power Company.'

Varuna's fingers tightened on the receiver.

'Kab? When?'

'Fifteen minutes ago. The request came in from one Syed Ali Hassan. Colonel, Defence Intelligence Agency.'

Varuna was silent for a moment. He felt the beads of sweat pop on his face. He kept his voice even with an effort.

'Kuch mila? Did he get anything?'

'Very little. Only that Sarvabharat carries stuff over the border for TH. Even the connect between the two came only because the customs manifests on the Bhutan border are automatically fed into the national security servers. But I thought it was important enough to bring it immediately to your attention.'

'Yes. You did right, Sarkar. Activate all our eyes within state security. I want anything unusual to be reported back to me immediately. At once, samajh gaye?'

'Of course, sir.'

Varuna placed the hand piece back in its cradle. His hands trembled slightly. Shit. *Shit.* That this Hassan – whoever he was – hadn't got much from the nat-sec grid was not the point. Something had triggered the search in the first place. It played Varuna's deepest fear: a potential security breach. He'd have to call it in on priority.

He waited a full minute, calming himself, then reached for the secure cell and punched in a single digit. The call was answered at the first ring. The same thick voice, the scrambler echo giving it an eerie, unearthly quality.

'You're calling early, Varuna.'

He quickly described Sarkar's call. The other side listened in silence. After Varuna stopped there was still no response – a blank echo that went on for so long that for a moment he thought he had lost the connection.

Then the voice came on again, and, for the first time ever, Varuna thought he caught just a hint of something in the mechanically disguised voice – a reflective quality – as if it was talking to itself.

'Syed Ali Hassan, S. Chandrasekhar, Meenakshi Pirzada. The team that took out the Shadow Throne …'

'Sir?' Varuna said puzzled.

'Nothing. I trust you have ordered all our eyes to high alert?'

'Immediately, sir. Sarkar is fully aware of the priority here, and will start a low-key comprehensive sweep of external security – especially the intelligence agencies and the military. I am calling in our Rakshak internal security team for a briefing at 10 a.m. We will intensify surveillance of all members of Pralaya. Any unauthorized contacts or anomalies will be reported to me on a 24/7 basis.'

'Good.'

Varuna hesitated. It was important to know what set off the IB enquiry, but Varuna knew better than to ask. So he said,

'What of this Colonel Hassan, sir? Do you wish surveill … ?'

'No. Hassan has a nose for spotters and his handler in Indian intelligence is a man we have to take very seriously. Leave it to me, Varuna.'

'Yes, sir,' Varuna replied, enormously relieved. With the leader looking into it personally, the problem was as good as solved. He'd seen it innumerable times before. Whoever these people were, they were as good as finished.

His eyes automatically sought out the shifting number on the screen. 060620121200, 6th June, 12.00 p.m. Seven days and counting.

*

Hassan strapped on the shoulder harness, picked up his gun and chambered it, checking the breech for smooth action. He tucked it into the holster and pulled a linen summer jacket over it. It was a sweltering morning and even a lightweight jacket was a chore, but there was no other way to hide the gun.

He called out to his mother. 'Ammi, main nikalta hoon.'

Fatima Hassan was a big woman in every way. Widowed early, she had single-handedly brought up her son and three daughters. Now she waddled out, her heavy figure covered in a black abaya, a woman in her seventies but with a surprisingly unlined and youthful face. She did her ritual blessing; touching his cheeks and cracking her knuckles against her temples.

He kissed her absently. She saw the familiar faraway look and knew that some new problem obsessed him, so she said nothing. Hassan spoke very little of his work, but no one could be both a cop and a military man at the same time, so Fatima had made her own shrewd guesses: ones borne out horrifyingly a few years ago when he'd returned barely alive. As soon as he left, she would start her morning prayers and her dua was simple and uncomplicated these days: the happiness of her three daughters, but especially – and always – the safety of her son.

Hassan liked exercise and avoided lifts when he could, preferring the stairs instead. As he took the steps down from his third floor flat to the parking lot in the basement, he thought about the conversation with his friends. A journalist and a history professor – on the face of it an unlikely duo to take on a criminal investigation of this complexity. But he knew their capabilities. Chandra – dogged, persistent, with enormous reserves of physical courage; and Meenu with her flashes of insight that lit up the trail just when it seemed to go hopelessly dark. Together they made for a formidable combination. But against this enemy's power and ruthlessness, they would have no chance if they went in without any help by way of intel or on-the-ground support. And he could not be by their side, nor bring official resources to bear upon the case. They would be utterly alone. He had almost changed his mind about allowing them to go ahead – when they had mentioned Dharma.

Dharma. That would make a *huge* difference.

Dharma was a state within a state – and in many ways even more powerful, for he made his own rules, was his own master. If he agreed to help, the chances of finding Gopal and breaking the gang behind the trafficking would get a massive boost. But would he? Why would he agree to add missing orphans to what must already be an endless list of pressing priorities?

Well, time would tell. He put it aside and switched his thoughts to the upcoming meeting at the Cabinet Secretariat. Nalini Pant's cryptic mail message had come in an hour ago, and reading between the lines, Hassan got the sense that Pant had developed some leads on the weather crisis. He felt a flare of mingled hope and excitement. First Dharma and now this call from his boss. Maybe their luck was beginning to turn after all.

He pushed the basement door open and moved toward the off-white Ambassador in his parking slot. It was unbelievable that the military still clung on to these jalopies. His eye fell on the front passenger side tyre. It was flat as a board, the tread bulging over the side of the rim. *Shit.* He must have driven over something sharp last night. Without breaking stride, he pulled out his keys and swerved to the rear of the car and flipped the boot open.

He bent down to reach for the spare tyre when he felt just a whisper of moving air behind. There was no thought, no time for conscious reaction; Hassan dropped to his knees and swung his torso around at the hip, his right leg scything in an arc. His leg cut the lead attacker's legs from beneath him, tumbling him to the floor. Two other ski-masked figures were advancing swiftly from beyond the falling figure. He had a fleeting impression of their bulk and beefy builds, muscles bulging through their T-shirts. They bore down upon him, hands raised up, clutching something. Hassan continued his pivoting motion, brought up a hand as hard as spade and slashed down at the fallen man's throat. There was a bubbling shriek and he went still.

The other two carried short, black clubs. They neatly side-stepped the fallen man and came at him from either side. He instantly knew these were pros. They were calm and completely unfazed that he had managed to take out one of them so quickly. Hassan was still in squatting position, and they gave him no time to regain his feet. Both switched the clubs to their right hands and hammered down at his shoulders. Hassan flung himself backwards, but the assailant on his left caught him with a solid crunch to the thigh in the downward arc of the blow. The pain spiked like fire up his leg, but he crushed it, put all his weight on his right leg and pushed himself upright. The other man was already swinging the club. Hassan ignored the coming impact, instead dragging at the Walther in his shoulder holster. The club hit him squarely on the collar bone. A blackness rose before his eyes, but Hassan was mentally ready for the pain. He rode it, pulled out his gun and fired. The report of the gun exploded in the basement; the bullet took the man centre chest and he flew back and crashed to the floor. Hassan started to swing the pistol left, but found his wrist clamped in an iron grip. A powerful twist to the shattered shoulder and Hassan grunted in agony, the pain so intense, the gun fell from his nerveless fingers. The club came down again, aimed carefully and with the full force of the arm behind it. The weakened bone cracked clean into two. Hassan staggered, tried to bring up his good arm, but the club was now a missile; it smashed him yet again in the face, splintering his cheekbone. Blood gushed from the split skin, flooding his eyes, blinding him. He tried a weak counter which was knocked aside easily. A knee came up and smashed into his ribs. He fell, his body aflame even through the fog of a fading consciousness as savage blows rained down on him … and then he knew no more.

12

Delhi. 30th May. 8:30 a.m.

AS WE DROVE BACK TO OUR PLACE, I THOUGHT ABOUT OUR conversation with Hassan. I'd rarely seen him so stressed and preoccupied. The weather shift seemed to be developing into a much graver threat than I had been aware. With Hassan effectively out of reach, Dharma was now the key. I rang Dharma's office and left word asking if we could meet him as early as possible. I'd expected to be told that they would revert, but instead I was put on hold for less than a minute and then informed that Dharma would see us at his home tonight.

I was instantly on tenterhooks, see-sawing on a medley of emotions. Would Dharma agree to help us? How would I manage the evening with Vaishali? And what of Meenu, who'd been dealt a hammer-blow that neither of us could have even remotely imagined?

Meenu, who was behind the wheel as usual, suddenly said, 'She has a reputation as a sexual predator, you know.'

'What … ?'

'Vaishali Dharma has the hots for men.'

I said incredulously, 'Meenu, I can't … you seriously expect me to believe that? How would you even know?'

My voice had risen without even my being aware of it, but Meenu said quietly, 'I'm simply repeating something I had heard about her quite a while ago. From someone I consider a reliable source.'

I said tightly, 'Bazaar gossip. It's garbage, like the stuff you read about film stars.'

'How would *you* know? It's not as if you've met the woman before. I mean, had you even heard of her before last night?'

I said nothing, just sat there feeling the slow burn of anger against Meenu. I could understand her angst, but not this tainting of another woman. It was so unlike her, but I wasn't about to provoke an argument that could get out of control.

Meenu went on, 'After you went to sleep last night, I did an Internet search on her. There's practically nothing on Vaishali. Just a couple of references to some charity event she attended. It matched with what my friend said – Dharma makes sure she's shielded from the media.'

'So? Did you get a lot more about Dharma – I mean on him personally?'

Meenu was quiet, then she said reluctantly, 'No. There's very little on him too. Just the usual business chatter on his companies.'

'The Dharmas are just protecting their privacy, Meenu. It's exactly in line with what we know about them. I think it's unfair for you of all people to rush to judgement.'

And then it was as if a dam had burst. Her face crumpled and the tears started to flow. Whatever resentment I'd fleetingly felt instantly evaporated. One part of me felt her pain as if it was my own. I wanted to hold her in my arms and tell her that I would never leave her. But I could not. I was consumed instead by the thought of the evening to come, like a fevered drug addict quivering in anticipation of the next shot, knowing it may well tip him over the edge into madness.

Gradually her sobbing subsided. She drove quietly, but the tension and despair still came off her like a physical wave. And then her phone buzzed. I picked it up and saw 'private number' on the screen. Caller ID blocked. I pressed the answer button.

'Yes … ?'

'Chandra, did you meet with Hassan? He said both of you were expected over at his place this morning?'

It had been quite a while since we had heard from Pant. The absence of any greetings or hellos, and the edge in his voice brought me up sharp.

'Yes … we did … Left him at about twenty minutes ago…'

Pant cut in. 'He was to call me at quarter past eight and there's no sign. His official mobile is switched off. Something he'd never do. We have an important Cabinet meeting at 2 p.m. Do you know anything that could account for the delay?'

'No. He told us he was due to meet you at ten.'

'That's correct. His mother says he left almost as soon as you both did.'

'Did you check the car? He keeps it in the basement garage.'

'Yes, it's the first thing I did. Sent one of my men over. Car's still there. Engine's cold, no sign it's been used this morning.'

I stiffened, sitting up straight in my seat. 'Anything else?'

There was silence over the line.

'Pant?'

'Better not to speak on the phone. Come to the office, Chandra. Bring Meenu with you.'

Pant maintained a second JIC office on Lodi Road, close enough to his main Raisina Hill HQ where the Cabinet Secretariat is located, yet far enough to maintain a semblance of anonymity. Word had been sent down in advance and we were ushered through the security barriers.

Pant was waiting for us. As Meenu and I sat ourselves down, I found myself looking across the desk at the familiar face once more. The intervening months since his elevation must have been ones of ceaseless strain, but this was a man who lived constantly on the edge of precipices. Nalini Ranjan Pant had been catapulted to the position of Chairman JIC a year ago in one of those unplanned events within the government, and it was due to him that the once defunct office of the JIC was now a powerhouse within the national security apparatus; a position that had been secured amidst the notorious turf battles among the myriad agencies within Indian intelligence.

But this time the glint of humour behind the glasses was missing, and I instinctively felt an undercurrent of a deadly seriousness radiating from the still figure.

'Hello, Chandra … Meenu … Thanks for coming in at short notice. Kuch chai ya coffee?'

Meenu asked for some green tea and I a glass of water. Pant waited in silence for the drinks to be brought in and served. When we were alone, he wasted no time on pleasantries.

'I asked you to come for the reason that I believe Hassan has been snatched. This time, however, that culprit is one of his – and your – making. We are in the midst of a looming national security crisis of unprecedented proportions, and thanks to you both, one of my best operatives has been put out of business.'

Hassan missing. My mouth felt dry, and a sudden dread swamped me. Gopal … Pagal bhai … and now Hassan. I stared at Pant, a thousand questions flooding my mind. The intel chief's manner was professorial, but in his tone was a cold anger that touched a raw nerve, and despite myself, I could feel my own angst rising. Pant displayed no personal anxiety, but seemed to view Hassan's disappearance merely as a professional setback. Meenu had also stiffened; she put down her cup and made as if to say something.

I put my hand on her arm to restrain her and said carefully, 'When you say "put out of business", do you mean dead?'

'I say exactly what I mean – that he's not available for vital intelligence work at a time when I need him. We have no means of knowing at this time if he's dead or alive. And all because the two of you managed to send him on some wild goose chase after a low-priority target.'

Meenu shook my arm off. Her voice was taut with suppressed fury.

'I can't believe I'm actually hearing this. Since when did kidnapped children become "low priority", Mr Pant? What if it was your own child? I'll bet you'll sing a very different tune. Just because it is a poor orphan and …'

'You'll lose, Meenakshi,' Pant said. 'I have a daughter who is the only family I have left in the world, and if she was taken by one of the gangs, my statement would be no different.'

Pant reached into a folder, drew out a sheet of paper, and tossed it across the desk. I took it up and held it so that Meenu could also read it. It was a recent extract of the NCB data on missing children. With the exact same stats that Hassan had just quoted to us; they'd probably accessed the same sheet.

'Hassan tried to persuade me to give him some time on the side to track down the child. I told him what I am telling you now. I just couldn't spare him. Besides, in a country of 1.2 billion people, this is one problem that is as old as time, driven by slavery, sex … crime and plain parental neglect. So bringing back Gopal … one boy … isn't going to save the others.'

'That's an incredibly callous thing to say,' Meenu cried out.

'Perhaps, but that's the truth. And it's a point with which your friend happened to agree.'

We sat silent. Hassan, in fact, had said it in almost exactly those words, but we didn't want to tell Pant that. I felt acute fear and guilt. My friend – my incredibly brave and intrepid friend –

was once again in mortal danger. If his involvement with us had led to this, we were squarely responsible.

Meenu shook her head unbelievingly. 'My God … I don't think I'm actually hearing this … monstrous …'

'Wait, Meenu. Wait for a moment,' I said quickly. 'Two of the people we care about are missing … Gopal and now Hassan. This isn't the time for an argument that's going nowhere. Look, Pant, we did tell Hassan about our search for Gopal. Surely he'd want to know, seeing how close he was to the boy. He heard us out, visited Kala Mill with me, and that's it. Just this morning, he as good as told us he couldn't be involved anymore.'

Pant said, 'I regret the children's fate. I worry for Hassan. But I'm even more worried for the country. But what if I told you that we are on the brink of a catastrophe – possibly millions of deaths? That Hassan is … was … crucial to our attempt to try and prevent it?'

The room suddenly seemed to darken. We both stared at him.

'What are you saying, Pant?'

'I'm saying mass famine, disease and death. It will strike the old and young first – those who can least fend for themselves. Then it will overwhelm us all.'

Pant sat slouched as usual but there was a core of passion in his voice that I'd heard only once before … when two years ago I had read out a set of numbers to him – numbers that had subsequently prevented nuclear Armageddon in the subcontinent.

'The weather change,' I said hoarsely.

Pant nodded heavily. 'Yes, weather change. But not just an act of nature, of the inevitable global warming that is still being debated in seminars. I'm talking about something altogether more evil – aimed at us … at India.'

Seeing our uncomprehending faces, he added, 'I'm talking about the ultimate weapon – weather.'

It took me a while to figure out that he was actually serious. Meenu beat me to it.

She cried, 'You mean some kind of weather manipulation? But that's impossible!'

'I thought so too, and so apparently did the experts. It did not even feature in our calculations. The warning signs stared us in the face but we were blindsided. We would have still been in the dark, except for one chance report that came my way. Thanks to it, we stumbled on a clue to the truth.'

Without waiting for a reaction, he turned his laptop towards us, moved the cursor and clicked. The screen went white and grainy – some sort of screen malfunction. I was about to mention it when Pant motioned to the screen. I saw then that it was a video, taken from what was apparently a mobile phone. The camera was panning. Whoever was holding it was shooting up a steep slope of ice. The grains on the screen were snowflakes, swirling and whipping across the line of sight of the lens. A moaning hiss emanated from the speakers, seesawing in intensity, which I made out to be wind whipping.

The shot was jerky, panning up and up. Along the edges of the screen, green smoke was visible, growing all the while till it filled the glass, and through it I thought I could see a box on a shelf … no … some sort of contraption on spindly legs. The camera was jerking about, the hands holding it barely in control when a shooting blue light lit up the screen. I heard a choking gasp, and the image began spinning crazily. The light continued, so intense that it seemed to burn up the screen. Then there was a keening cry and the screen went dark as the video ended.

Meenu and I looked at each other. Neither of us were sure what it was that we had seen. Pant said, 'This video was shot by a lone French trekker on the lower slopes of Saltoro Kangri in the Pakistan Karakorams. August 2010. On the evening of 5th August to be exact.'

'Pakistani side … You're saying that Pakistan … ?' Meenu said.

Pant held up a hand to forestall her. 'The video was taken on their side. I actually had to ask … beg Gul Mohammed in the ISI for it.'

Before we could digest this startling piece of information, Pant rose to his feet and walked up to a big chart on the wall. Pins of various colours were stuck all over. 'After seeing that video, I reorganized the board. The blue pins represent lightning bursts observed and reported by locals on the ground; the red pins are LAWs – that's Localized Anomalous Weather events for you.'

We stared at it. The blue and red pins were twinned everywhere in a dense cluster in the Himalayan region. But as we travelled south, the reds were starting to show up solo – without the blues. Indore and Salem, which had seen unusually severe LAWs, were also marked with a lone red.

Pant said, 'We don't know enough about those two biggies – the ones that caused very serious damage. Two explanations are possible: either the lightning event was unnoticed or the enemy has developed the power to strike from a much longer distance. After seeing the video, I believe it's the second. What if I told you that within thirty minutes of the video shot, Leh was hit by flash floods of a type and magnitude never seen before?'

The Leh flash floods. I still remembered them, a freak disaster that had wiped out most of the town. And if I had understood Pant right, it was man-made. *Man-made.* It was straight out of a comic book, or a plot from a science fiction novel. Impossible to believe.

As I sat struggling with it, Pant spoke into the receiver. 'Send Dr Das in.'

Hardly had he completed the sentence than the door burst open and a figure flew into the room with the force of a projectile. It proved to be a bald, dishevelled man of about sixty with a pencil moustache. He sat in the spare chair and slapped the thick stack of what appeared to be computer printouts on the desk.

Then, unexpectedly, he leaned across and shook our hands enthusiastically.

'Ah, you must be the math interns I ordered from TIFR. You both seem older than I expected, but that's all to the good. The calculations that I ordered have just come in from PARAM. Even the supercomputer took its time … the simulation algorithm has proved much more complex in terms of the variables we had to factor in, but I think we have found a possible energy source.'

Pant said softly, 'Are you saying we might know how they're doing it?'

Das nodded. 'I think so, but it still leaves open several possibilities.' He thrust the computer printouts at us. 'You've arrived not a moment too soon. These are the simulations that …'

Pant cleared his throat and said, 'Sorry to disappoint you, Doctor, the interns are on the way. Mr Chandrasekhar and Ms Meenakshi Pirzada here are my field agents. Chandra, Meenakshi, this is Professor … Dr Das, the head of the Indian Met and a leading global expert on weather prediction. He's the man who's making the vital calculations we need – to prove that the localized weather phenomena we've been experiencing are man-made.'

'Thanks to you, Mr Pant, thanks to you and your team. It's that really remarkable video grab of yours that forced us to rethink all our basic assumptions.' He slapped his forehead. 'My God! We were blind, blind as bats.'

I said, 'It's seems incredible … and so improbable. On this humungous scale. Surely we've got to be wrong on this one?'

It was as if I had switched on a light. The man's eyes sparkled with enthusiasm. He clearly wanted to respond, but instead he turned to Pant and said,

'May I speak freely?'

Pant nodded. 'Yes. They're Colonel Syed Ali Hassan's deputies in counter-intelligence.'

Before either of us could react, Das had launched into his exposition.

'First of all, weather weapons had been recognized as a distinct possibility when forty-eight countries signed off on ENMOD – the Environmental Modification Convention – formally the Convention on the Prohibition of Military or Any Other Hostile Use of Environmental Modification Techniques. ENMOD came into force in 1978. So it will interest you to know that the world has recognized the possibilities of this technology decades ago. In fact, cloud seeding, which you are familiar with, is a simple form of weather modification.

'It's the military uses of climate that are much less known, and ENMOD hasn't prevented research being carried out in the field. Have either of you heard of HAARP?'

If we had, it was usually Meenu. But she shook her head mutely.

'HAARP stands for High Frequency Active Auroral Research Programme. The first site for HAARP was set up by the US Military and the Defence Advanced Research Projects Agency in 1993 in Alaska, but has subsequently seen massive scale up in scope and also secrecy. Some other countries including Russia and China are also into HAARP work, which basically consists of beaming a high energy wave into the ionosphere – the outermost layer of the atmosphere which is to be found in the region of 100 to 300 kilometres above the earth.'

We listened closely. Like Meenu, the weather scientist was also a born teacher.

'You have to understand, that to us – the Met science community – HAARP type work has always sat on the fringes of the far more serious work of weather prediction and, of course, understanding climate change. Ostensibly, HAARP focuses on enhancing efficiency of radio-frequency communications which the ionosphere directly impacts. But over the years, it's spawned a whole community of conspiracy theorists, and persistent claims that the real motive behind HAARP type technology is military.'

Pant interrupted, 'That is localized weather change – in some ways the ultimate weapon – to be used against an enemy both in times of peace and war. It can disrupt enemy communications and electronic weaponry by electromagnetic waves through the higher atmosphere. Or cause acid rain, disease and death on an unimaginable scale.'

Dr Das got animated, hands stabbing as he made his points. 'But the technological challenges are so immense as to defy description. That's one reason why HAARP projects are generally government-backed. At this time the countries that are most into HAARP are the big three: the US, Russia and China.

'Global warming and weather shifts arising from phenomena like the El Nino have effects well beyond their immediate vicinity. For this reason, meteorology is more a global collaborative effort than ever before. All of us in the field know each other – a tight-knit community that shares data and information all the time.

'And that makes what we're experiencing well ahead of anything we believed possible in weather manipulation. The precipitation of rain with specific acid content, the sparking of hot winds … all with extremely precise geographical targeting … This is technology that is decades ahead of its time, developed by person or persons unknown working in isolation. None of my colleagues have guessed at it for the simple reason that they believe it is impossible.' The met scientist paused to wonder at the marvel of it. 'None of us. Unbelievable!'

Meenu said, 'If it's so hard to believe in the first place, what makes you suspect it is someone with a HAARP weapon? Couldn't there be some other cause?'

'By a painstaking process of elimination,' Das replied. He pointed to the printouts. 'When all the probable natural causes were eliminated by a series of calculations and simulations, we started to look at the outliers. Here, let me take you through some of the calc …'

The scientist again reached out for the papers, when Pant hurriedly interrupted.

'The most important of which was the steady accumulation of sightings on the ground of lightning bolts … literally arcs of fire … that were observed to be of unusually long duration. Exactly what a HAARP weapon would generate. Correct, Dr Das?'

Das nodded. 'Lightning strikes last for a few seconds at most. It was these ground reports of electric arcs that lasted a minute or more that piqued our interest. The one that triggered our new line of investigations was Mr Pant's mention of an intelligence report on an arc of unusual power and duration in the vicinity of Saltoro Kangri in the Karakoram Himalaya in August of 2010. It was followed immediately by unprecedented flash floods in Leh – a region that had not experienced such a phenomenon ever.'

Meenu said, 'HAARP electrical power beams operating across a distance of … ?'

'Saltoro Kangri sits around 150 kilometres northwest of Leh. Incredible, but no other explanation fits. When we started investigating with this new hypothesis in mind, small but odd perturbations which had escaped our attention earlier now acquired new significance. When we did the correlations, we discovered patterns that cannot be explained by chance alone.

'But we still need to pinpoint the power source. Given that the acid rain and other anomalies have been experienced across a wide land mass from the north to the south, we suspect mobile generators. Assuming even very advanced technology, a single HAARP event would need to be powered by at least a 3 MW mobile generator bank, or even higher.'

Meenu said to Pant, 'Were any special anomalies experienced in and around Bhutan?'

There was a dead silence. Pant's eyes grew even larger and owl-like behind the thick lenses, and both he and Dr Das had gone still.

Finally Pant said carefully, 'How the hell did you guess? The information is classified.'

Meenu didn't reply directly. Instead she asked Das, 'Doctor, if a HAARP weapon can impact weather at a distance of 150 kilometres, couldn't a much larger and more powerful one influence weather in, say, Indore or even Salem?'

Das' button-eyes flashed. He then blinked rapidly and said, 'We understand almost nothing of the technical issues, mind you, but given what we've seen, I have to say yes. Especially if it's in the approximate vicinity of the south buttress of the Himalaya. The great mountain range is a sort of a weather amplifier for the whole Indian subcontinent. What happens there impacts the entire Indo-Gangetic plain. But to take it as far south as Salem would require another station to boost the HAARP EM wave.'

Meenu and I started to say simultaneously, 'The Trans-Him …' Then I said loudly to drown her voice, 'Dr Das.'

Pant said quietly, 'Dr Das, from now on you are doubly bound by your oath of confidentiality. So far it's been mainly a scientific investigation, but now you are about to receive state secrets directly and if we find they have leaked from you the penalty is life imprisonment or death. Do you understand?'

The met expert blanched, sweat popping all over his face. He drew out his kerchief and mopped his face. He said weakly, 'Mr Pant, I'm a scientist. I understand little of intelligence work. If you prefer, I can wait outside till you …'

'On the contrary, Dr Das, you are required more than ever now. But nothing you hear should ever leave the room. Chandra, Meenu … what were you about to say?'

'The Trans-Himalaya Power Company. It's the company that employs Sarvabharat Transport,' I said.

Pant looked blankly at me.

'Has Hassan told you anything about our search for the missing boy?'

Pant shook his head. 'No. Not in any detail. I'm sure he didn't want to bother me with it. He did say that a big sophisticated organization was behind child trafficking, and that the two of you were pursuing some clues. So when he vanished, I assumed it had to do with that. Am I right?'

Meenu had the faraway look which said her brain was ticking away at full speed. To give her time, I quickly sketched out the events of the last few days to Pant – who listened with intense absorption.

Then he leaned back, speaking almost to himself. 'Let me summarize. Gopal's mobile pinpoints a truck belonging to a transporter who does work almost exclusively for a large power utility. Both companies have a shadowy ownership. Hassan discovers this how? By accessing our central intelligence databases remotely from his residence in your presence, at around seven forty-five this morning. We have it from his mother that he left home at around 8:30 a.m. as planned. And then he vanishes into thin air and it's the last we hear of him ...'

Pant opened his eyes suddenly and fixed us with a penetrating glare. 'Which means we have a mole tapping into our servers within national intelligence. No sooner does Hassan access our server, their spy reports it. Within an hour, our most experienced operative is kidnapped – or killed. Questions: Is it the trucking company or the power company that's connected to child trafficking? Or is their connection really with the HAARP weapon? I can think of no obvious link between the boy's disappearance and the climate change plot.'

I said, 'So it could be a pure coincidence? We just stumbled on to the trucker which led us to the power company?'

Pant said, 'Let's say that Sarvabharat is running a legit logistics business providing services to companies like Trans-Himalaya. But they also have a lucrative child trafficking operation on the side. Maybe the choice of a Bhutan customer is deliberate. Maybe they're using Bhutan to ship the children further north – to the flesh markets of Central Asia, maybe even the Middle East.

'But Trans-Himalaya itself is into a whole different ball game. I'm pretty sure China's behind it. They have the financial resources and the organizational muscle within Nepal and Bhutan to set up a HAARP weapon programme under cover. It's the perfect weapon to keep us severely weakened, perhaps permanently – without seriously destabilizing us and risking unpredictable consequences. The beauty of the strategy is that its workings can – and will – be camouflaged under the barrage of climate change. Knowing them, they will even trigger a few events on their own soil to deflect any possibility of suspicion. The Bhutanese are none the wiser. All they know is that this is a serious investment in their power infrastructure by the Chinese and the customer is their other giant neighbour – India. All in all, a neat little arrangement. The more I think about it, the more probable it all seems. So … I'm prepared to lay a pretty bet that the Trans-Himalaya Power Company is owned by our Chinese friends. It explains the ownership maze. But the child disappearances don't fit in. Logic says they've nothing to do with it.'

Pant paused a beat, reflecting. 'Yet … I don't think this is a coincidence, Chandra. I could be wrong, but somehow … somewhere … I think a link's there, though for the life of me I can't imagine what it could be.'

I felt excitement stirring within the sea of doubt and confusion that still claimed me. It all seemed so huge … a labyrinthine plot of such magnitude that my brain could only dimly grasp it. But if Pant sensed a connection, it was good enough for me. 'My God, Pant. Two separate strands weaving into a single enemy. What's to be done now?'

Pant slumped back in his chair. He removed his specs and rubbed the bridge of his nose tiredly.

Then he said in a flat tone, 'We can't take them on. At least, not frontally. This is an organization of almost limitless reach and power. And if they've gotten into our servers, I suspect other arms of the government have been penetrated.'

Meenu added, 'We can't be *that* impotent, Pant. Shouldn't we escalate it to the Cabinet? This is the greatest crisis the country has ever faced and coming from you they'll surely have to act?'

'With what? What proof do we have it's a HAARP weapon? And that they're behind it? The Cabinet will need some credible evidence at a minimum. Otherwise, the Chinese will simply deny it and sit back and wait it out. They'll doubtless point to other disasters within their own borders. We'll be laughed out of the room by the international community. Our politicians for sure won't take that risk. Whoever thought of this one deserves a Nobel Prize for Armageddon plotting. They'll bring us down to our knees without firing a single shot.'

We absorbed this in silence. My thoughts raced as the purport of his words hit home.

I said, 'Well, if the Indian government is ruled out on this one, we're left with only one choice.'

Pant looked at me sharply.

'Dharma Enterprises.'

13

HASSAN WAS DROWNING IN THE BITTERSWEET ACHE OF IT ALL. The Air Force pall bearers marched in rigid lock-step down the airstrip carrying between them the coffin that held the man he worshiped most in world: Air Commodore Nurul Ali Hassan. His mother's face was devoid of colour and she swayed just a little, all the while crushing his little hand in hers. The sobs of his three sisters tore at him even as one part of him perversely swelled with pride at the manner of his father's passing. The papers were full of it that morning: the definitive air engagement of the war, where the No. 18 Squadron's commander and ace pilot had taken down four of the enemy fighters before being shot down over the Kashmir skies one midnight in December 1971.

A fast-forward of the memory … the trauma of the burial; flashes of the medal ceremony at Rashtrapati Bhavan; the return to a routine of a life crushed by loss. The coalescing of resolve had happened in his teens and had been sudden, but total – that his would be a life dedicated to the memory of that sacrifice.

But now that tall, beloved figure was beside his bed, smiling down at him. He was saying something, but Hassan couldn't hear the words. He tried to bring his arms up, to reach out, to hold his father fast and never let him go. But his arms were pinned down and a rock was upon his chest, crushing him, making it hard to breathe. He writhed and twisted. The figure beside his bed was beginning to dissolve, and in its place, there was a white, intense burst of pain.

'Abba … Abba … !'

He awoke suddenly. His skull was on fire as if stuffed with hot coals, and through the agony, he felt a powerful taste of sour onion in his mouth. And it was this last that brought him to his senses. Sodium Pentothal or a variant. A powerful knock-out drug designed to induce an almost comatose loss of consciousness. He was familiar with it from the pharmacological course mandated for all field operatives as the most commonly used of the truth serums.

He reached deep within himself, seeking to re-establish control, starting with the breath. Gradually, he turned his awareness to his surroundings. It was black, dense as pitch. He could see nothing, feel nothing except that he was lying on something hard and that it was numbingly cold. A faint smell of antiseptic hung in the air. It was nothing he could put his finger on, but he somehow felt he was not alone. It was deathly quiet, yet there seemed to be furtive movement all around.

He tried to turn and instantly came up against restraints. Both his hands and feet were strapped to whatever he was lying on. A hospital gurney? Even the small movement set off waves of nausea and, despite the chill air, he broke out in a sweat. Knowing it to be the after-effects of the drug, he waited till his pulse slowed, then deliberately set out trying to reconstruct his last memories. His assailants had clubbed him down and beaten him savagely. His last memory was a savage punch to the kidney which had knocked him out. His body should normally have been screaming in pain, but one of the side effects of the pentothal was that it dulled certain pain receptors even as it stimulated others.

Whoever they were, they were good – bloody fucking good. Either the timing of the hit was a coincidence or they'd set it up within an hour of his querying them on the server. Either way, this was an organization with capabilities far beyond a child-trafficking gang. That he wasn't killed but sedated and transported meant interrogation; his captors clearly intended to extract information. Hassan's in-built sixth sense for danger told him that what was coming would test him to the limit of his physical and mental strength. He started to systematically test his bonds when suddenly the lights came on.

He let it flood his closed lids and opened then slowly, letting his pupils adjust. The first sight that met his eyes triggered his pulse and again sent a wave of nausea rippling through is gut. Hanging above him was a giant man-sized creature. Two glass eyes the size of cricket balls stared down at him from a rounded head, and from its box-frame of a body several arms sprang out like those of a malign deity. Each ended in three metallic digits like fingers, but sharp, talon-like. It was a sort of robot, suspended by cables from the ceiling, but horribly life-like and menacing. Something stirred in its eyes, and he saw it was himself reflected, strapped down and helpless.

He was in the centre of the cubicle, laid out upon a hospital stretcher-type bed. Though it felt like broad daylight, the space was completely enclosed, a cubicle perhaps 10 square feet, illuminated by concealed LEDs that closely simulated natural light. Most of the floor space was taken by medical equipment. Some he could recognize: ECG monitors, a dialysis machine, anaesthesia dispensers and metering pumps, and an array of neatly laid out surgical instruments. Others he could make nothing of – complex instrumentation all connected to a large computer screen on which bunches of numbers – line after line – were scrolling down in a continuous stream. To his left, the entire wall was taken up by a bank of multi-coloured vessels with tubes snaking out in every direction into plastic bags that were clearly for intravenous feeds.

The door opened and two men entered to stand on either side of the bed. Both wore white lab coats but there the resemblance ended. The figure to his left was a tall, white-haired, distinguished-looking man in his late fifties. Whereas, the one opposite was of middle height, with protuberant teeth, skin splotched with white patches of leukoderma. His eyes were filled with malice. It was he who spoke first.

'Well, well. Who have we here but the Indian government's master snooper Mr Hassan. Poking his nose, as usual, in dangerous places. But this time there will be no escape, my friend.'

Hassan kept his face neutral with an effort. *Shukla!* One of the few who'd escaped the dragnet after the Shadow Throne conspiracy. The man was wholly evil. He switched to the other, who was regarding him impassively.

The tall man said, 'Colonel, your reputation precedes you. We do not make the mistake of underestimating enemies. You will give us the information we want one way or another – or you will die extremely painfully. On this very bed you're lying on. What's it to be?'

Hassan swallowed, trying to work some saliva into his dry mouth. The men waited without saying anything.

His voice finally came out in a weak whisper. 'Where am I? Who are you?'

His captor smiled mirthlessly. 'You are outside India, far from any aid. Your government cannot help you even if they knew your whereabouts. As to who we are … You tell us what we wish to know and we will do the same. A fair trade of information. Saves you a lot of blood and pain and saves us time.'

'What do you want to know?'

'How did you come upon Sarvabharat and Trans-Himalaya? How much does Indian intelligence, especially Nalini Ranjan Pant, know about the two companies? How involved are your friends Chandrasekhar and Pirzada in your investigations? These are the simple ones – but they will do for a start.'

Hassan had been gathering his strength for the last several minutes as the drug was starting to slowly wear off. But when he answered he kept his voice deliberately weak and his expression fearful.

'Look, sir. You have enough reach into our servers to know we have very little on you or your companies. What tipped us off was something we found on a man you'd killed: a beggar called Pagal bhai. He had a piece of paper with a vehicle number scribbled on it. We traced it to Sarvabharat and the database showed a connection to Trans-Himalaya. That's it. Chandra and Meenakshi know nothing. They're still clueless about the boy who's missing from their school. Where have you taken him? Is he alive?'

Shukla chuckled, his buckteeth glistening yellow in the light. 'Aapne kamaal kar diya, Hassan ji. The answers are rolling off your tongue. Very different from when we actually tortured you last time we met. Aap patthar jaise the. Like a stone.'

The tall man nodded thoughtfully. 'Shukla's told us about your high tolerance for pain. But we're specialists, Colonel. We can take pain to levels you've never even dreamt of. Your answers are pat … very quick. A little stimulation is in order, though we've been asked to keep you intact till your friends join you.'

He stepped back. That was when Hassan saw that he held a remote in his hand. There was a small beep and a red light started to flash at the centre of the robot's bulbous eyes like a live bindi. Its two frontal arms started to move with a faint whine. They dropped down over Hassan's face, the fingers spreading and clamping down on either side of his head immobilizing it completely. Hassan's mouth opened in a silent scream. His body bucked, struggling crazily against the straps. The pressure on his temples instantly intensified, till it felt like his skull was being crushed, destroying his strength. He moaned out aloud in agony.

'Few terrors are greater than loss of sight, Colonel. Our mechanical friend here will do it layer by layer and literally peel away your eyeballs.'

Shukla laughed loudly. 'Woh video bhi lega … We will film you and enjoy your screams again and again.'

Two of its side arms extended forward, the wrist joints flexed down ninety degrees and the talons came together to form a single sharp drill that pointed directly at his eyes. Then they started to descend, stopping just an inch from his face.

The tall man said, 'I'll leave you to think about it. The next time I come back, it'll be to take your eyes – unless you tell me exactly what I wish to know.'

*

Delhi. 30th May. 3 p.m.

And so it was that our campaign to save the country from a terrible fate began yet again. By the strangest quirk of fate it was our search for a poor orphaned boy that pointed us towards the dark core of an even greater evil, and I took it to be a sign of the perverse luck that we desperately needed, for it brought into the equation the formidable and subtle intellect of Nalini Ranjan Pant.

Pant had decided that it was too risky to bring in the government frontally, even if it was possible, given that we were working on the basis of pure speculation. But that did not mean he was helpless. The JIC head had considerable power, but would have to exercise it with care so as to keep their plans hidden from the all-seeing gaze of the enemy. He himself would stay on in HQ to swing to our assistance the state apparatus within his control; for he had no doubt this would be needed before long.

So it would be the three of us – Dr Das, Meenu and I – who would form the covert team against the enemy.

It was with some difficulty that Pant managed to explain the mission to the bewildered Das, stressing that his task would be the most important one: to dismantle or cripple the HAARP field if we ever managed to get close to it – a forest of directional antenna towers surrounding the power station that would be needed to focus the power to a specific point in the ionosphere.

I had to acknowledge that apart from his technical skills, Dr Das lived in his own world and a more unlikely secret agent there never was; while Meenu and I were strictly amateurs. Without Hassan to lead us, it was a near hopeless mission, as even Pant acknowledged – unless we managed to rope in Harshvardhan Dharma.

This time I was not alone in my quest. Meenu was with me, and that should have brought comfort, even with the desperately high stakes at play. During the course of the day, I had tried to ask myself what Hassan would do in our place. One thing was sure: he would have been utterly focused on the task at hand, on thwarting the enemy to the exclusion of all else. I should have been doing the same. Instead, I was a seething cauldron of emotions on the verge of bubbling out of control. Fear of the unknown that we were heading for, and a profound fear for my friend's fate were part of it; but so too were guilt and anticipation filled with wild imaginings. I was already like a moth circling a flame.

*

Delhi. 30th May. 8 p.m.

In a city where to have it was to flaunt it, Dharma continued to surprise. He lived in Vasant Vihar, but in a modest-sized, single-floored dwelling. The only concession, it appeared, to his wealth was that it was at the dead-end of a cul-de-sac and the plots around it were empty, so that it stood by itself surrounded by a sea of leafy green. The gate was fastened by a simple latch and when we let ourselves in and rang the bell, it was Dharma himself who answered the door.

'Hello Chandra, Meenakshi. Glad you could make it.' He stood aside and waved us in. The small foyer led into the drawing room. Dharma seated us and said, 'I'm sorry but we don't serve alcohol, but I can give you coconut water with ginger and pomelo; that's pretty special.'

We both murmured a 'yes' and Dharma retreated inside. *Where was she?* I was wound up tight as a drum. I looked around, vaguely registering that the room had very little on show. The furniture was leather strapped on wood, and looked well-used. A few artefacts placed here and there, some scattered pictures on the walls: Gandhi in a reflective mood, an arresting pencil sketch of Ramakrishna Paramahamsa and a photograph of a tribal woman. The place had a lived-in air where comfort obviously took precedence over looks – the sort of place I would normally have felt immediately at home; but as it was, I sat in a fever of anticipation.

Dharma came back with a tray carrying three tall glasses. 'We give the servants off on Wednesdays; allows Vaish and me to indulge ourselves in the kitchen,' said he by way of explanation. The coconut water had a pinkish tinge from the pomelo and proved to be delicious. Dharma sat opposite us in silence, smiling. He seemed to be in no hurry to make conversation, and here in the privacy of his home, his presence filled the room with a kind of radiance that enfolded us anew.

It was Meenu who broke the thrall.

'Mr Dharma ...'

'Harsh, please.'

'Harsh. I wish this could be just a social visit, but it's not now. We need to speak with you about something vitally important. You're going to find it hard to believe, but you're our last hope.'

Dharma's expression changed. He sat up straighter, a hint of wariness in his manner, and waited.

Meenu glanced at me, and I nodded. With her natural narrative style it was better she laid it out to him. And so it was that for the next hour Meenu and I sat with one of the most powerful men in the country and explained how our search for one missing boy had led us to a plot on a scale that boggled the imagination. Through it all, Dharma continued to say nothing, but I got the sense he was absorbing everything, processing and filing the information away as Meenu spoke. He was mostly impassive, but I could sense his growing astonishment – and incredulity. Now and then his eyes flicked from my face to hers, as if he was trying to make up his mind about us. I didn't blame him. If two strangers I'd just met were to give me this same story, I would have laughed them out of the room. Hearing Meenu now, even I, who had been a part of it from the very beginning, found myself wondering if we could be totally wrong about this thing – if there wasn't some other perfectly rational explanation.

Meenu's antennae must have been even more tuned than mine to Dharma's reaction, for she said quickly, 'I'm not asking you to believe us or take us at face value. All we're asking is that you meet Nalini Ranjan Pant at Joint Intel. Committee and Dr Das of the Indian Met. You can then make your decision on the reality – or not – of the threat.'

It was exactly the right thing to say. Despite himself, I could see Dharma hesitate. 'I don't know this Dr Das ... but Pant is another matter altogether. The man behind the unmasking of the Shadow Throne …'

The Shadow Throne conspiracy was highly classified, with less than two dozen people in the country being aware of it – all high up in the corridors of power. That Dharma knew of Pant and his role in that chain of events spoke volumes of his reach within the government. His voice trailed off, and then he said, 'But really, Meenakshi, all this stuff is so … weird. Even if I thought it possible, the science itself is so ahead of its time that I can't believe the Chinese could have broken through on a HAARP weapon before the Americans.'

But Dharma's mien was changing. The affable persona now acquiring new form and character, like a blade being drawn from its scabbard. But before he could say more, the air was suddenly touched with the musk of sandalwood, tripping my pulse into overdrive. And then she was in the room.

Vaishali dropped into the couch opposite us and drew up her legs. The muted light played on her sari of maroon silk. She had pulled her hair to one side, letting it fall in a thick lustrous mass over her left shoulder. *Yamini, my wife.* Smiling at me from across the room. I knew I was staring at her, but I could do nothing about it. My mouth was dry and I was trembling inside … To my horror, I was losing control, a dam ready to burst.

'Chandra … Chandra,' Dharma's faint and insistent voice finally penetrated. With difficulty I turned to him.

'Can I tell Vaish? There are no secrets between us and I can assure you of her discretion. Besides, I'm going to need her if we are to take on this threat.'

I nodded weakly. He turned to Meenu. 'Meenakshi, do I have your okay on this?'

Meenu said, 'I take it that means …'

'I'm going to reserve judgement till I get to see the JIC Chairman. And this Dr Das.'

Meenu pulled out her mobile. 'Pant knows we're meeting with you and is waiting for our call. We have no evidence to back up what we have just told you, and the government's network is compromised. He thinks that taking matters to the Cabinet will not help us either. Matters are coming to a head, and we're looking to you to take the lead.'

Dharma nodded. 'Make your call. Ask if I can meet him first thing tomorrow. We'll have to set up a safe house for the contact; the fewer people know that I'm involved the better.'

Meenu punched the keys on her cell and was soon into an extended conversation with Pant. Dharma had turned to his sister and was talking to her in a low voice. Like he had done, she too listened without comment, glancing every now and then at me, as if trying to read something there. I tried to look away, but her eyes were dark pools that drew me like a magnet, drowning out any shame or embarrassment I might normally have felt on staring at a woman. *My wife, come to life again.*

Meenu hung up and waited for Dharma to finish with Vaishali. She kept her face averted from me, resolutely ignoring what was patently apparent, determined to stay with the matter at hand.

'He'll see you tomorrow as early as you wish. This is his number. He'd greatly appreciate a call from you tonight.'

She held the phone out to him and Dharma stored the number into his cell. Then he snapped the cover shut.

Vaishali said in a low voice, 'It seems so incredible ... someone acquiring such power over nature. Like a Frankenstein magnified a hundred times.' She shuddered, looked out of the drawing-room window into her garden.

'Magnified a thousand … a million times, if it's even half-true, that is.' Dharma said softly. 'I'll call Pant after dinner. I suggest we park this matter till then and enjoy our evening – or what's left of it anyway.'

Vaishali rose to her feet in a graceful movement. 'I'll go see to dinner.'

They served us themselves; Vaishali tossing the chapattis on the tava and then onto our plates, while Dharma heated up the rest of the food. They set the dishes on the kitchen counter and we helped ourselves. The meal was simple vegetarian fare – delicious, served on old-fashioned ever-silver plates that were the staple of our childhood. We all ate with our hands.

As the evening wore on, I could see why, despite his reclusive tendencies, he seemed to evoke such universal admiration. Some of it was surely his enormous wealth, his business empire and the way he'd placed it in service to the nation; but I could also see that some of this love and respect came from a persona that was arrestingly magnetic. To see him and be with him even briefly was to fall under his spell.

Not once did he even indirectly refer to himself. Instead, he seemed eager to learn and talk about my views as gleaned from my writings and despatches. Dharma had read enough of them that he was well aware of my left-of-centre leanings and anti-corporate views. This seemed to not disturb him in the least. Instead, he debated them with me vigorously with wit and charm. He seemed serious and interested in what I had to say, and so our dinner conversation flowed easily. Even Meenu who'd been stiff and wound up was starting to relax. Through it all, there were two of me, the one making a conversation on the surface, while on the inside, another part of me stayed intensely aware of the woman on the other side of the table.

Dinner ended and we helped clear away the food. On entering the living room again, Meenu commented on the photograph of the old tribal woman.

Vaishali smiled and said, 'That's the Baiga lady who brought up Harsh and me.'

Dharma was quiet for a beat, then said, 'My father was a civil servant in Madhya Pradesh where I was born. She was our ayah, but when our mother died at Vaish's birth, it was she who brought us up. I think my inner life comes in large measure from her.' He looked at me to see if I'd understood.

I nodded. I had read a bit about the Baiga. They were the most shamanist of the Indian tribes, possessed by an imaginary spirit world as real as the physical one they inhabited.

Dharma said to Meenu, 'The Baiga have changed beyond all recognition, but I began to collect their artefacts early – as soon as I understood their importance. If you enjoy folk history, you might be interested to see my collection.'

Meenu nodded and replied a shade reluctantly, 'I would love to see them.'

'Great. Please come with me.' Dharma stood up and led the way inside, leaving me and Vaishali alone. My pulse throbbed. Did Dharma do that on purpose? He must have noticed my reaction to her; on the other hand, there was nothing manipulative about him, of that I was convinced. My thoughts where still whirling inside when she said, 'Coffee, Chandra?'

I nodded, barely aware of myself, intoxicated by the nearness of her presence. She reached for the tray on the table and the action loosened the sari so that I could see the swell of her breasts clearly beneath the silk blouse. All the while she talked softly, yet animatedly. I understood nothing of what she said, the words floated by like ghosts in a dream. I knew only that light was suddenly dimmer, and that among the rounded shadows of the room my wife was with me again.

Suddenly, to my horror, my eyes filled and before I could control it, tears began to roll down my cheeks. She lifted her gaze and her dark, kohl-rimmed eyes pierced me like a lance. She put down the tray and moved around the table. She took my face in both her hands and regarded me gravely. Her fingers brushed my cheeks, wiping away the tears. Then she kissed me.

I wrapped my arms around her and crushed her lips to mine, drinking deeply of her, intoxicated with a wild happiness. We remained like that for an eternity. Then I broke contact and looked at her hungrily; tightened my grip around her once more, gluing her to me, scarcely able to believe what was happening. Meenu's depiction of Vaishali rose up in my mind; nothing else seemed to make sense.

Vaishali suddenly twisted out of my embrace and turned away. She wrapped her hands around herself, swaying on her feet. She remained like that for a while as if struggling with something. Then, she said huskily, 'Chandra, let's not get into something we'll both regret. I've never done this before … thrown myself at a man I've barely met.'

I had to know. I said in a low voice, 'Then … why me?'

She looked at me and I saw that her eyes were mirrors of my own, suffused with passion and fear. 'It started with your wife's death.' Seeing my astonishment, she went on quickly, 'It was reported in the papers, with a photograph of the two of you. Harsh showed it to me. We were both shocked by how much I resembled her.

'I was already reading whatever I could find of your work. I can't explain it, but I was already attracted. Seeing your wife's picture was some sort of a tipping point. I know … that was over two years ago. But you vanished soon after and when you reappeared there was someone else in your life.'

Imperceptibly her face hardened, a woman making a decision. 'Chandra, I won't come between you and Meenakshi.'

I half-rose from my chair, to get around to her, but she was already moving to the kitchen. With shocking suddenness, her face became bland. She turned to me and smiled, then said pleasantly, 'Coffee, Chandra?'

I felt a spike of pure panic. *Why was she … ?* I started to follow her when Dharma and Meenu walked into the room.

I kept my face down, not daring to look up. She had obviously heard them coming. Not a moment too soon. Had we been seen? Meenu's face was carefully neutral, and for once I could make out nothing. Dharma spoke just enough to say that Pant himself had called and fixed to meet him the next day at 8 a.m. We sipped our coffee in silence. A sombre mood had settled over us, preventing any small talk.

'Pant says there have been some new developments and that we don't have a moment to lose. I'm going to start making some discreet enquiries through my networks. I have a long night ahead and so if you'll excuse me, I'll get to it right away. Vaish, don't wait up for me. Chandra, Meenu, please stay as long as you like. Thank you for a stimulating evening and I'm sure we will all meet again soon enough.'

At that, Meenu and I stood up quickly and made our excuses. It was late and time we got home too. We shook hands and as I took Vaishali's in mine, our eyes locked and I had a fleeting glimpse of something hot and primal lurking in their depths.

I barely registered the trip home. I had inhaled deep and was in the throes of a drug-high. Never in my wildest dreams had I imagined that the night would turn out this way. Yamini's and mine had been an extended courtship; my chronic shyness and her absolute need to make sure I was right for her had seen to that. Tonight was anything but that. Vaishali and I had thrown ourselves at each other like charged magnets brought within touching distance. My obsession was easily explained, but what of her? Could what she said be true – that she was drawn to me by my work, and the picture of my dead wife? What could have possessed her that she should return a stranger's passion with equal desire? For all her wealth and stunning beauty, could it be that she too was lonely, and my tears a trigger for a deep and repressed need for love's expression, or was Meenu right – that she just a wanton woman who took on and discarded lovers with equal ease?

But these were questions that floated up unbidden from a deep subconscious, only to be instantly swept away as wisps of smoke in raging wind. I was like the doomed lover in one of Zauq's poems who knows only that he feels he is drowning in hot honey, and his ecstasy is shot through with a burning grief. One look at the woman next to me was enough to tear at my soul. She sat silent at the wheel, leaning away from me, face stark in the flitting street lights. Comfort and joy in each other's presence was gone; we were suddenly strangers, spiralling helplessly into a void where oblivion awaited us as surely as day follows night.

14

5th June. 2:30 p.m.

ACCORDING TO THE BROCHURE STUCK IN THE SEAT POUCH, THE Dassault Falcon 8X sits at the ultra-luxury end of the long-range executive jet market. The jet's noise at full thrust must have been deafening outside, but here in the cabin it was all a velvety quietness, a world of plush leather seats that folded back into beds, personal TVs and a well-stocked bar panelled in genuine walnut.

From 35,000 feet up in the sky, at the extreme rim of the horizon, where the azure blue sky met the curvature of the earth, I could see a series of sharp, silver teeth glistening in the rays of the westerly sun. The great Himalaya was where we were headed now in a race against time to save the country, and if we could in the process, save a child – and Hassan. Despite the grandeur of the scenery, I felt full of foreboding, weighed down by a sense that we were too late. Everything I had seen at Kala Mill told me that Gopal was dead or trapped in a fate worse than death. Probably so was Hassan. We were up against an elemental force that dealt in mass death and extermination. On that scale, individuals, counting for less than nothing, had no chance at all. Not even when faced with the destructive threat of the Shadow Throne conspiracy did I feel as miniscule and impotent as I did now. But even if we were too late to save our friends, perhaps we could yet find and expose the enemy. And in that mission, I had a sliver of hope – one that grew by the minute – Harshvardhan Dharma.

Nalini Pant and he had first met last week, and it became obvious as the meeting progressed that the two men had each taken the measure of the other, and each had come away impressed. It could not have been otherwise. Both were supremely competent professionals; Pant with his subtle, devious mind and an uncanny sixth sense; and Dharma the man of action with limitless resources. I thought back to that the all-important briefing in an anonymous hotel room – well away from JIC headquarters.

'Your main point of destination is an antenna field,' Pant had said, pointing to what resembled an enormous wind farm on the satellite map. 'It's the nucleus of any HAARP Ultra Low Frequency (ULF) generating station and powers the EMF low frequency waves into the ionosphere. The field is set upon a plateau overlooking the valley, about 140 kilometres north-east of Thimphu. Dr Das?'

The meteorologist nodded nervously. He had the air of a man about to take a bungee dive: terrified and excited at the same time. He said, 'If, as we suspect, the Leh flash floods were triggered by this station, they must have something hugely powerful up there, and the sheer size of this field matches up.'

Dharma said, 'Understood. How will we actually take down the field?'

'Antenna fields are only the receiving and redirection components of a HAARP station. We have to destroy the generator – or at least some component of the generating station, like the step-up transformers,' Das replied.

Pant said, 'With explosives. I will have two commandos accompany you, Mr Dharma. They're trained saboteurs and will be fully equipped for the task at hand.'

I said, 'Is the installation guarded?'

Pant nodded. 'I had one of our local "eyes" in Bhutan pass by the valley dressed as a local herder. Armed security guards everywhere and there's an electrified fence around the whole valley. Another indication that Dr Das is correct about this being not just a regular power station. Inserting you into the facility is going to be a challenge as we have very little to go on. Given the sensitivities with the Bhutanese and Chinese, you'll have to be on your own. The one option we have is to have you visit the station in some official capacity but without arousing suspicion.'

'I think we can do one better,' Dharma said. 'In the last two days, I've had my corporate guys do a careful and very discreet probe into Trans-Himalaya. Turns out that their marketing team sits in Delhi, which makes sense if their aim is to sell power in the Indian market. The company has been aggressively pushing for business: they've been talking to all major buyers in the power market, including my energy distribution subsidiary. The Chinese have planned it brilliantly; the company is operating under a completely legit cover.'

Pant nodded. 'For all intents and purposes, it *is* a power company. I'm sure the real agenda is hidden from all but a few at the apex of the organization. Are you saying you can use this to make an official visit?'

'Yes. If you agree, we can arrange it so that my technical team makes a first recce on the pretext of a power station audit. One of my engineers can be tasked with getting a general layout of the place. I can have them put out to the Trans-Himalaya guys that I intend to visit Bhutan on a holiday and would like to use the chance to visit them myself.'

'Isn't that a bit over the top … ? I mean the Chairman of Dharma visiting just for a power purchase deal,' Meenu asked.

Dharma smiled. 'We are one of the largest private power distributors in the country, Meenakshi. And should they check, they'll find that I keep a home in Bhutan and am there on holiday once or twice each year. This year too we'll announce I am there for a break with my friends. A business visit mixed with pleasure won't be hard to explain.'

'I like it,' Pant said simply. 'It provides a plausible cover for all of you. The commandos can be your personal bodyguard detail. We'll conceal the explosives in either of them.'

Dr Das said earnestly, 'Mr Pant, this technology is simply unique … way beyond anything the world has ever seen. The potential for advancing the science is unlimited. Before we blow up the station we *must* lay our hands on it. Most of the circuit and control data, the algorithms and the transducers that feed the signals to the instrumentation and control equipment will be in the central control room. We should try not to damage it beyond repair.'

Pant said carefully, 'Point taken, Dr Das. I have been giving the very same matter some thought. This is a good time to define your mission. It has three objectives. The first priority is to destroy the HAARP station or at least disable it seriously enough that it buys us time to take permanent counter measures. The second is to secure the technology. If, as you say, this mainly resides in the computers at the station, they will have to be seized and taken out if possible. The third is to rescue Colonel Hassan – if he's there at all. But, though it pains me to say this, the first objective overrides the others. The fate of the nation is at stake.'

Dharma said, 'What's the timeline on this, Mr Pant? How quickly do you want us to move?'

'No later than one week from now. Will you be ready?'

Dharma nodded. 'I'll send my advance technical team in for the "commercial" negotiations and a recon. We'll follow into Thimphu as soon as they clear my visit. I presume Chandra, Meenakshi and Dr Das all remain their true selves?'

'Chandra and Meenu, yes,' Pant replied. 'The Chinese may run a check and it may actually help our case if we declare them to be who they are. But I think it's better if we change Dr Das's appearance and identity. Your regular mobiles won't work since much of Bhutan is in the grip of an electro-magnetic disturbance. Mr Dharma, I'm sure your private networks can try and get around this. I'll be available on my secure cell 24x7. One other matter so that there is no misunderstanding. I can provide you no further backup. The Indian government disowns all knowledge of you or your presence in Bhutan. If you are captured or exposed in any way there is nothing we can do. Best of luck.'

*

Now, as the Dassault sped east, eating up the 1,200 kilometres that separated Delhi from Bhutan's tiny airfield at Paro near the national capital, I looked across the aisle where Dharma crouched over the table with Dr Das. They were poring over the INSAT 4 defence satellite maps of Bhutan provided by Pant, talking to each other in low voices. My mind went back to the debriefing with Pant. Gopal and the missing kids had not featured even peripherally in the conversation. They were now a sideshow in the scheme of things. Even Hassan was a distinct third priority. I wondered at the cold-blooded streak that must characterize the mind of a spymaster. Hassan had that same ruthlessness. I had to admit to myself that both men applied that quality as much to themselves. Especially Hassan. Again and again, I'd seen him undaunted, ready to abandon himself if it meant the destruction of the enemy. It seemed we had now well and truly abandoned him along with the children. Or had we? Was there even any connection between them and Trans-Himalaya? Would we even see them there? We had no means of guessing in advance, but I felt that if we found Hassan, I could not – would not – leave him to his fate. But if I had to choose between him and the mission? The prospect was just too terrible to contemplate.

Sombre as these thoughts were, my eyes slid to the forward seat where Vaishali napped and once again I felt the thrill shoot through me like an electric bolt. Just as a delicious dream lingers on in our emotions well after the night itself has passed, my lips still tingled with the soft crush of hers and her musk surrounded me, heady and wild. I thought back to her last words to me, words which pierced like barbs and instantly I was seized by an awful fear. If Meenu stood between us, what would be my choice?

She dozed restlessly in the seat next to mine. Meenu had been Yamini's closest friend. She of all people would know, would understand. Vaishali held me in thrall because she was my wife, miraculously restored to me. Had she been the most beautiful woman in the world, she could not have touched me if she did not carry so much of Yamini with her.

But that was logic. It would do nothing to still her inner demons. Her face was drawn and thin. Lines had begun to appear on her forehead and at the corners of her mouth – lines that were not there just a few weeks ago. I longed to reach out and hold her, but it would have an empty gesture. She needed an act of renunciation that I was helpless to give.

*

The Dassault touched down at Paro, Bhutan's tiny airport to the west of the capital, Thimphu, at four o' clock in the afternoon. Appropriately for this tiny country – which was dealing with a changing world in its own deliberate and reflective way – there were two oldish Toyota SUVs waiting for us on the tarmac, and, with them, a small crowd to receive us at the foot of the disembarking stairs. Most appeared to be from the Dharma organization, but two were Bhutanese immigration officers in uniform. Our passports were taken, stamped and handed back to us within minutes. The Dharmas got into one vehicle with a couple of their staff and Meenu and I into the other. The bags were loaded up with quiet efficiency and soon we were on our way.

Dharma's home in the hills was some distance east of the capital Thimphu – and we had a drive of about two hours left. Meenu and I looked out through the window with interest at this country we had never visited but had heard so much about. The road was in decent condition, and led us through verdant, thickly forested mountain slopes. There was a chill, and a pine laden scent in the air. We passed yak herders and peasant women in traditional Bhutanese dress with cane baskets strapped to their foreheads. Away to the far right, a gompa perched precariously on the hillside. The monastery's ochre walls and red roofs were touched by the gold of the setting sun. It was all perfect, as close to the Bhutan I had built up in my mind; the quaint, tiny country that was famous for keeping its 'gross national happiness' at the centre of state policy.

Yet, it was not all a picture postcard. Bhutan had expelled a large number of Nepali settlers from its southern borders as 'non-Bhutanese' though they had lived in this country for many years. The result was insurgency in parts and as recently as a few years ago the country had experienced some bomb blasts. There was also a simmering dispute with China to the north on the border.

I pointed the monastery out to Meenu. 'We must do some of the gompas together if we ever bring this thing to a successful end.' She whipped her head around and looked at me strangely, but I was too busy taking in the countryside to pay attention.

Dharma's home turned out to be an old dzong or medieval fort, built in the early eighteenth century by a local warlord. Massive walls ringed a large courtyard, in the middle of which was a mansion. Irregular shaped lawns of neatly trimmed grass and local rhododendron in a riot of colour interspersed the dressed stone of the courtyard, and enormous fir trees – rather like the minarets of the Taj – in each of the four corners. The dzong had been beautifully restored, the eye for detail everywhere apparent, clearly every bit of it was faithful to the original. We were at the bottom of a meadowed valley surrounded by steep hillsides covered with spruce, pine and fir trees. A small distance away I could see a swiftly flowing stream, the blue of the water flecked with white where it splashed and bubbled over the rocks.

Dharma waited for us on the steps. Seeing us take it all in, he said, 'My one indulgence, thanks to Vaish. I still haven't got used to it. When we first stumbled on this valley, the building had fallen apart from an earthquake and we decided to restore it. But now that it's done, we've fallen in love with it. Let's get settled in and meet over dinner. There's a quite bit we have to go over.'

I took a deep breath of the air redolent with pine. The sheer beauty of this paradise lightened for a moment the grim nature of our quest, and acted like a balm on the turmoil inside me.

The interior plan was much as I had expected; a large open atrium surrounded by a corridor from which individual rooms could be accessed. Our luggage was being carried in by one of the many servants and we followed him to a spacious bedroom with a four-poster bed. It was a little after six o' clock now, but there was enough residual summer light for me to appreciate the stunning panorama: an expanse of garden merging into a meadow ringed by hills.

My eyes travelled up the slopes, where I saw that the sea of green was abruptly broken by a grey patch more than halfway up the mountain. It looked to be a high stone wall, but in this muted evening light, it was hard to make out much more. Small black dots buzzed in a tight circle over it like a swarm of bees.

Meenu had followed me in. She took the room in with a sweeping glance, walked up to the bed and sat down. I waited for the servant to withdraw, then sat down beside her and looped my arm over her shoulders. She didn't respond, but neither did she move away. We sat like that for a long time in silence. Then she disengaged herself gently, stood up and turned to face me.

'What now, Chandra?' she said simply.

It was a question that was hammering at my brain too, driving me to distraction. 'I don't know,' I said. 'I love you, Meenu. Nothing has, or can, change that. But seeing her … back … like this … I'm not able to control my …'

Meenu leaned in and kissed me. 'Then don't,' she said.

'What?'

'Don't. You're the most faithful man I know, the man I love, the man who makes me completely secure. But this time you are up against your own fidelity – the love for your wife. You're smitten by Yamini, not Vaishali. That makes it very hard to fight.'

I couldn't believe what I was hearing. 'You're saying I should …'

'Yes,' Meenu nodded. 'If you resist Vaishali, it will tear you apart. I can't bear that – to see you in this pain. But promise me this: that you will stay focused till all this is over. You know the stakes; Dharma may not be able to overcome the enemy alone and he will need all the help he can get. We can give that to him only if we remain undistracted. Can you promise me that?'

I stood up and took a step back. Relief, shame and confusion swept through me in equal measure – the bewilderment of a child that has just been given a forbidden gift by a parent. There was no trace of resentment on Meenu's face; even the earlier sorrow and resignation were gone, replaced instead by a serenity that was even more disconcerting. Was I losing her? I felt a stab of cold fear; the terror of a rat that senses doom, but still cannot leave the trap alone. I struggled to make sense of my feelings, but before I could say more, a servant knocked on the door to announce that we were wanted in the living room.

Meenu said again, 'Will you promise me that, Chandra?'

I nodded, not trusting my voice.

The main room of the residence was a cool, airy hall. Traditional Bhutanese wooden chairs were arranged in a semicircle on the thick carpet. Dharma and Das waited for us there, a large map spread out on the table at the centre. A side table was filled with plates and dishes with food. Of Vaishali there was no sign.

Dharma said, 'This is a working dinner, so please help yourselves and then let's get started.' He waited till we had served ourselves and moved back to the centre table.

'The commandos from the army's Special Operations Group are landing tomorrow by a separate military plane and will join us presently. My staff have sent word to the power plant that I will visit accompanied by my friends, all of us being on holiday. Dr Das is being given a separate identity as my personal secretary and we're also slightly changing his appearance. The two SOG men will be passed off as my bodyguards. A couple of senior guys from my power company will be with us. As far as they're concerned it is in fact a quasi-business visit, and so they're sure to ask the right questions in the most natural manner. Whoever is behind this will be watching our visit very closely and I don't want to take the slightest chance. It will really be what it's purported to be – a commercial "feel out the supplier" visit.'

'When are we going?' I asked.

'The day after. The facility is a short distance north of here. We'll chopper in.'

'What's the plan, Harsh?' Meenu said.

'The plan is to aim for two targets. The first for sabotage and second for seizure. Dr Das?'

'The antenna field,' Dr Das said, laying out a large satellite photo on the table. 'This has been taken from 2 miles up and is a bit hazy, but you can see the array of metallic masts, a bit like your cell phone towers. The antennae at the top are oversized and act as focusing dishes for the energy beam. The power from the generators is first fed into a sub-station that steps up the voltage to create the energy burst of the HAARP weapon. If we destroy the sub-station transformer, it should cripple the system.' He pointed to what looked like a tall multi-storeyed building on the sat map. 'These transformers are massive, and from the look of it, that's the building that most likely houses it.'

'The transformer building is a little to the north and west of the main office complex,' Dharma continued. 'The first part hopefully should work out: to get the commandos in with the explosives. The Dharma Power Company's advance team was apparently searched thoroughly; so this time they've been instructed to send a clear signal to the Trans-Himalaya higher-ups at the facility that searching me or my party will not be acceptable. Played the "big shot with a big ego" angle. But then comes the hard part. Three key questions: how do we get the commandos to slip away without sounding the alarm? How can we seize the second target – the control room or least the contents? And third, how do we get away?'

'Can't the explosives guys get into the facility from outside? The field's a big area, and some part of the perimeter should be vulnerable to penetration. That seems a lot less risky than taking them with us,' I said.

'Good point, Chandra. That was my first idea too, but when I saw the map of the place, I changed my mind. The field is enormous – at least a couple of square kilometres – and our guys have to cross the entire length to get to the transformer building which is much closer to the main complex. Traversing it with video cameras and security guards patrolling everywhere is going to be impossible. The place is also without cover of any kind. No, I reckon our best bet is the headquarter complex itself.

'Anyway, let's just park that problem for a moment and assume one of the two of our SOG guys manages to slip away and set the charges. The timers will be set for one hour. By the way, the explosions will be localized but very powerful – aimed at completely destroying the equipment without bringing the whole place down.

'The moment they hear the bang, you can be sure the staff will be distracted. Dr Das will use the confusion to make his way to the main control room accompanied by the second commando. There they will neutralize the people in the room by any means necessary and seize what they can by way of the computer hard drives, papers and so on. Pant has made it clear that with this our work's done. Then we have to get out.'

'Not quite. What of Hassan?' I said anxiously.

Dharma nodded gravely. 'I haven't forgotten him. That's why we need you and Meenakshi. I'm on a semi-official visit and have to show enough interest and engagement in the plant facility, to keep the conversation going along. That'll limit my movements, but also hopefully distract the attention away from you. Your job is to keep a sharp eye out – especially you, Meenakshi. Pant was categorical about that; he said you could see things which would escape almost anybody else. I have my doubts that you will see any trace of your missing friend, but if you do spot anything unusual …' Here Dharma paused and I could sense his invisible shrug. 'We'll just have to improvise on the spur of the moment.

It's impossible to prepare for all eventualities. Who knows – you may be needed to carry out the computers and electronic stuff. Pant was categorical that takes priority over Hassan.

'Now, as to our exit plan. It's the best reason for us to take a helicopter. The power plant has a landing pad and the chopper is our best chance to get away fast. We're still reviewing the visit action sequence and you'll both get a clearer briefing before we start off.

'One last thing. Chandra, you're not just a journalist. You're a hugely respected voice. I'm telling you now that Pant's Chinese hunch has been confirmed by my own digging over the last few days. I intend to make over the full evidence to you as soon as we're back. Anything we seize at this station that points to China's involvement is that much more ammunition for you. We need to expose them once and for all, and build the weight of world opinion against what they're capable of.'

I nodded grimly. If this wasn't a case of targeting innocent civilians in covert warfare, I didn't know what qualified. At the very least, the Chinese had to be brought up to the court of international justice.

I said to Meenu, 'Anything else you can think of, Meenu?'

'No, nothing. A hundred things can still go wrong, but under the circumstances, Dharma's come up with the best plan we have. Seeing as we have a day before the visit, do we have time to do some exploring? There seems to be some sort of a ruin up on the hill. Perhaps, I'll just hike up tomorrow and take a look.'

Dharma said, 'Please don't do that. That's a gompa, a monastery; it was badly damaged by an earthquake in this valley and abandoned almost a century ago. I've taken up the restoration at the request of the local abbot, but till we start the work it's prone to collapse. So anywhere but there. We have a couple of nice climbs on the other side and I'll have some guides organized for you.'

He looked up and his brows drew together in a tiny frown. 'Hello, Vaish. You just missed the briefing.'

Vaishali had changed into a Bhutanese dress; the cream blouse setting off the earth-coloured kira or sarong-like ankle-length skirt to perfection. Standing there, with her hands on her hips, head tilted to one side in enquiry, she simply took my breath away.

'Sorry, Harsh. I was a bit woozy from the flight. Just had to freshen up and take an aspirin. You know I don't enjoy flying.'

Dharma was instantly by her side, feeling her cheeks and neck. 'No fever. Are you okay?' She nodded. 'What's that I heard about the gompa?'

'Meenakshi wanted to trek up there, but it's too dangerous. I'm sending her with some guides to the other side of the valley. Why don't you join her if you feel up to it?'

'I'd love to, but let's see how I feel tomorrow. What I need right now is some fresh air. Anybody care for a walk?' She said it to the room, but her eyes were on me.

Dharma said, 'I need to see to a few things with Dr Das here, if you don't mind.'

I reflexively turned to Meenu, but she beat me to it. 'I need to lie down a bit myself, Vaishali. Chandra, why don't you go ahead and I'll see you later?'

Her face was bland to the point of being almost wooden, but this time I barely noticed, gripped by a painful excitement.

Vaishali waited for me to join her and we walked down the steps together, across the courtyard and through the main gate. The brook running through the meadow had cut a natural gully and the land sloped gently down towards it. The grass felt like a velvet carpet beneath our feet as we strolled to the water's edge and sat down.

Night had fallen and the hills around us had the aspect of sharp cardboard cut-outs etched against the inky sky. A magnificent lone deodhar tree stood across the water and from the copse of bushes around it, I could hear the hooting call of a crow-pheasant. Vaishali said nothing and I could have said nothing even if I had a mind to, for it was as if there was an electric charge building between us, waiting to spark across the intervening space.

She said, 'Chandra …' Her voice cracked and suddenly we were in each other's arms. The emotions I had kept dammed within me burst forth in a tidal wave of want and longing. Our lips met in a crush of passionate desire and I felt all control slipping away as we drank deep of each other. We fell together onto the grass in a tangle of limbs. She unbuttoned her blouse and tore it away. Her bra came loose and her breasts sprang free, full and bursting. She drew my head down, working my kurta loose and then pulling it over my head. Her hands worked her sash free, unwrapped her kiri and flung it to one side. She was wearing nothing underneath.

My chest pounded like a sledgehammer. I was seized with a wild exaltation as I beheld my wife unrobed in all her loveliness. Then she was reaching out, grabbing my belt, moaning incoherently. It may have been that act that awakened a small spark, a glimmer of an understanding deep within that if I came up naked against her, I would be lost, and that my promise to Meenu would be swept away by the roaring gale that possessed me.

I took her wrist, and gasped, 'Wait, wait … Yamu … Vaishali … wait. Please.'

She ignored me, pulled my belt away, tugged at my waist. Her eyes were closed and her breath came in shuddering gasps. I held her wrists, waited for her to reach a semblance of control, teetering upon the abyss myself, barely in control at the sight of her body writhing next to me.

Finally, she opened her eyes; they were drunk with desire, uncomprehending.

'Vaish, please. I can't go all the way just now. I can't … we hardly know each other. You said it yourself: that we shouldn't get into anything that we'll both regret and …'

She cut me off and said softly, 'Yes, I said it. But I don't care. You're the man I've waited for all my life and now I'm not going to let go. It's not been easy for me too, Chandra. Men circling me all the time, knowing exactly who I am. But I know you. More than you can guess. You don't give a damn if I'm a Dharma or not. So, no, I not going to allow the possibility of regret to come between us. I want you in my life … and I know you want me equally. Don't deny it.'

Through it all, she'd made no attempt to cover herself, and it was all I could do keep my eyes on her face. Now she sat up slowly, took my hand and kissed it and brought her face to mine, hot breath singeing my skin, seeking my lips. I found my arms raise of their own accord to her breasts, ready to cup them in my hands, but with a supreme effort of will, I continued the upward movement to her shoulders. I held them and pushed her back, even as one part of me wondered if I was crazy. Promise or no, the woman I'd fantasized about for weeks was in my arms ready to give her all, the moment itself crying out for the culmination of pent-up desire.

Finally, I twisted her about and she fell to one side. She lay there for a moment, then slowly raised herself. Her expression changed, a new wariness flooding it.

'Is that girlfriend of yours holding you back?'

'Yes … no … it's not just Meenu. It's what's going to happen in the next …'

I stopped. Her face twisted, contorting in a spasm of despair and then it was gone, leaving behind a pale mask. 'No … it's her – Meenakshi. I know your type. You'll never leave her.' A sob wracked her, a dry, gut-wrenching sound that made me long to comfort her, but this time I dared not. Instead, I sat there and stared at the ground, trying to make some sense of it all. There was a rustle of movement and I looked up to see her reach for her kira and swiftly wrap it about her, then pull on her blouse. She got to her feet: a ghost silhouetted against the remains of the day, her features in deep shadow. Then she turned and walked away.

I sat there, numbed for the most part, but conscious of an inexplicable relief. After a while, I got to my feet and slowly trudged back to the house. The hallway was dark and empty. I pushed down the lever and gently opened the door to the bedroom so as not to wake Meenu, but to my surprise she wasn't there. I called out her name and then went across to the bathroom. I knocked on the door.

Her voice came through softly. 'Who is it?'

'It's me. Is everything okay?'

'Come in and shut the door behind you.'

I pushed the door open. The lights in the bathroom were off. Meenu was standing up on a bathroom stool by the window. The curtains were drawn except for a small gap through which she was peering out. Her head was fixed to what appeared to be a bulky black object.

'What're you … ?' I exclaimed in astonishment.

She held up one arm, motioning for silence. Then she beckoned me forward. Closer up, I could see it was an olive-coloured scope not unlike an odd-shaped binocular. She stepped down and handed me the scope. 'Focus on the mountain slope, around eleven o'clock, up near the peak,' she whispered.

Thoroughly intrigued, I stepped up on the stool and did as she asked. The world went green. How in the world did Meenu get hold of an infra-red night scope? It took me a while to zero in on the spot and when I did the grey walls jumped out of the trees like an apparition that had been conjured from thin air. The monastic ruin stood on the very edge of a precipitous ledge cut into the mountain, perched at an impossible vertical. At this distance, even with the magnification, it looked like a toy house stuck on green wallpaper. The retaining walls were imposing, but gap-toothed, with chunks of missing stone. The monastery soared away from behind them, three or four stories high, set with tiny square windows like the portholes of a ship. The whole place had a bleached aspect, devoid of life except for the birds. I remembered seeing black dots circling over the mountain, and while a few still did, most were perched on the wall now like silent sentinels. Now and then they spread their wings, huge flaps with extended wingspans. Vultures … ?

'Lammergeiers,' whispered Meenu in response to my unspoken thought. The great raptor of the Himalaya, and the largest of the Indian vultures. The parapet was thick with them. 'Look at the periphery … three o'clock.' I swung the glasses right and caught it almost at once – a tallish machan-like structure, and inside, what appeared to be a gun on a mounted tripod. A guard in a peaked cap stood behind it.

Meenu tapped me on the shoulder and pointed to the bedroom. I handed her the scope, stepped off the stool and followed her, the aftermath of the tryst with Vaishali replaced by a frisson of curiosity and excitement. Meenu was on to something, but I had no clue as to what it might be.

She went to the door, opened it, looked out into the corridor, and then and shut it noiselessly. Then she plonked herself on the bed. Her face was flushed, her eyes sparkling with suppressed triumph.

I went up to her and said, 'Well, Ms Holmes, what was *that* all about?'

She smiled and said, 'It was all about a piece of paper.'

'What paper?'

'During the drive here, when you pointed out the monastery for me, you used the Tibetan word "gompa". That was what Pagal bhai was trying to say the night we last saw him, and that's what we and Gopal heard and scribbled down – except for some reason, the man swallowed the "g" and what we – and presumably Gopal – heard was "ompa."'

I stared at her. *Gompa.* The word was close enough, but the rest of it was pure fantasy. 'That's a hell of a stretch, Meenu. The man was a poor beggar, half out of his mind. How would he know a word like that, let alone bellow it out like he did?'

'That's where the paper becomes important. We should have seen it as part of Gopal's message – the cell phone *and* the paper. The mistake we made was to let that piece of paper slip out of sight; it got overshadowed by the mobile phone. The mobile led us on Pagal bhai's trail, we found his body, and the very next day the phone also gave us the truck number. We got so caught up in all that stuff that we forgot all about the paper – because we couldn't make any immediate sense of it.

'The first word on that paper was the same as the one we heard Pagal shouting that night. So Pagal had to be the source. Gopal wrote down what he thought he heard from Pagal exactly as it came out from the man's mouth.'

I thought back to the childish lettering, Ompa. The reproduced sounds of a gibbering man. 'Maybe, but I still don't see how this has anything to do with ...'

'Listen, Chandra, isn't it logical to assume that the child met Pagal and discovered something? Something so disturbing that he started to miss his classes? We saw three numbers after Ompa on that chit. We thought they were 6-1-0, and couldn't connect them with anything. But they're actually letters – *G-I-D.* "Giddh" in Hindi means vulture.'

Long ago, in Japan on an assignment, I had suddenly woken up in the dead of night in my hotel room high on the thirtieth floor. My bed was shuddering; out the glass pane window, the lights of Tokyo were trembling; the entire city was gyrating in a cosmic death dance. It lasted no more than twenty seconds, perhaps half a minute, vanishing as quickly as it had appeared. I had run to the bathroom and retched out my innards. Now in a room in that remote Bhutan valley, I felt the same terror rise up as I dimly began to comprehend what she meant.

'You mean ... Pagal bhai was here ... up there ... in that place?'

'I agree it's a bit of a reach, but yes ... I think he was and then he escaped. And before you think I'm the crazy one, let me tell you that Pagal was most likely an autistic savant, one of those mentally challenged people capable of flashes of supra-normal intelligence. Some weeks before Gopal had vanished, he had asked me about madmen – if they could also sometimes have magic, jadu, in their brains. I think he was referring to Pagal. If he was, Pagal may well have got out and made his way back.'

I sat limply on the bed beside her, trying to digest it. 'When did you start to put it all together?'

'The first premonition I had was when you said "gompa". It right away brought to mind Pagal and his yell … Gopal's scribble, but I dismissed it as just a coincidence. But then we came to our room and I spotted that place on the slope. A gompa again – but with vultures. And watch towers. With armed guards. Again, there could have been a simple explanation, but one I thought worth testing. At dinner, I brought it up, said I wanted to climb to the gompa. Dharma instantly shot it down. The excuse he gave was that it was dangerous and he's restoring the place. But if it's an abandoned ruin, why ring it like it was a high-security military facility?'

My chest felt tight, constricted. I could hardly breathe. 'Dharma … ?'

She nodded calmly. 'Yes, Dharma. And now the whole thing begins to make much more sense. The power, the resources, the sheer organization to mount a weather-change threat over the subcontinent. And think of it; he owns a clutch of power utilities all over the country. Who better to orchestrate something on this scale?'

'But why, Meenu, *why?* Why in God's name would he do something like this? The man is worshiped in the country by millions! He's been their saviour time and again … !'

I was on my feet in agitation, thoughts whirling chaotically as I struggled to come to terms with what I had just heard. Then a cold hand clamped down on my heart; I swayed and might have fallen had Meenu not shot out her arms and steadied me. *Vaishali … Oh God … no …*

I felt an inarticulate cry build within; a searing spike of anguish that engulfed me whole. My mouth opened to vent it, but Meenu's palm was clamped over my mouth; her other arm hooked around and pulling me down onto the bed, on top of her.

'Shh … shh … Chandra darling … sweetheart … It's okay, it's okay. Breathe, just breathe.'

Meenu was saying something else, but I barely registered. I clutched at her like a drowning man, burrowing into her like a mole into the earth, shuddering all the while like a man with the plague. I lost all count of time as she kept talking to me: a steady, soothing flow of words till I gathered myself again, and slowly became aware of the present.

I turned to her then, but I felt swollen, gorged with an unbearable shame, unable to lift my eyes to hers. I felt her palms on my cheeks, lifting my face to hers. I took her in, truly seeing her for the first time in days. The beloved face, thinner now, the cheekbones more prominent. My eyes began to fill, but she quickly wiped them with the tips of her fingers.

'Now, darling, bawling is strictly my prerogative. Don't you dare take that away from me.'

'Meenu, can you ever forgive … ?' She cut me off, stoppered my mouth with a tender kiss.

'Chandra, for you it was always Yamini. Remember that. It was never Vaishali. And what was I to do – break you in two? Remember that, and you'll know there's nothing to forgive.' She paused as if weighing something in her mind, then said reluctantly, 'In all fairness, I can't say for certain that she's a part of Dharma's plans. Maybe she doesn't know.'

I shook my head. 'No, Meenu. She knows. They're closer than twins. Down there … by the brook, she almost made me lose control. She was playing me. I'm pretty sure that was well thought through. But I managed … to hold out.'

She looked so blazingly happy, I was suffocated anew with remorse. I thought of those torrid moments with Vaishali. I had the love of this extraordinary woman and yet I'd treated it as callously as I would some throwaway trinket.

Meenu said gently yet firmly, 'Chandra. Stop blaming yourself. You've got to put it behind. We're out of time.'

I stared at her. Slowly, the questions began to crowd my head – the most mundane at the top of the list. 'How did you get night vision binoculars?'

'You know my Dad was in the armed forces. He was actually in the paras, and when he passed away a few years ago, this scope was among his things. The rules said I had to return it, but I never did and no one asked. When this trip came up, I threw it in my bag on a vague impulse.'

Then her expression changed. She swiftly looked about her and said, 'Chandra, we're in Dharma's house, smack-bang in his valley. If he so much as suspects we're on to him, we're as good as dead. We've got to seize the initiative before it's too late. Any ideas?'

I thought swiftly. 'Have you told Pant yet? Any chance he might suspect?'

'No,' said Meenu. 'Dharma's reputation is so unique that it must have blinded even Pant. Otherwise, he'd have taken us into confidence – of that I'm sure. And as for informing Pant, my cell is dead – no signal anywhere in this place. Convenient, don't you think?'

I nodded grimly. 'Which means we're cut off. Meenu, I want to get up to the gompa. To take a look. The way they've ringed it, it's got to be important to Dharma's plans. I think we'll find some answers there. I'll leave right away. But you have to find a way to explain my absence to Dharma in the morning.'

Meenu nodded reluctantly. 'I agree, though I don't like the idea of your going alone. That place looks impenetrable. Guards everywhere, and god knows what else.'

'What about Pant's commandos?'

But even as I said it, I knew the truth. Those commandos were done for. We'd never see them again. The two of us were completely alone.

I paused, as another thought struck me. 'We still have Das. You get him to understand what we're up against. See if the two of you together can cook up some story – hold things together till I get back. Maybe you could even get access to a phone that works. I don't think it'll take me more than mid-day tomorrow to do the recon and return.'

She didn't argue further. Every moment brought the danger of discovery closer and raised the already desperate stakes in a game where the enemy was immeasurably more powerful. We were completely outmanned and outgunned. Our only hope would be to seize the initiative and somehow hang on to it.

She came swiftly into my arms, and held me fiercely. 'Look after yourself, my Karadi,' she whispered. That was Yamini's nickname for me, and to hear Meenu use it for the first time made our understanding complete. Then she pulled out something from beneath her kurta and pressed it into my hands. I looked down at a can of ManKiller, an Indian variant of Mace – a pepper spray so strong it was officially banned, but the rapes and molestations graphs ensured that it did a roaring illegal business in Delhi and other metros.

'Bring it back; it's the only brahmastra we have at the moment.'

'I will. Keep them distracted tomorrow.'

I slung her night vision glasses over my neck, swung my legs over the window sill and dropped to the courtyard.

15

Bhutan. 5th June. 11 p.m.

I CROUCHED BY THE WALL, TAKING A MINUTE TO GATHER MYSELF. Lumpy clouds the colour of curdled milk were scattered across the sky and behind them a waxing moon played hide and seek, dappling the earth with an ever-shifting chessboard of light and dark squares. I supposed that if one had to make one's way unseen across an exposed valley floor, this was the night to do it. I crept forward, keeping close to the wall and peered cautiously out in the direction of the main gates, which were wide open. I hadn't seen any guards during the day. This was Bhutan, and the valley was also pretty much Dharma's territory; with the servants about, I guessed he had no need for special security.

I ran noiselessly across the courtyard and out through the twin gates and into the meadow. The mountain rimmed the northwest corner of the valley and I veered left along the path to the brook. Soon I was at the water's edge, at the very spot where Vaishali and I had sat together less than two hours ago. *Two hours.* It now seemed an aeon ago, another age, and it wasn't even me but another man that had lain entwined with her: a bewitching, dazzling spider of a woman who had woven her web of silk around him and pulled him deep into her lair.

I mentally shook myself, pulled off my socks and shoes, and entered the brook. As the shock of the ice-cold water hit me, all vestiges of Vaishali were washed away in the swift current.

The water was no more than a foot or a foot and a half deep, and 12 or 15 feet across, bottomed with round pebbles. I waded through and scrambled up the opposite bank. The crossing had been quick, but this was glacial melt coming from the high snow peaks on the horizon, and the water had been like an ice-pack that numbed my feet and set my teeth chattering. I rubbed my feet hard with the socks, then looked at my watch. Close to midnight. It was getting on to mid-summer, and I reckoned I had about six hours till daylight. The grass was soft underfoot and I set off at a weaving trot trying to stay in the shadows, avoiding obvious patches of lit ground.

I kept this up for an hour, steadily narrowing the distance to the base of the mountain. If there were sentries in the valley guarding the approaches, I would soon be within sighting distance. A group of chortens loomed out of the darkness. These mounds of stones, local shrines erected along well-used walkways, were indications that I was on the right track. I crept forward carefully. The stone pyramids were usually carefully, even artistically, constructed with delicately balanced stones. But here the shrine looked abandoned and uncared for, the prayer flags uncharacteristically missing. Clearly no one had visited them – or more likely – had been discouraged from doing so. The local belief was to skirt them from the left and as I did so, I caught a flicker of light ahead. I ducked behind one of the shrines and peered out.

A lamp glowed from the window of a guard hut – perhaps at a distance of around seventy-five yards. I brought up the night vision goggles. A signboard with official-looking letters in daubed paint said – in Bhutanese and English – DEFENCE LAND: KEEP OUT. The silhouetted profile of a sentry expanded into view. From the angle of his peaked cap, it appeared he was looking down: probably reading something. It was clear what he was guarding – the platform of a lime-washed stairway directly opposite, curving up the hill.

I sat back to think through the options. So far as I could see, the stairway was unfenced on both sides; I could circle wide behind the sentry and climb alongside the track keeping out of sight under the trees. The hut was well out of normal vision range and with my dark clothes, I would be near invisible. Backing away quickly, I tacked left and proceeded at a crouching run across the intervening space. The tree line came up and I plunged in, climbing fast. The floor was carpeted with springy pine needles that made for slippery walking but at least it muffled my progress. I bore right and up, digging in my toes for grip. A good forty minutes of hard climbing and I was breathing heavily, sweat running down my face and back, despite the sharp nip in the air.

I remembered the guard tower Meenu had pointed out; its twin would be very close now. I crept forward cautiously. A puff of breeze swept down the mountain bringing with it a whiff of cigarette smoke. The trees were thinning out ahead and I spotted it at the edge of a clearing. The tower was of fabricated steel topped by a roofed cabin open on all sides for clear sighting. Just beyond the tower, the pale grey walls of the gompa loomed 30 or 40 feet up the mountain. The stairway was clearly visible; the only entry into the complex that I could see. Scaling the walls was out of the question; they were sheer and smooth and well-nigh unclimbable.

The cabin was unlit. The KEEP OFF board below and the lack of any illumination anywhere else on the mountain were definitely part of a deliberate attempt to keep attention away from the monastery and the hill. I scanned the tower through the night vision lens, but this time the angle was too acute and the line of sight was obscured. All I could see was the muzzle of an automatic rifle poking through the front window.

I cast about and found some tennis ball-sized stones lying about on the ground. I collected these and placed them in a mound near my feet. I picked one up and tossed it hard to the left. The stone curved up into the air and fell with a distinct crash through the trees. I lobbed the next, then I crouched down and waited.

The man reacted quickly. I saw the gun retract; a dark body leant out holding a pair of binoculars to the eyes. He stayed like that for a while and then withdrew. I got ready with another stone when I saw him emerge on the step-ladder. He did another cautious sweep of the forest with the binoculars, and then he started to climb down. He jumped off the last few steps, and keeping the gun at the ready, advanced in the direction of the sound. I edged slowly to my right as he moved away, then ran towards the stairway, vaulted over the small stone siding and raced up the steps. The wall of the monastery loomed up and I slid into its shadow. The risers were taller now, each step more than a foot high and climbing at a steep angle. It was the old Buddhist way, the pilgrim having to work harder as he got closer to the Holy Ones inside the temple. I started up the steps, pushing myself harder, heaving myself from one step to another with manic energy till each breath rattled through my throat in great gasps. The steps twisted into a dog-leg, and stopped at an arched gateway with a thick wooden door. I came to panting halt. My watch said half-past two. The moon sat serene and untroubled in a gap in the clouds, shining down on the valley stretched out below in a mottled mosaic of green and silver. Far away to the south, I thought I saw the glint of the stream and just beyond, the twinkling of the dzong's lights. I thought of Meenu alone in Dharma's lair, and momentarily felt a flare of panic. For all her resourcefulness, she was within arm's reach of a man who could at any moment simply reach across and crush her. We were like two ants scurrying across the path of an advancing beast whose weight and power was so great as to be beyond its comprehension.

I thrust the thought away and advanced to the doorway. There was no sign of a lock. I pushed at it, but it remained firm. I set my shoulder against the shutter and thrust harder and this time it swung inwards. I let open just a crack and peered through.

The dungeon-like central keep of the monastery reared up in front of me, four stories of it, bathed in the light of the moon. It looked somehow crooked, the top stories listing to one side. Deep cracks and fissures criss-crossed its facade, giving it the appearance of being put together with a child's building blocks. The gompa seemed so unsteady, so ready to fall apart at the smallest push that it matched what Dharma had said exactly. For a moment, I wondered if we'd misread the whole situation. Maybe this was, in fact, defence land. Maybe there was nothing sinister here and that we were making a monstrous mistake: could Dharma actually be the man the world thought him to be?

Something stirred on an upper story. I swung the glasses to my eyes and saw that it was a lammergeier ... now another and another ... birds were roosting on the window ledges. The vultures were enormous. At this range, I could clearly see their mask-like faces and the short beard-like tuft below the beak. The nooks and crannies of the ruin were thick with them, a massed crowd of grey sentinels, and a waft of breeze brought the smell of something rotten, dead and decaying flesh.

I was still looking through the binoculars when I thought I saw a wink of light from one of the windows. I quickly lowered my glasses to catch it better but it was gone. One of the birds gave out a mournful whistle and the others took it up. Their sounds soon echoed off the walls. By the light of the silver moon, there was such a demoniac aspect to the ruin that a primal terror took hold of me. I stepped away from the door, ready to bolt, when I heard a dull thud. I swung round and put my eye back to the chink in the doorway. The entrance to the main keep had opened and a figure was framed in the doorway. Then it stepped through, closed the door and appeared to be locking it. When he turned and I could see it was another of the security men. He fixed the strap of his carbine crossways across his chest, ran down the steps, turned to his left and commenced walking with a steady tread across the paving. A clink sounded with each step he took, an impact of metal on metal.

The sight settled me instantly; the fear of the supernatural vanished, replaced by a fresh sense of purpose. Ghosts were one thing, men of flesh and blood were quite another. His measured walk told me that he was almost certainly patrolling the perimeter. I waited till he turned the corner and vanished from sight. I pushed at the door just enough to let me slip through, reset it to closed position, and darted to the main door. The thick panelled wood was inset into the building wall and afforded a natural cover. I drew the can of ManKiller from my pocket, pressed myself to into the alcove against the wall, and waited.

The minutes ticked by, stretching endlessly. I half expected the door to open suddenly behind me. The itch across my back grew steadily, the tingling of hundreds of tiny insect feet scurrying over the skin. I felt the sweat popping through the pores. I grit my teeth and willed myself to stillness, but the itch was growing unbearable and my muscles were seizing up with the tension. Just when I readied to shift position, the familiar clink of metal cut through the night air, followed the creak of leather. I pressed back against the door, gripping hard at the can of ManKiller. The guard came on with that same steady tread. He didn't turn in my direction, but looked straight ahead, swinging his arms military style. I waited till he crossed. *Now.* I pushed off the door like a sprinter and ran after him on tip-toes, accelerating. He sensed me when I was less than five yards behind and pivoted a half-circle. His eyes widened with shock; he clutched at the rifle with both hands, swinging it around to point in my direction, but I was upon him, can at level with his face. The hiss of spray cut off the warning cry that was forming in his throat. I almost felt a pang as I clamped my hand around his mouth, for he was already blacking out with the fiery pain that is the equivalent of inhaling concentrated chilli powder.

I pulled him into the shadow of the wall, stripped him down and quickly put on his uniform. ManKiller guaranteed to knock the victim out for about an hour, so as insurance I pulled his arms behind and tied his wrists with strips of cloth torn from my discarded shirt and stuffed his mouth with more of the fabric. Then I grabbed his weapon and keys and ran back to the door.

After trial and error, one of the keys fit and the door swung open. I stepped into a thick, soupy darkness. I pulled the door to closed position, careful to not shut it completely, then stood there, listening. My senses were tuned to an unnatural pitch, vibrating like a tuning fork, and the cavernous building seemed filled with whispering echoes and the restless, shifting movements of an animal menagerie. I waited, fearful and undecided. But soon the claustrophobia welling up inside decided it, and I slid the mobile out of my pocket and pushed the torch button. Before me was a small, foyer-like entry space with a stairway to one side. I crept to the left, cupping the beam with my palm to cut the radiance. The steps were narrow, winding up steeply. I stared at them: another climb, now leading me deep into the bowels of this ruined pile. I turned off the light and started up the steps. The walls closed in, no more than a couple of feet apart and the opaque blackness fed into my claustrophobia, but the cold steel of the automatic rifle was a powerful antidote. I gripped it tighter in the crook of my arm and kept going. The air, already cold and still, turned almost frigid as the stairway spiralled up, twisting like a corkscrew. Then, without warning, the walls vanished, the steps levelled off and I was pitching forward, out of balance. The rifle clattered to the floor and the sound was like a bomb going off, shattering the tomb-like silence. In panic, I rolled and scrabbled around, grabbed the gun and brought it up, ready to fire. I knelt there, expecting doors to open, running footsteps and raised voices. But there was nothing, just silence – and an odour. The chemical, antiseptic smell of a hospital.

I got to my feet and switched on the mobile's torch with trembling fingers. It seemed pointless to play hide-and-seek now that the din had advertised my presence loud and clear in the building. Before me was a corridor; arrow straight and yet so long I couldn't even guess the end of it. I could just dimly perceive how enormous this pile of rock and stone was. The floor gave off a dull gleam in the light, tiled with some sort of a plastic material with a complex, slip-proof pattern. To the right of the passage, the wall was set with doors at equal intervals; heavy steel jobs, grey-painted and industrial looking, with grip bars for handles and pneumatic swing controllers bulging from the top. The bottom lintel was about six inches high, like the entrance to a ship's cabin.

A few years ago, I had stumbled upon a giant industrial complex dedicated to weapons of mass destruction – buried deep within the Afghan mountains that were home to the Buddhas of Bamiyan. Here, deep inside another desolate, abandoned abode of Buddhism, thousands of kilometres to the east, I was gripped once again with a fateful sense of déjà vu, a sense of being close to something that would rip into the very core of my being. As if in answer to my thought, a muffled cry came to my ears, then a shuddering moan. The hair stood up on my arms and neck. I switched off the torch, cocked my rifle and stepped onto the tile. It had a spongy, rubbery feel – as if I was stepping on a live creature. The first door to the right had a long lever-like handle that slid down with a click on my touch and swung back noiselessly. I stepped over the jamb. So intent was I on what might be on the other side that I hardly registered the door swing back on its own and settle into place with a gentle click. My senses were already reaching out, quivering.

It is dark here too, but the smell of chemicals is now mixed with another reek, a stench of putrefaction and rot so overwhelming that the gorge rises in my throat. I finger my mobile to switch on the light, but I hesitate, unsure and terrified of what the beam will reveal. For all around me are sounds: myriad hisses and suppressed grunts and cries, muffled flurries and movements, scratching, scrabbling, ferrety sounds that are everywhere and nowhere at once. My hands shake and tremble as I turn on the light. I bring up my weapon though I know deep inside it will be of no use against what I will encounter here.

Before me is another long chamber mirroring the corridor outside, except it appears to be lined with cubicles. They run along one side of the room, narrow box like cells with opaque bottoms and glass on top, like telephone booths. I move up to one of them and shine the light through the glass.

I stagger back like I've been struck. It feels more like a hammer blow. I cannot register what I see … think I see inside that booth. I am clammy with sweat and the blood pounds inside in an escalating drumbeat that feels like it will burst through my body. I drop the rifle and use it as a prop, leaning on it, momentarily robbed of strength. Slowly, I force myself forward on rubbery legs, brace myself and look into the cubicle once more. My breath suspends itself.

A man is sitting on a chair-like contraption. I can see he is a male only from the fact that he is naked, for in other respects this form is barely human. Tubes sprout from him like weeds: from his head, his open mouth, from his arms and legs and abdomen. Dozens of them twisting and turning but all climbing like creepers to the roof. And the face … the face! It is a visage from hell, unbearable at this range. I raise a trembling palm to my face, use it as a physical shield and view him through the lattice of my fingers. All flesh has been stripped away from the head leaving a slimy glistening skull with protruding eyeballs that stare lifelessly ahead. The mouth is a lipless slit vomiting the tubes, but in between the pink slab of a tongue pushes through.

The skin is stretched tight over the rest of the skeletal body, translucent as tracing paper, and through it I seem to be able to make out his internal organs by the light of the beam, a sort of human anatomy mannequin in a biology class – except that this is a thing of living flesh. I bring the beam closer and suddenly the figure in the chair writhes convulsively; the eyeballs like giant marbles move this way and that and fasten upon me and they see me – aware. It knows I am looking. The mouth opens wide and there is an agonized grunt that ends in a whistling hiss of air. The tongue is alive, slithering from side to side pushing against the tubes. Then the eyes swivel away from me as if the beam pains him and the body slumps and stills.

There is a roaring in my ears now. I am not able to breathe, either in or out, my lungs have locked down, and there is a red hot burning in my chest, as if it is filled with hot coals. I reel back and then I am falling … falling into a void without end.

When I came to, it was to a sensation of lying on a block of ice. The mobile lay a few feet away, the light facing up, casting a ghostly glow on the pale-coloured ceramic floor, glassy-smooth and freezing to the touch. The carbine was level with my eyes, the barrel pointed at my face. Near the roof, I could see more tubes now, hundreds of them, climbing out of the booths like industrial cables, and onto a common tray at the top which ran along the length of the corridor and disappeared into the shadow on the far side.

I lay there feeling a complete and total lassitude. I was drained of strength even to move. Nothing seemed to matter, not even the thought that I might be discovered at any moment. I just lay there, waiting for the numbness of oblivion. An aeon passed, but deep down, a spark awakened, a thought that brought me jerking, shuddering, to full consciousness. Suddenly I knew with utter certainty that Hassan and Gopal were here. I rolled over, pushed myself up with my hands. My body still felt limp and drained, and I kept slipping. Every instinct was to be gone, to run from the horror that surrounded me. But I was here, and I could not ... *would* not leave them to their fate.

And so began another time – I say time, for I had no means of knowing whether they were minutes or hours. All I knew was that I moved from cubicle to cubicle, from creature to creature caged within, each barely human, all hideously disfigured, covered with poisonous boils and eruptions, some blind, others with stomachs sliced open, intestines on display, some so leached of blood they appeared to be shrivelled larvae of a monstrous insect. Each cage had its occupant: male and female, young and old, and in some there were infants. The wonder and horror of it was that each was alive; and in their twitching, crying, grunting and moaning it was as if all the pain in the world was collected and then stuffed into this one room.

Each time I discovered that the occupant of a cell was not Hassan or Gopal, or any of the other children I knew at school, an explosive cocktail of guilty relief filled me, a see-sawing of emotion that took me to the edge of total collapse. Only one single door was left at the end of the room – the one into which the cable tray carrying the tubes led. I pushed the latch down and entered.

This was a smaller chamber. The common bus-bar ran all the way to the middle and then the tubes fell in thick bunches into a massive instrument bank. The whole thing hummed and whirred, digital displays and lights flickered and flashed in a continuous pattern. Lining one side were several oversized monitors on which green lettering scrolled down like rain. There was enough light coming off the screens as to paint the room with a faint, luminescent glow.

I registered all this only peripherally, for the instant I entered, all my attention was drawn to a glass cabin at the far end, enclosing a hospital bed. With a still form laid out on it. Suspended over the bed was a crouching, multi-armed creature. I cocked my rifle and stood stock-still. It was some sort of a robotic contraption, eerily life-like, the multiple arms ending in a sharp talon-like spike. It radiated an animal malevolence, its very appearance making plain its purpose: to inflict pain. I crept forward, breath suspended. I had no need of the torch. The glow from the monitors illumined the shaven skull, the waxy death's head with its lean, angular profile. I had found Syed Ali Hassan.

And then the lights came on.

16

Delhi. 5th June. 8 p.m.

THE INTER-DEPARTMENT GOVERNMENT COMMUNICATION mocked Nalini Ranjan Pant from the top of his desk. He read it again, coldly and carefully. It was from the Cabinet Secretary, countersigned by the Ministry of Home Affairs, in effect transferring Pant as Additional Secretary (Co-ordination) in the Home Ministry. No word of his replacement, not even the courtesy of a call from his bosses. Pant was a professional. His lifelong training called for a separation of feeling from fact, and his dedication to the mission of guarding the country against all enemies was absolute. He was also a seasoned in-fighter – he had to be to survive in a world of backbiters and monumental egos all manoeuvring for power within the government of India's labyrinthine bureaucracy. But this time he seethed with uncharacteristic anger. The country was under grave threat. There was *no one* within state security who held all the threads to the crisis facing the nation as he did. He had taken a few trusted men and women at the top into confidence and they had all been appalled. They had also all agreed that without proof, the state was helpless to move against a neighbouring country – that too China. He had receiving their full – if unofficial – backing to use Dharma for striking at the enemy's plot. To remove him now, he knew, just did not make sense. Ergo, it was a deliberate move. He picked up the phone and punched a number.

'Cabinet Secretariat, Amitabh Patel.'

'Amit, Pant here – from JIC. Still the night owl, I see.'

'Hello, Pant. Nowhere near your late-night standards, but everyone's busy these days. Don't ask me why. We're mostly creating work for each other in the finest traditions of bureaucracy. Long time no hear. Sab thik thaak hai?'

They exchanged pleasantries for a bit, and then Pant said, 'Amit, I need a favour. I've been transferred from JIC to Co-ordination at Home.'

Patel's voice went up. 'Wha … ? Who the hell issued that order? And that too to you … ! I can't believe it, Pant. And to Co-ordination! It's a ticket to nowhere, dammit.'

Pant said, 'Amit, keep your voice down. You know me. I don't care where I go as long as I can contribute in some way. But this is not the right time.' Pant paused and said deliberately, 'What would you say if I told you that this can seriously impact national security – that it's the worst possible moment to shift me?'

There was a pause at the other end. Then warily, 'You're saying it's been done deliberately? By whom?'

'I'd have said it's our big neighbour to the East, but I doubt they have the kind of clout and penetration to pull off a governmental transfer. So it's a bit of a puzzle. Can you do a little digging for me? But carefully. Don't get any antennas up.'

'Give me a few minutes. Let's hope it a goddam bureaucratic foul-up.'

Pant sat back in his chair, took off his glasses and rubbed the bridge of his nose. The Chinese had penetrated their servers. That wasn't new. Hackers on both sides were pitting themselves against each other in a war fought in server rooms – the new battlefields of the covert wars of the twenty-first century. But if the Chinese were behind his transfer, it showed a level of influence that was altogether a new normal. But at least he was here and could fight a rear-guard action on his front. For Bhutan he could do nothing at all, and that was becoming a serious worry. It would now be more than two hours since Dharma and his group would have landed in Bhutan and yet there had been absolutely no news. All mobiles seemed off-signal, but Dharma should have had no problem in setting up comm. and giving him a situation report by now. Perhaps they hadn't reached their destination … but it bothered Pant. He looked out the window, pondering. The Rajpath curved gently up to the imposing Rashtrapati Bhavan atop Raisina Hill. Government and private cars were plying in and out of the parking, the impatient honks and jockeying for place in a display of Delhi's indiscipline at its crassest. It looked superficially normal, but the setting sun had leached the sky to a peculiar tint and the tri-colour hung listless from its pole on the ramparts of the North Block opposite. He'd observed over the last few days that the crows, parakeets, the monkeys and stray dogs – all of the ubiquitous animal life around Raisina – had vanished. Not a breath of non-human life stirred. He recalled reading somewhere that the animal and bird life in the Andamans had exhibited strange behaviour even as the tsunami had started to swell thousands of miles away. It was as if the natural world had sensed a coming catastrophe.

The telephone shrilled, breaking his reverie. 'Pant here.'

Patel's voice was almost a whisper. 'I spoke to Ahmed in Personnel, you know the former Joint Secretary in OI Affairs. He owes me big time and I called in the favour. The transfer was initiated direct by no less than the Home Minister. But I have to give our fellow babus some credit for spine. The Cabinet Secretary and Home Secretary both have objected to the transfer, and what's more, have recorded their objections on file – "… highly regarded and indispensable officer at this time … Irreplaceable etc …" and have recommended that you be retained in the interests of national security. So there are quite a few people batting for you, Nalini …'

'But ... ?'

'Grapevine is that objections have been overruled by the Home Minister, backed by senior sections of the PMO – but this is off the record, of course. No one's putting pen to paper, and no one seems to have a clue about who's pulling the strings at the ministerial level.'

'Thanks, Amit. You don't know how useful you've been.'

'For you, Nalini – any time. I know when you ask, it's not for yourself but the country ... and we desis have to hang together, yaar,' the JS's tone was light, but Pant sensed the seriousness beneath.

Pant disconnected and quickly dialled another number on the red secure line. The CS picked up the phone at the first ring. 'Yes?'

'Sir, Pant here. How much time do I have?'

The CS did not hesitate. Pant and he knew each other well. 'I was just going to call you myself. The fact is that they don't have a successor. So I'd say it's a play to get you out of the way rather than bring any specific body in. Still ... I'd say a couple of days before you are well and truly out. I'm sorry Pant, we tried our best.'

'I'm grateful, sir. But can you get me a week? You recall my briefing on the weather threat. The mission's underway as we speak. But I need time.'

'Any progress report from the field?'

'No proof yet, sir, but yes, if anything it's bigger ... far bigger than we can imagine.'

'Damn.' The CS swore under his breath. 'I'll see what I can do. Get onto it, Pant. Do whatever it takes.'

'I intend to, sir. Thanks.'

Pant replaced the receiver, momentarily warmed by the fact that he was not altogether friendless in the bureaucracy. Powerful players were on his side, but they were all outmatched at the moment. It was time for desperate measures, a time to act on a plan that had been stewing in the back of his mind for some days. He took out a key and unlocked his side cabinet and extracted a bulky looking phone from within.

*

Islamabad. 5th June. 7:45 p.m. PST, 8:15 p.m. IST.

In the Islamabad HQ of the Inter-Services Intelligence – known to the world as the ISI – Gul Iftikhar Mohammed prepared to wind up another fraught day. Thus far, the communications nightmare showed no signs of easing; the vital north-east frontier with arch-enemy India was a silent black box from which not a squawk had emerged the last few weeks. The early phase was the most harrowing. The army had panicked. Ever since Kargil, an ever-present fear of a punitive Indian attack was never far from the defence establishment's mind. Two strike-mountain divisions had been moved to the front, and strategic nuclear force status taken to Alert 1. The Indians had responded by massively reinforcing Siachen and thrusting forward aggressively toward Dras. Gul recalled the tense meeting at Army headquarters not two weeks ago, when the Pakistani general staff wanted to take the Indians head-on, with the intel bureaucracy balking strongly. It soon got into a shouting match and it had taken all of Gul's persuasive powers to keep things from spiralling out of control. In the end, it had been a very close thing and it was only his reputation within the military that had carried the day.

Gul grimaced to himself. That rep was fraying. The Shadow Throne affair was a triumph in one respect, when he'd managed to avert a nuclear exchange between the countries, but that victory had turned to ashes in his mouth when he learned that he'd been manipulated all along by his nemesis in Indian intelligence – Nalini Ranjan Pant. To add insult to injury, he had been gulled by that Indian into the open and Pakistan's nuclear deterrence had been seriously compromised. But he was realistic enough to admit that he'd have done exactly the same thing had he been in Pant's shoes.

To his credit, the Indian had made repeated attempts to reach out to Gul this past year – one intel professional to another – to urge cooperation on common national security issues. Then Pant had called in ten days ago and made the urgent and unusual request for a video grab found on a dead trekker's mobile near Saltoro Kangri. ISI analysts had immediately analysed it for clues, but it was all very mysterious: a humanoid-looking machine generating what seemed a lightning bolt. Pant had assured him that the Indians were as concerned and suspected a 'third hand' behind what he hinted was a communication-jamming device. Gul had set aside his resentment and cooperated. Unless it was deception on a massive scale, all intel indicated the Indians were equally on a hair-trigger, suspecting Pakistan or China.

An urgent knock on the door broke into his thoughts.

'Come in.'

It was his aide, sounding breathless. 'Sir, call on the scrambler from New Delhi. Caller is Chairman, JIC – Nalini Ranjan Pant.'

Gul stared at his aide. *Think of the devil.* 'Transfer the call, Abdul.'

He picked up his receiver and waited for the scrambler echo. 'Hello?'

'Mr Mohammed, Nalini Pant here. How are you, sir?' The voice was exactly as he remembered, precise – almost pedantic and professorial. The bottled up anger and embarrassment surfaced yet again, but he crushed it; he would not give his foe that satisfaction. Instead, he said coolly, 'I'm well, Mr Pant. Anything to report?'

The Indian's voice on the scrambler had a distorted quality that made it hard to gauge the tone, but Gul could sense the edginess. 'Mr Mohammed, I want to once again assure you that the radio comm. blackouts are not of our making. But we're closing on the culprit.'

Gul said nothing, letting the silence build. Then grudgingly, 'I find it hard to believe that. Your DGMO hasn't called us once, and you're moving your forces up at Dras. What are we to make of this?'

'That's only because we were unsure about what was causing it, and the first suspicion fell on you. I'll be frank and tell you that we're convinced it's not you and it's certainly not us.'

Gul said coldly, 'Well, it's certainly not the Chinese, if that's what you're getting at.'

There was a long silence at the other end, then, 'Are you sure?'

'Yes. You know how closely we work with them. They've not gamed us before and they are not about to start now.'

Pant said, 'There's some evidence that they're developing technology for ionosphere disruption – stuff that would kill electronic communications.'

'Well, I can guarantee as one professional to another they're not behind it. They've been monitoring troop movements on both sides, and are as nervous as both of us. We've been inundated with calls from the Chinese Tibetan Army Command. They're worried that things are getting out of control. So, no, Mr Pant, I can guarantee you it's not the Chinese.'

Something like a long sigh came over the line, an *Aaaah* … as if the pieces had suddenly fallen into place for Pant, and Gul had the sense that what he'd said had somehow profoundly affected the other man.

'Okay … What if I said that it's not China, but a powerful non-state organization within India that is likely causing the disruption?'

'What?'

'Mr Mohammed, I can't explain over the phone, it'll take too much time and you're not going to believe it. I suggest we meet at the border, any place of your choice.'

When Gul made no reply, Pant said urgently, 'Sir, you're right to bear a grudge, but I beg you to put it aside for both our countries' sake. It will not stop with India, and what is happening poses an existential threat to Pakistan.'

'What … the EM radio disruption … ? You've got to be joking …'

'No. I'm talking weather manipulation. That video you were good enough to give me … A trekking team was buried in an avalanche on the mountain and your ranger rescue teams found an electrocuted body in the valley below. Within hours, on the evening of 5th August, Leh was hit by flash floods never experienced in that region. We've since seen a number of electrical spikes each followed by a freak weather disturbance, but we never connected the dots till a few days ago. Two of our cities have been hit with acid rain and hot winds. In each case, we've had mass deaths and disease. We're sure more strikes are planned and on a much larger scale. Just give me a chance … Hear me out and then take a call.'

What the hell was the man talking about? None of it made any sense. But the entreaty in Pant's tone shook the Pakistani. As a seasoned intelligence officer, Gul's experience told him that Pant wouldn't play him twice; that would burn all bridges between them and would be dangerous for both countries. He made his decision.

'When do you want to meet?'

'Now, if possible. There's not a second to lose.'

'Longewala, then. It'll be more private and away from the crowds at Wagah. No later than midnight. And come alone.'

17

Bhutan. 6th June. 5 a.m.

THE ROOM FLOODED WITH LIGHT AND BECAME AS BRIGHT AS day, hammering at my eyes. I staggered back, disoriented, hiding my face in the crook of my elbow. A metallic voice boomed out from the room outside, amplified by Tannoy speakers:

'Attention. Attention. Security to holding chamber 41. Attention … Att …' The words cut off as if someone had pulled a switch and I heard a pneumatic hiss. Heavy footsteps sounded on the tiles; the latch clicked and the door swung open. Framed in the doorway was a short and stocky uniformed figure, bulletproof vest, SMG, baton – the works. The submachine gun was up and pointed directly at me, the safety off. I had reflexively brought up my own weapon, but these were professionals. He jerked his thumb to his left in an unmistakeable gesture, and I saw another man just out of sight behind the cover of the doorway. Even if I took out one of them, I would have no chance against the other. I lowered my weapon and he nodded. His Asiatic features were stolid, giving nothing away, and I had a fleeting impression that my presence was no surprise. I turned to have one last look at Hassan. The bluish cast of his face was even more pronounced in the harsh light and I could see no rise and fall of his chest, no sign of life; he could have been an embalmed cadaver ready to be mummified.

I turned on my heel and walked out. The guard relieved me of my gun and the pepper spray, and then patted me down thoroughly. The other one clicked on a pair of handcuffs and I was marched out between them. The cubicles were quiet, but it was a silence more horrible than the earlier noise. Perhaps it was my imagination, but I felt the miasma of a terror so acute, the very air vibrated with it. I knew that whatever these captives were subjected to, it came with the light, and the sounds and vibrations of footsteps.

We exited onto the long external corridor, and walked to the end to a lift door. One of them swiped his card on an electronic access control slot and the door slid back. The guards stepped back and motioned me in. The lift powered us up and came to smooth halt. The doors opened to reveal a perfectly circular room, enormous and imposing. Fully 50 feet in circumference, the far wall was taken up with floor-to-ceiling glass. At right angles to the glass wall and dominating the room was a massive Bhutanese carved table with a single executive swivel chair set behind it. A space-age communications console occupied one half of the desk with a bulky sat-phone handset that stood upright in its holder. Otherwise the desk was bare. The space on the left corner had been converted into a plush sitting area: a leather sofa set with matching couches and a centre table set upon a glowing Persian rug. The walls just behind were hung with abstract oils on canvas that completed the ensemble. I was dimly aware of the impeccable aesthetic visible everywhere in the room, but here, in such a place, there was an obscenity about it that was indescribable.

I walked slowly to the table. Faint silver shimmered through the glass and I saw with a start the swelling outlines of forests and hills emerge from a lightening in the east. I looked at my watch. Five a.m. A hard lump formed in my stomach as I stared at the dial, unbelieving. I should have been well out of this place and descending the mountain by now! The chamber of horror below had robbed me of all sense of time and perspective. The extreme stress of seeing those hapless beings had driven every thought of the mission clean out of my mind: to scope the gompa and return well in time to chart the next course of action with Meenu. Instead here I was, trapped like a rat in a cage, and Meenu all alone in the dzong, growing increasingly desperate as time went by without any sign of me, and Pant far away, in complete ignorance of the truth about this monstrous enemy. For the second time in as many hours, my head swam and I clutched at the table top, overcome by foreboding and helplessness.

A small ping sounded from the electronic console on the desk and a red light flashed from the panels. I felt an awakening spark. *A telecommunications link.* I hobbled over and snatched at the receiver with my manacled hands. I put it to my ear and locked it in place with my chin. No dial tone. I punched likely looking buttons for the external exchange. Nothing. When I exhausted all of them in feverish haste and was about to grab at the sat-phone, the door opened.

They stepped into the room, and we faced each other for a long, suspended moment. Dharma and Vaishali stood on either side of an ashen-looking Meenu. Guards tailed just behind. Dharma wore his habitual smile, his expression warm and friendly. Vaishali's face was subtly changed in a way that gave me the shivers. She was still the intoxicatingly sensuous woman, but her eyes were that of a serpent, venomous hatred barely hidden behind the half-closed lids.

Dharma chuckled and said, 'Surely you don't think you can use my own sat-phone to warn our friend Pant? I'm afraid we're well beyond the old James Bond scenarios, Chandra.'

I said nothing. Dharma wore a kurta-pyjama and had draped himself in a light shawl. He looked like a benign Gandhian activist. He pointed courteously to the sofa. 'Come,

Chandra, sit. Make yourself comfortable. We have much to talk about. I'm sure the journalist in you is interested in what we have built here.'

It struck me that we were alone. What if I were to take him down? I flicked my eyes to the guards, gauging distance. Dharma shook his head regretfully. 'Your face is like a mirror, Chandra. I can almost see your thoughts. You would be finished before you even took the first step. Think of your friend Hassan and your lady love here. Act the hero and you will see them skinned alive before your eyes.'

Suddenly, I was shaking. Rage bubbled inside like volcanic lava that I almost choked with the intensity of it, the ashes of failure black and bitter in my mouth. Meenu said, 'Chandra, we weren't to know. Das is with Dharma. He turned us over.'

I stared at her uncomprehending, half stupefied. *Das … that absent-minded scientist …* Dharma laughed gently. 'My, my. You seem shocked. For a journalist who's been awarded a Magsaysay, Chandra, your naivety never ceases to astonish. All you had to do was google the man to know that he's one of the world's leading experts on weather change. Yet you couldn't put it all together. Nor could my worthy foe in Indian intelligence – your friend Pant. No doubt he was fooled by the good Dr Das as you were. Except for your woman here who managed to stumble on a few clues that we let escape.'

Dharma's tone was laced with a certain good-natured contempt, and lurking just beneath, for the first time I sensed the play of a titanic ego. So completely hidden had it been that I had no inkling of it in the past weeks, but now it was surfacing. This was a man who was playing God. In a sense he *was* a god; he had power, great and terrible power. He had conquered a nation, had it eating from his hands, and was now manipulating it onto a path of destruction. He alone could decide the life or death of millions and he knew it.

Meenu's eyes were on me and her message was plain: keep him talking. Not that I needed any prompting. I knew we were going to die, and with that realization, my anger was gone. I might as well be angry at the universe, for all the difference it would make. But I understood what Meenu meant. Play for time and perhaps we would still get a chance, however slim. And truth be told, the same journalist within me that Dharma had so decried was on fire. I was doomed, but I was still at the very centre of the greatest single act of mass destruction to be unleashed upon the world by a diabolic genius. In its very perversity and scale, it tempted the imagination almost beyond enduring.

It took very little to totter over to the sofa and slump onto it. I held my head in my hands: a man overwhelmed. One of the security men opened my cuffs and re-fastened them to the armrest.

Dharma said, 'I would be exaggerating if I told you that Dr Das is happy with all that we're planning here. But where will a man, as obsessed with his science as he is, ever get a better chance to put it into practice? So he has made his own pact with the Devil and bound himself to me. And you, Chandra. You would like to have your scoop, wouldn't you? The greatest story of them all. A new world order – created by one mind, brought to a complete, logical perfection.'

There was about him a radiation of energy so potent, that it crushed me, made me a child again. I regarded him with wonder and fear, as one might a demoniac spirit of the netherworld.

Dharma nodded as if pleased. He pointed Meenu to the seat beside me and took Vaishali by the hand and crossed to the large divan opposite. He sat cross-legged, back erect, in a guru-like posture.

He reached forward and picked up the remote and pressed a button. Instantly the roof lights dimmed. The glass panel windows flickered and burst into life as TV screens, except these were CCTV feeds. The white walls had also become a series of split-screens now and the whole panorama was a 360° visual of a control room out of *Star Trek*, the command module of a spaceship, giving us the eerie impression of being in the centre of the room projected all around us. It was a control room; around us were maybe thirty people in front of consoles – screens, lights, read-out panels. To one side, a massively tall computer bank covered the wall. Cabling and electronics were visible everywhere.

A lean figure clad in a white lab coat stood by one of the consoles, looking down at some print-outs. The bald head came up. It was Dr Das. He gave no sign of having seen us, but Dharma raised his hand and received a deferential nod. That was when I realized that the video was two-way. Dharma said in his normal tone, 'Can we have the target screens on, Dr Das?'

The screen darkened and then burst into life yet again to reveal a high-definition panoramic fish-eye lens view of a city. It took me a few seconds to take in the wide avenues and the palatial bungalows before I recognized Lutyens' Delhi. With barely a pause, the screens began to change every few seconds, panning into different areas of the capital. Civil lines, Old Delhi and the Ridge, the bustling streets, the markets and crowds of commuters everywhere, scenes of Connaught Place and then back to South Delhi … India Gate and Rashtrapati Bhavan … RK Puram … it was all there in a flashing kaleidoscope of a living, breathing city caught in real time. The images were so clear and the effect of the IMAX screen so dramatic that it was almost as if we were right there, mingling with the crowds.

Dharma said, 'Welcome to Pralaya. Delhi is going to be the opening scene of our next drama. And, you, Chandra, are going to be the chief guest at the function we plan to organize there. Not physically, of course … shall we say … a virtual guest?'

His dark, deep-set eyes were fixed on me, assessing my reaction. The shifting screen images mottled his face making it seem chameleon-like. 'Chandra, I really don't like you in cuffs. But I need your cooperation, your unstinted cooperation. And I'm hoping you'll give it to me. Let me explain.' He leaned back in his chair and said, 'Pralaya – you know what that means?'

'The flood?'

'Yes and no. It actually means dissolution. Of the world. A cosmic event that destroys the old so that a new order may come into being. In the scriptures, Chatur Yuga or the four ages on earth ended in a great flood, so I suppose water is as good an agent of Pralaya as any.'

Dharma now leaned forward. 'Chandra, it is the sole objective of Pralaya to bring in a new world. A world whose starting point is here – the Indian subcontinent. Collectively, India and Pakistan alone house 1.6 billion people, more than a quarter of the world – *a quarter.* We should be ruling the world, but what is happening instead? We are rudderless, lurching along without purpose, with a leadership that is craven and without a will to rule.

'The irony is that there has never been a better time for India to assert her role in the world. The West is in long term decline. The financial crisis, the rise of Islamic terror, and refugee influx that threatens to rip apart their social fabric – they are caught in crisis after crisis and every move they make to address their growing malaise only deepens the downward spiral. Look at what they have unleashed in the Middle East. Entire peoples – even erstwhile moderate elements – seethe against the West.

At home, a bankrupt capitalism that divides society ever more starkly into those that have everything and those that have nothing. Each crisis spawns another even as governments flail around helplessly.

'And it's not just Europe; America too is flailing. It is a second-rate power in decline, struggling to come to terms with its loss of dominance. Its politicians have become irrelevant. What of China, you may ask. And I will reply, what of China? Superficially, it presents the aura of a confident, rising nation, but for all its military and security apparatus, it hasn't been able to crush something as puny as the Tibetan resistance. Tibetans are standing up in larger numbers than ever, and the whole of Xinjiang is in eternal simmering revolt – this despite the presence of thousands of troops.

'Think of it. The Americans fielded the most modern army the world has seen to date against Iraq – a country smaller than Florida. What was the result? A complete rout. Instead of the slam-dunk that they expected, they had to pull out, licking their wounds, leaving a country dangerously fractured and exposed, with the results we are all seeing today.

'I have studied the mechanics and the dynamics of power for thirty years. Nothing has obsessed me more, Chandra. Nothing. And if I have learnt one thing, it is that power in today's world has no meaning in the abstract. Of what use is a giant nuclear arsenal when your opponent knows you can never use it – when both he and you know that the consequences of using it would be too great? At best you have a draw in the chessboard of power. Power is power only when you can use it without fear of the consequences. Or even more to the point: that power is the greatest which may be used without consequences, and it therefore subject to no limits other than itself. The country which possesses that power will be unconquerable. It will instead conquer the world.'

Even as Dharma spoke, the morning sun lit up Delhi. I could almost feel the warmth of its rays, so extraordinary was the quality of the images surrounding me, investing them with an impossibly real immediacy. Delhi was here; and we were in a space-time continuum hurtling into an Armageddon that I was dimly beginning to perceive.

Dharma said, 'Pralaya was conceived by me as my instrument of domination. It is beauty personified. A weapon of ultimate power, yet so subtle, so disguised, that it appears only as a force of nature. A force unleashed by the greed of man – for Pralaya will be perceived as an inevitable consequence of global warming itself. And for the destruction and mayhem it will bring, the countries of the world will take the blame only upon themselves.'

I saw his brow unclouded, his face shining like one who has beheld an eternal truth and has come back to expound it to a world that awaits the Word. This was a message from the deepest abyss of Hell, yet I could not help but listen, utterly fascinated, as he proceeded to expound. For Pralaya's weapon, perfected over years and with an unlimited budget, was disease rain and wind. With chilling calmness, Dharma called it DRW, a HAARP technology so advanced that it could manipulate the heavens to create cloudbursts in combination with wind – and aim them with the precision of artillery or bombs. Grafted into the atomic structure of the elements of DRW would be specific pathogens; pathogens designed to create lingering diseases – immune to conventional drugs.

'Delhi, for example,' Dharma's arm swept around the room. 'A city waking to a sunny summer's day. Yet in less than six hours, the sky will darken, and a giant cloud, pregnant with rain, will appear over the sky. There it will wait for a bolt of lightning that will slice its womb open and let loose the showers of Pralaya. If left unchecked, do you know the numbers that Yama will claim this day, Chandra? One million and some change. *One million in one hour of disease rain.* As the God of Death rampages through the city, there is only one hope for the government, for the people of Delhi. Only one organization stands between order and chaos.'

'Dharma Foundation,' it came out from my throat in a hoarse exhalation that carried within it a complete inevitability.

'Yes. Only Dharma Foundation possesses the cure, and the power to provide succour to millions in their hour of despair. As the DRW strikes, the government is thrown into panic; its aid organizations prove hopelessly inadequate, and even where it is able to reach, it is clueless about the peculiar diseases that seem to be breaking out, carried by winds that operate ever so gently as to defy all detection except by the most sensitive instruments. Even then, the Dharma organization will not pretend to be omnipotent – lest suspicious eyes fall upon us. No, the beauty of DRW is that the pathogens are so mixed as to create the right statistical mix of lingering disease, mortality and curability. Believe me when I say it; our work on induced disease within the human cellular organism is ahead of even the giant drug multi-nationals – far, far ahead. And do you know why?'

I could not reply. My tongue was stuck to the roof my mouth, blocking the air passage, choking me. Dharma must have seen it in my eyes for he nodded. 'Yes. I see you're getting it now. We're the only ones to use humans on a large scale for all our work. Do you know that our laws are such that it takes decades before we can scale up from lab cultures to experimental tests on human beings? That's decades of progress stopped in its tracks. By using humans direct, we leap-frog the clinical trials, all the other mind-numbing regulations, and the results are there for the world to see.' He laughed. 'If only they *could* see.'

There was a long pause. Dharma let the silence build, eyes burning into me. I got the feeling he was sizing me up, and all of a sudden, my brain was working again, recovering from this shock. The man before me was insane. That was the only word for it; if sanity was to be understood in terms of the elementary sense of right and wrong then Dharma had long crossed the bounds of reason. But omnipotence was a powerful aphrodisiac and could saturate the brain into a kind of intoxication to the exclusion of all else. As could desire. I glanced across at Meenu for the first time since this extraordinary narrative began and I saw mirrored in her face the cocktail of shock, awe, fear and revulsion that I had gone through. Throughout his speech, Vaishali had her gaze adoringly fixed on Dharma; if he was crazy, what about her? What held her in his thrall – committed her to something so totally evil?

I said, 'So where do Meenu and I come in, Dharma? Was all this drawing us into your inner circle a coincidence?'

Dharma said quietly, 'Nothing, absolutely nothing that happens around me is a coincidence. One of my experimental subjects escaped from this valley some months ago, and we have been on his trail. But we were also on your trail.'

Seeing me start up in surprise, he nodded. 'I said nothing about what I do is coincidence, but perhaps what I meant was that even coincidence bends itself to my purpose. My network reported Hassan's raid on the Kala Mill compound almost the minute it happened. Your presence with him was also noted. We understood why; that you too were on the trail of the same boy who'd been in touch with the man who escaped. Our paths were starting to converge. The incident of The Shadow Throne is unknown to the Indian public, but I have deeper connections within the Indian government than you can possibly fathom. In certain important quarters, you will be flattered to know that the reputation of the team of Nalini Ranjan Pant, Meenakshi Pirzada, Syed Ali Hassan and Chandrasekhar is very considerable. Especially of Pant and Hassan.

'The moment the report reached me, it was time to neutralize the threat. I cast my bait – a bait I knew you could not possibly refuse.'

'Vaishali,' I said, hardly daring to breathe.

Dharma laughed – a grating sound. 'Yes, Vaishali, my pit viper. She put her fangs into you. Yet another coincidence that she was your wife reincarnated. An irresistible combination, I should have thought. But you surprise me, Chandra; you managed to resist her charms. I wonder how that dumpy matron of yours pulled you back from the brink.' He shrugged. 'Well, no matter. I have the three of you in my power, but the fourth is free and in some ways he is the most formidable. You will help me deceive him – freely and willingly.'

He took up the remote and the screens changed. The long room again, with the booth-like cells. I felt the bile rise in my throat. 'We're going to strap your beloved into one of them and then we're going to do some experiments on her while you watch.'

18

I LUNGED OUT OF MY CHAIR BEFORE THE CUFFS BROUGHT ME UP short, the steel biting painfully into my wrist. Dharma signalled to the sentries and got to his feet. The guards started to drag a kicking and struggling Meenu to the door, herding me close behind her. Soon we were back in the experiment chamber. I had somehow imagined that the creatures inside were strapped to their chairs, but to my horror some of them were on their feet, beating at the glass and crying soundlessly. One – I could not make out if it was a male or female – was leaking blood from the eyes and nose, leaving red streaks on the glass.

No human being could be proof against a sight like this and the guards, familiar as they were with this terrible corridor, were no exception. I felt their hold on my arms loosen just a little. I let myself go slack and suddenly twisted, using the full force of my arms and shoulders to pivot around. Before they could react, I had torn free from their grip and launched myself at Dharma. I almost got to him, when the stock of the rifle smashed into my back and sent me crashing to the floor. I lay stunned, the pain so overwhelming I thought for a moment that my back was broken. Arms caught me on either side and I was hauled unceremoniously to my feet.

Dharma regarded me sorrowfully. 'Chandra … Chandra. I wonder if all these histrionics come from watching too many Tom Cruise movies. Cruise at least had his spiffy assistants and a bundle of aces up his sleeve. You, on the other hand, hold an empty deck. So please … spare yourself. Believe me; I will cause you a lot more pain if you try any more stunts.'

'You bastard.' I was breathing heavily; my uniform was soaked with sweat from the shock of the blow. 'You murdering bast …'

Vaishali swung her arm and struck Meenu viciously on the face. The rings on her fingers raked across Meenu's lips, splitting them open. The blood welled and ran down her chin and onto her chest, staining the kurta red. Vaishali pointed and we were hustled down the corridor to the room at the end – the one where I'd seen Hassan.

Hassan was exactly where I'd left him – still and corpse-like. The robot was suspended above him as before, arms extended menacingly, as if waiting to spring into action at any moment. I felt my arms yanked behind me and before I knew it, a chain was looped over my cuffs and fastened to a railing on the side wall and secured tight. The door opened and now, for the first time, I saw the technicians that worked their hellish science upon human beings. Both were women in white lab coats and caps, faces hidden by surgical masks. They looked neither left nor right, but kept their heads down as they brought in a stretcher.

The door to the glass cabin hissed open and the women swiftly wheeled the stretcher inside. There was a flurry of movement beside me and Meenu was suddenly crying out and struggling. I started to shout and curse, but within seconds she had been taken in and laid on the stretcher, and strapped down by her ankles and wrists. A chest strap came on, then one on the forehead, immobilizing her completely. The techs pushed tubes into Meenu's arms and linked them to a complicated monitor that separated her and Hassan. Then they walked out silently. A beep sounded and then a mechanical whine as the robot came alive. It started to move sideways along the mounting rails till it was directly over her. Meenu was looking at it like a trapped bird views a snake. Then her eyes swivelled to me and I was throwing myself desperately against the railing not caring that my wrists were at breaking point, the cuffs ripping into flesh. I came to a shuddering halt and we stared at each other through the glass. Her face was waxen yellow. Her terror was naked, beyond bearing, but I forced myself to hold her gaze, to give her what strength I could.

Dharma said something, but I barely heard him, focusing all my senses on Meenu.

'Chandra, look at me.' I turned and for the first time, Dharma stood revealed in his true colours. There, in the cold light, his face was like that of a wolf, feral and pitiless. He pointed to the IV sac plugged into Meenu. 'I've got something special for her. HLP 34. It's a pathogen that causes incurable leprosy. I will trigger the dose unless you do exactly as I say.'

How many times as a journalist had I piously pronounced judgements on this or that issue? How many times debated and pontificated, talked down to my readers, produced pat solutions to the problems of the world? In one overwhelming moment, faced with the terrible fate of my loved one, everything I had done and said in my life till then – my carefully constructed image of a writer of conscience – vanished as if it had never been. I didn't hesitate. I gave myself over to Dharma – body and soul. Completely. I would do anything to spare Meenu this fate.

Tears spilled down my cheeks. 'Please, Dharma,' I said in a broken voice, 'I'll do whatever you say. Please don't harm her. Please. I beg you.'

Dharma's face was still and expressionless now as he took me in carefully, assessing. 'She'll remain strapped on that bed till the Delhi strike is over. Her fate depends on how you perform.' He said to the guards, 'Bring him to my room.'

'Wait. Give me a moment with her. Please.'

I think he saw the depth of my despair, how close I was to collapse. He nodded curtly to the guards. 'One minute only. Then bring him to my room.'

He turned and left, followed by Vaishali. Meenu was lathered in sweat despite the chill of the air conditioning; blood had coagulated into a purplish mass over her mouth and jaw. She had herself under a semblance of control but from the rigidity of her expression, I knew the effort it must cause her. I dragged my cuffs along the railing till I was close to the glass. The guards moved up, but I ignored them and pressed my body against it, arms spread, giving her as much of myself as I could, willing my strength into her. The seconds ticked away on the wall clock, and digits turned 07:00. My minute was up and I felt the guards pull me back.

It was then that Hassan opened his eyes, turned his head and looked straight at me. I jerked back in shock, but the movement was masked as I was being drawn away and out the door. I threw a glance back but Hassan was once more was corpse-like and still.

As the lift hummed its way to the upper floor, my thoughts bombarded each other frantically. It was no more than a second; could I have been mistaken, the stress and the reflected lights on glass somehow creating a vision warp?

The lift doors opened, and as I was hustled along the corridor, I struggled to bring some semblance of order to the chaotic thoughts that buffeted around my brain. Even if he was alive, surely he would be wasted, utterly useless? Though his expressive eyes had been anything but wasted. I tried to recollect that fleeting moment. Hassan's thin face had become even more skeletal, but his gaze had been sharp and focused. It was a look I remembered well from our most desperate hours together. When he had taken me in hand and forced me to commit an act of desperate daring that I had never dreamed I was capable of.

My thoughts and feelings were starting to coalesce. Hassan was alive, helpless but alive; and I had no doubt what he would expect of me: to neither ask or receive mercy but to fight the enemy till my dying breath. But what of Meenu? Could I ever find the strength to condemn her to a horrible fate? It was an impossible dilemma, one I had no idea how to resolve.

We were back in that circular room where Delhi continued to flash by on the screens in real time. There, for the next hour, speaking in a clear passionless voice, Harshvardhan Dharma laid out Mission Pralaya in all its awful grandeur: weather strikes across thirty cities in India and three in Pakistan.

It became clear to me why I – and by proxy – Hassan and Meenu were being allowed to live. I was to be the instrument of his deception. First, I was to misdirect Nalini Pant, point him in another direction and keep him going along a false trail till the Pralaya strikes were done. The second target of my duplicity would be the people of the subcontinent.

A massive disinformation campaign had been worked out to the smallest detail. Media reports, interviews, video coverage, internet news and blog saturation, social media chatter … it had all been prepared and scheduled to leak in a precise sequence, a cascade of news so choreographed as to produce the maximum effect and complete believability. Over the last year, skilfully planted reports were already warning stridently of the dangers of climate change citing scientific research, and quoting 'experts', pointing more and more to weather shifts as a part of a pattern of natural disturbances to the earth's systems as the world got hotter.

'You see, Chandra, the whole thrust of the media reports is to shift the attention away from any HAARP speculation, and to ensure that the Dharma Foundation consolidates its role as the saviour of the country. In the aftermath of the devastation, I will engineer mass protests and calls by popular voice for an early election. The government will be in no position to refuse – in fact it will resign of its own volition. In the polls, I will win 99 per cent of the popular vote. The statistics of death will permit no other outcome; the thirty cities I have targeted have almost 20 per cent of the Indian population. From there, word will have spread at the speed of light, bathing me in its golden glow and voters everywhere will carry me on their shoulders to power. I will emerge supreme, Chandra – the power behind all power.

'You may ask: why target Pakistan? Because the two are conjoined at birth: they can never be separated. India today, Pakistan tomorrow and Bangladesh the day after. I have to shatter the entire subcontinent in order to rebuild it. The seeds have been planted within these countries already – small but active political groups that work diligently among the people, disdaining the inefficiency and corruption of the mainstream parties. They only await the moment.'

Gone was the modest and benign image, this was instead a messiah explaining his message – a grand plan for humanity itself – for it was plain to me that he would not stop with the subcontinent. Once he had gained mastery over it, Asia, Europe and then the Americas would follow. What he had in mind was nothing less than a new world order. Coming from anyone else this would have been laughable – a pipe-dream of a madman – but the precision with which each piece of his plan fitted into the others gave it the character of a monumental jigsaw puzzle, an extraordinary feat of practical imagination. The financial costs of achieving his vision would be beyond any one man, though Dharma himself was one of the richest of men. But even here, the logic of Pralaya threw up its own answer fully formed.

Dharma Foundation was both the disease and the cure. The drugs that Dharma alone possessed would, after Pralaya, be worth billions and make him a Kubera beyond imagination. The Dharma

Foundation had built its presence in every nook and corner of the country for this ultimate purpose, and the tremendous scale and vision of the man were now visible in their full and terrible grandeur. The technology for disease rain and wind, the experiments on humans, the fortune from the drugs – all the pieces meshed smoothly with the inevitability of a giant cosmic force against which no power on earth could stand.

'But I must make the people believe. Believe that the world is gripped by dissolution due to humanity's own greed and wantonness. Believe that there's no alternative to a new rebirth. You will carry that message for me. You will be my Goebbels, Chandra. You will manage my media campaign and be the voice of Pralaya that the world will see. You alone on my side are worth my entire media corps.'

Dharma pulled open the drawer on his desk and produced a thick folder which he threw on the table. 'First, you will call Pant and tell him certain things I want him to know. Then you will go through our media releases both for timing and content. I want you to master the campaign and then I want you to throw your weight behind it. I know you will not disappoint me, Chandra, knowing the consequences.'

*

I leafed through the folder, one part of me absorbing the contents, the other feverishly trying to see a way out, to come up with some sort of a plan, however desperate. Each time my mind went back to Meenu lying in that cabin, I found myself overcome by fear and my will weakening.

The intel man had almost para-normal sensory receptors and I was sure that in my current state I would give the game away – and forfeit our lives in the process. But Dharma had known this;

he'd had the scrambler echo set so that my voice would come out comprehensible but distorted.

Pant had picked up at the very first ring. He would have had a scrambler at his end too, but his voice came through clear and he sounded both relieved and upset. 'What the hell happened, Chandra? You were supposed to report in the moment you got in.'

'Some malfunction in Dharma's equipment. We couldn't set up comm. Even now the network is patchy and it's best I be quick. Dharma's made enormous progress in just days. We made the visit to the power station. First, it's the Chinese – just as you expected. Second, the HAARP station is not here but near the Tibet-Ladakh border. This Bhutan thing seems to be a genuine power station. Third, they're planning something big, but not for a couple of months at least.'

Pant's elation came through loud and clear on the speaker. 'If that's correct, it's a huge break. But how did you get all this?'

'Dharma. He wants to brief you directly.'

'Is he there?'

I glanced across the room at Dharma, who'd been closely following the conversation. I'd already been supplied the answer.

'No, Pant. He left for Leh.'

'You mean he's gone to the HAARP station?'

'Yes, I think so. He did say something about concrete evidence to present to the Cabinet. He'll call you from there or first thing when he's back.'

'So it's just you and Meenu there?'

'Yes – and Das.'

Pant said nothing for a beat, then, 'Any sign of Hassan?'

'No, Pant. Nothing.'

A sigh came over the line. 'Okay. Tell Dharma we're already in his debt; just get him to call me, and soon.'

We disconnected. Dharma rose from his chair. He nodded. 'Good, Chandra. But just as well we had the scrambler.' He pointed to the folder on his table and left.

The file confirmed what I had already suspected. Dharma had already purchased enormous influence with the national media through his corporate largesse. Many influential newscasters and journalists had started to carry weather and climate change reports that all but indicated that we had reached a tipping point. Others were rehashed quotes from influential international journals such as *Lancet* and *Nature* which reported on the emergence of extraordinary viruses that seem highly immune to the normal antibiotics. I marvelled at how these were twisted just enough and taken out of context to present a grim picture, setting up the country to accept ready explanations for Pralaya. I had no great belief in my own infallibility as a journalist, but I was realistic enough to accept that if I added the weight of my reputation to Dharma's plan, the result would be a smokescreen that would effectively draw a veil over Pralaya and the mastermind behind it.

The initial euphoria at seeing Hassan alive was beginning to fade. The seconds were ticking away and I could see no way to break free. And even if I did, what could I do? This time I up against an enemy who was truly omnipotent, against whom I had no chance at all. I remembered the earlier discussions with Pant about taking down the HAARP weapon. Das had himself suggested destroying the step-up transformer. Was he right or had that just been part of the misdirection? I had no idea of the technicalities of the project, but it seemed logical that the voltage of the power station had to be boosted to be fed to the HAARP weapon. Also, it was just possible that Dharma would not chance misdirection with Pant, whose antennae were as sensitive as an insect's.

The map we had studied showed the transformers housed next to the HAARP field on the other side of the mountain. Too far for me to get to without external aid. And then what? I had no explosives with me; was it just a matter of randomly pulling out wires, smashing control equipment?

So many questions, zero answers. The panic reared itself yet again. I held my head in my hands and squeezed hard as if to contain it, to prevent it from spilling out and overwhelming me.

The door opened and shut. The scent of sandal, the rustling of silk and I knew without looking up that she was in the room. For a long moment, we stared at each other. Vaishali's eyes were lit by a burning glare. She advanced on me and hit me across the face, once and then again. I rocked back with each blow, but did nothing to defend myself.

'I was ready to give myself to you as I've done with no man. And what do you do – spit on me, turn against us. And … all for that … that woman. You bastard.' She was almost choking with rage and mortification.

I had myself well in hand and hardly felt the blows. Ever since my capture, I had assumed that Vaishali had worked deliberately to trap me, playing her part in Dharma's plan. But instead of a cold, scheming seductress, I beheld a woman raw with emotion, breast heaving as she struggled to contain it.

Acting on pure reflex, I put every ounce of sincerity I could into my voice. 'If you believe anything about me, you must know that I loved you. I really did. But when Meenu voiced her suspicions to me … when she sent me to look at the monastery … Vaish, please. Did you really think I would accept this? This is the work of a monster. I cannot believe you of all people would have anything to do with this … mass murder.'

'Look at you, snivelling and feeling sorry for yourself – and that bitch of yours. My brother will soon sit on the throne of the world. And I will sit by his side. Together we will rule. And you …,' she said contemptuously, 'where will you be? In the dung heap of history.'

I hung my head and said nothing, the picture of dejection and misery. I let the silence build and then I got to my feet and in a swift movement, clasped her to me and kissed her. She struggled in my arms, pushed hard against my chest. I felt her hands come up to rake me and braced myself, but her fingers instead entwined in my hair, pulling me down fiercely, lips crushed against mine. We drank of each other greedily; but my passion was entirely manufactured. Inside, I stood apart – for the first time, cold and clear, assessing.

I said softly, 'Vaish, I love you. I want to be with you for the rest of my life. Can you believe that, despite everything that's happened?'

Despite my attempt to put feeling into them, the words came out cheesy and insincere and I braced myself for the worst. She pulled back and looked at me searchingly. 'Do you really mean that? After all that you've seen?'

It took all my self-control to cover my soaring relief – and astonishment. I had just seen human beings subjected to the vilest experiments, listened to a twisted genius planning mass extinction on a scale that would exceed the Holocaust. Meenu, Hassan, and everyone I knew or cared for would soon join the corpses strewn on the streets; and yet Vaishali was ready to take my pathetic performance at face value. It came to me then that she must be lost in some fantasy of her own making; that behind the facade of a well-publicized simple and private lifestyle, there well may have been a wild side. This was very likely a woman who all her life was used to getting the men she'd set her sights on. For such a one, even the possibility of rejection would have been impossible to comprehend. Yesterday's fateful evening by the brook would have come as a shattering shock and now she was pushing it out of her memory, grasping at any straw to reassure herself that her power over men was untouched.

I said feelingly, 'With all my heart, Vaish. Is it so hard to understand that I was anxious about the boy Gopal and about Hassan? That when I saw the … creatures being experimented on … I would lose my head? Oh, Vaish darling, I'm ready to be yours if only you'll save them – and Meenu.'

Surely she would see through this fresh nonsense? But she was quiet, nestling in my arms. I buried my face in her fragrant hair, keeping up the act – taut as a drawn bowstring inside.

Then she said in a voice muffled against my chest, 'If he hasn't already been used for the experiments, I'll have your boy spared. And Hassan. But that … woman … she'll be spared the leprosy, but she has to die.'

This time I couldn't control my shudder. She felt it instantly, pulled away and saw my expression before I could school it to neutral. And in it saw my soul bared: the terror – and loathing. She said, venomously, 'You fucking bastard. So … it's still about her. Let's see how you make love to her when she's a stinking leper.'

Then she stalked out of the room.

19

THE GAMBIT WITH VAISHALI HAD FAILED. MY WATCH SAID 9:35 a.m. Two-and-a-half hours for the Pralaya strike. I rang the bell and when the guard entered I asked to speak with Dharma. In less than five minutes, he came into the room. There was an unmistakable tension about him now that the moment he had planned for fast approached. He said nothing but stood waiting for me to speak.

'I've gone through the brief. It's a well thought-out effort, but I can't help feeling that a re-calibration and sequencing of the releases can multiply the impact several times over.'

'What do you mean?'

'It's simple reader psychology. Larger font sizes and headline banners on the opinion pieces help lay the ground, but too many of them and there's a danger of overplaying it. We need to let the stories stew in the reader's mind. Intersperse them with reportage of actual local weather anomalies with just a hint linking one to the other, and let the reader's subconscious do the rest. I think this plan is not subliminal enough. The best propaganda nudges the audience toward a pre-arranged conclusion without their even being aware of it. This plan is too "in your face" for my liking.'

Dharma thought about it. 'I think you can guess why I had to pressure you into working for me. You're exactly what I need. "The conscience of the nation." Isn't that what the Magsaysay citation said? Add to this plan your own voice over the public broadcasts and we have an unbeatable propaganda machine. How much time to rework the plan, Chandra?'

This time I was ready, didn't even have to pretend. I said with all the firmness I could muster, 'I have a couple of conditions. They're not negotiable.'

Dharma's eyes glinted with malice. 'Do you really think you're in any position to make demands?'

'Dharma, I have thought this over carefully. We are totally in your power, and after what we have seen here, I accept you will never let go of us. But I would do anything to save Meenu and Hassan from what you have prepared for them. So keep us as your prisoners; all I ask is that you do not subject us to your experiments.'

'And the second condition?'

'Release them from that chamber. You've made your threat clear. Why strap them down when you can do it at any time?'

Dharma shook his head immediately. 'No, I won't do that. Not until I see the extent of your cooperation.'

'Then let me be with them while I work. I need to see that they're safe. Believe me; you'll have no cause to complain about my work.'

He said reluctantly, 'All right. You'll be outside the chamber, but with a clear line of sight. My men will come for you in an hour, to bring you to me. You'll witness the true extent of my power, and you'll unconditionally come over to my side.'

I had no choice. I'd pushed him as far as he was going to go. 'Agreed.'

That this was a pact with the devil needed no reaffirmation. Dharma would destroy Meenu and Hassan the moment my usefulness to him was over. Especially Meenu; Vaishali would see to that. I was playing for time – but to do what? In a few hours, the world I knew would never be the same, but I was like a blind man in a maze, utterly unable to see any way out.

*

The tomb-like silence magnified the tiniest sounds, the squeak of the chair and crackling of paper and as I flipped through the charts. Now and then I glanced up to look at Meenu and Hassan. Meenu's face was flushed and she appeared to be in the throes of a slumber induced either by exhaustion or a drug. Hassan was as still as marble. A guard stood to one side, keeping a watchful eye. Ten-fifteen. Time was flying on the wings of doom. I sat there, gathering myself, then gestured to the guard that I wanted water to drink. This was the second time I had done so in ten minutes, but the room was so dry with the air conditioning that I figured the guard himself would be feeling it. The first time he had handed me the water, but this time I didn't wait but walked over to the water bottle kept on a side table. I drank and offered him a cup. He hesitated, and then advanced. He took the cup from me, raised it to his lips, head thrown back to receive the liquid. I struck with all my power; it was a blow I had seen martial arts movies: stiffened fingers driven straight to the exposed throat. I felt a shooting pain drive through my hand and my fingers buckled, but he dropped the cup and reeled back clutching at this neck, mouth working soundlessly. I gave him no time, but grabbed him close and kneed him in the abdomen, then hit him again in the throat. He folded and dropped to the floor, unconscious. I grabbed the gun, ran to the cubicle and punched the green button on the panel. The door slid back and I was in.

Hassan first. I stepped to his bedside and my mouth fell open. He was already wide awake, fully aware. Before I could react, he said in a thick, barely recognizable whisper, 'CCTV. Must be quick.'

The video cameras! I'd forgotten about them completely. *Why hadn't we been spotted yet?* I worked frantically on the Velcro strips binding his hands and feet, and as ripping sounds exploded to fill the room, I was sure we were done for: guards would pour in at any moment. Then he was free. I hooked my hands beneath his armpits and pulled him up as gently as I could. He grimaced in pain coming upright, sat there swaying as I held him gently by the shoulders. Slowly he brought his hands down on the sheets, propping himself up. I released him and sprinted to Meenu.

She was sleeping, breathing heavily through her mouth. I peeled off the restraints and shook her gently and then harder. No response. I placed my hand on her mouth and pinched her nostrils shut. Her eyes flew open flooding with panic. And then she was twisting violently, bucking on the bed. I could feel her mouth working frantically against my palm, and the tremors of a scream building up in her throat.

I bore down on her with all my strength and hissed, 'Meenu. Stop. It's me … Chandra. Hassan is also here.'

Her eyes flicked left and widened with astonishment; abruptly she became still. Hassan had managed to swing his legs over the side. He straightened up and stood there, swaying like a reed but on his own two feet. He pointed wordlessly to the tray on the right and made a slicing motion with his hand.

'Are you okay, Meenu?' When she nodded shakily, I removed my palm from her mouth and sprinted to the tray and snatched up a scalpel from among the bunch of surgical instruments. We had a gun and a knife, but they barely shortened the odds. Hassan took the scalpel from me and pointed at the body of the guard and gestured once more.

I looped the carbine across my chest, stepped out and began to strip the man of his uniform as fast as I could. By the time I raced back with the bundle of clothes, Hassan had managed to pull off his hospital gown. He let it drop to the floor. His naked body was all skin and bones, but when he started to put on the guard's uniform, I was stunned to see how fast he seemed to be recovering; his movements becoming stronger and more confident by the second. Meenu too had gotten to her feet. Her face was still flushed and sweaty, but to my relief, whatever they'd given her hadn't impacted her motor coordination: the adrenaline rush likely helping to dispel the drug's effects. She helped Hassan fasten his buttons, and together we started to hustle him toward the door. His feet trailed for a bit and then gained their traction hesitantly.

The door came up and Hassan pointed to my gun and shook his head. *No noise.* He stood there, taking deep breaths, clearly collecting himself, gathering his strength. I saw him palm the scalpel, thumb crossed loosely over the hilt. At his signal I opened the door and he stepped through without hesitation, head kept low. I saw him do a quick sweep, then Meenu and I followed through. Hassan had already spotted the lone guard to his right. His hand flickered in a hard, underarm throw and the next moment the scalpel thudded home just above the man's heart.

We dashed forward together. I paused just long enough to scoop up the weapon on our way to the landing at the end of the passage. Here he paused, breathing hard, holding on to my shoulder for support. 'My muscles … killing me. Need to loosen up.' He sank down on the steps and sat there, head bowed. As his breathing slowed, he looked up and said, 'Do you know when he's planning to launch the attacks?'

'Yes. Twelve noon today.'

He stared at me, then took my wrist and peered at the watch. 'Almost ten-forty. Just an hour and a half left. The antenna field and generating station are on the other side of this mountain. And the control tower and observation deck. *Fuck.*'

Then seeing that we were bursting with questions, he started to speak in short staccato sentences.

'Dharma couldn't resist giving me a full guided tour … soon after I was brought here. Have some idea of layout.'

'But, Hassan, how did you manage to recover so … you were lying like that for days … !'

'Isometric exercises. Meant for immobilized patients. Kept my muscles going. They shot me up with some pretty strong anaesthetics, but my body … I have a rare condition of immunity to many of them. Dharma's sleep drugs didn't take and I was awake most of the time. I was spared his nastier treatments; Dharma was planning to use me as a bargaining chip with you. The mental strain was the worst … thought I would go mad.'

He paused, catching up his breath. 'But I'm actually feeling better than I look. We've got to move while we still have some time.'

'Shouldn't we try and somehow warn Pant?' I said.

'And what can Pant do? Call in an air-strike on our say-so? He can't do zilch, Chandra. All he's got right now is us. The cable car access to the HAARP field is from the roof. I'll bet they are all gathered there already. Give me that gun.'

He started to mount the steps, and as Meenu and I followed him, I felt a surge of fierce joy course through me like a life-giving elixir. Hassan back, leading us once again. The odds and the clock were stacked heavily against us, but we had broken out and had not yet been discovered. As long as we remained on the loose we had a chance – even if it was one-in-a-million.

Hassan was panting, but he had speeded up, taking two steps at a time. The stairs levelled off and we were at a sharp corner. Hassan dropped to his knees and peered round the turn, keeping his head just over ground level. It was a trick I'd seen him use before. He pulled back, hefted the gun up. He looked over at us and nodded shortly. *Get ready.* He slid the gun round the wall and let loose a quick burst. The sound was deafening in the confined space and we pelted at full tilt for the lift, even as the guard was folding to the ground. Hassan grabbed the guard's SMG, handed it to Meenu, and punched the elevator button. It had hardly come to a halt before he was out. He yanked back the bolt of the door in front of us, and we stepped out onto the terrace of the monastery. Hassan banged the door shut and shot the external bolt.

I was fleetingly aware of the cool breeze, the stunning panorama spread out below – mountains covered with emerald-green forest and the snowy peaks in the far distance beyond. One end of the terrace was dominated by a concrete box from which a pair of thick cables snaked out and spanned the valley all the way to the receiving station on the far side of the saddle, with a cable car docked.

Hassan swore under his breath. 'Looks like they're across. Everyone must be on the other side ... Explains the thinning of the sentries here. We have to get the car back. You two try and figure the cable controls. I'll hold off anyone to tries to get through that door.'

All three of us ran for the cable shed. Inside, Hassan crouched beneath the window facing the single entrance through which we had come, the SMG hefted at the ready and aimed, Meenu's gun as a spare by his side. Meenu and I went up to the controls. Once glance told us everything. It was a simple three-button panel: Onward, Return and Stop. I punched the Return and instantly a rumble sounded and the enormous spool started to turn, reeling in the cable.

Almost as if on cue, we heard a clatter of boots and loud banging on the door. Hassan sent a burst of fire at the door and the clanging of the bullets on steel was followed by loud yells as the enemy realized we were armed. We were in a strong defensive position; the pursuit had only that single doorway to get after us and as long as we had ammo we could hold them off indefinitely. After that first shock, the opposition started to hammer at the door. By the sound of it, they were using their rifle stocks to batter at the bolt area and the hinges. Soon the sheet metal was beginning to bulge, and the door began to list at the top. The barrel of a SMG poked through the slot and a burst of fire raked us. Meenu and I had dived to the floor for cover. Multiple guns opened up, loud and deafening. The bullets thudded harmlessly against the pill box. I crawled right and took a look across the valley. The car was coming along at a fair clip; I reckoned the distance across the saddle at around 200 metres and it was almost half way across. In a fever of impatience, I willed it to move faster.

Hassan sent a long, vicious burst at the door and called out, 'How much longer?'

'Five minutes max,' I shouted back. The firing was increasing in tempo now, the door had opened wider, exposing them but also giving them a wider angle of fire to pin us down. The guards must have seen the approaching car and were desperate to stop us.

Hassan's face was pale, sweat pouring of his face. He said hoarsely, 'Okay, start firing with me. Let them know we have two guns.'

We opened fire simultaneously. The first and only time I had ever fired a gun was in 2011 in Afghanistan and that had been a SMG too. I was amazed at how familiar it felt in my hands: the shudder of the weapon as it spewed the bullets out, the barrel riding up automatically, before I corrected it and sent a hail of bullets at the door. More cries and yells and the door shut with a bang.

The clanking of the cable car was audible now, the hum of the geared motor at a higher pitch as it wound down while maintaining the torque required to bring the car to a halt.

Hassan let loose another hail of bullets, then ducked down and clipped another magazine into the breach. He started to speak rapidly between short breaths. 'Chandra, keep up intermittent fire. Here's the plan. I have the feeling I haven't been spotted by the guards yet. We've kept them pretty much pinned behind that door. Meenu, when the car docks, use the far side of the car as a cover to get the doors open. The two of you will get in. Chandra, that's when you pour on the covering fire, really give them a blast and keep them behind the door so they don't see me crawl to the floor of the car. I want you to ease up only once I'm in. I'm pretty sure the guys here will call their counterparts and we can expect a welcoming party waiting for us at the other end. Clear so far?'

We nodded. He broke off as two men burst out behind the door and charged towards us, yelling. I fired and they both went down in a heap. I sensed a suicidal rush was imminent.

Hassan went on calmly. 'The two of you need to be visible. When the car is about to dock on the other side, start shooting. Their first instinct will be to dive for cover before they start to return fire. That's the window for you to jump and get to the tree-line as quickly as you can. The idea is for you to draw them away from the car and me. It's also your moment of maximum exposure, and it'll be touch and go. If they return fire you're both done for. But I've a feeling they'll chase you down, rather than kill you. I'm betting Dharma will want you to watch his triumph.

'When you make it to the trees, start your climb immediately. Remember: the antenna field's on the other side. Make straight for it even if you have to reveal yourself. You'll need to draw your pursuers with you, so climb as fast as you can. The faster you go and the further – the better for me. But ultimately, they will overtake you. You'll be taken directly to Dharma: I'm sure of it. After that we have to play it by ear. I'll somehow have to evade the enemy and get to the control room in one piece before Dharma throws the switch or whatever he needs to do before the heavens explode. When you see me, or hear gunfire, drop to the ground instantly. That will give me the chance to plug Dharma, Das and the techs. We'll have to take our chances with the guards. But if they get me first, you've got to use the moment to take down Dharma. Clear?'

My head was spinning – too many instructions and all far-fetched and desperate, certainly my part of it. I was no action hero and I was in a panic that I would come apart just when I needed to act.

'I know it seems a long shot, Chandra. But it's all we have. So don't screw it up.' He smiled his sardonic smile and I felt a little lift of courage.

The car came to rest outside the shed with a grinding noise. 'Go, Go!' Hassan called, his gun chattering as he opened up. I fired in sync and the bullets twanged and ricocheted off with a high whine, literally blasting the door.

Meenu shouted, 'Door open!' I rolled over and crawled to the exit, and darted across the short open space to the car, dived in and started to fire from the cable car window. Hassan clicked off his weapon and was slithering like a snake towards the console. He hit the onward button and again the grinding started and the car began to move. I saw him stoop and open the control panel, reach inside and do something. We were pulling further away by the moment, gathering momentum, and still he stood there. I kept up a withering barrage of fire, then stopped to yell a warning when he ran and launched himself off the terrace edge. For a moment I thought he wouldn't make it, then I felt the car dip sharply to one side with his weight, and in the next moment, he swung himself inside.

I loosed off another burst, but now the terrace door shivered open and the guards poured out like a wave. Meenu and I ducked as the car was hammered by a hailstorm of bullets. I returned fire from the window but with limited effect. Meenu cried out, 'We forgot the console! All they have to do is stop the car and get it to return.'

My blood turned to ice as I saw some of the soldiers sprint to the shed. I saw one of them press the button and braced for the car to stop, but nothing happened; we continued our traverse. Hassan gasped, 'I've disabled the other two controls.'

The car had picked up pace and we were swinging down the saddle. I could see the receiving station looming ahead, and behind it, a jeep bumping its way down the steep slope, seemingly in a dead heat to reach the docking station at the same time. I fired at the jeep. At this range, there was no chance of hitting them, but I figured it might slow them down a bit. The jeep swerved; I saw muzzle flashes as the fire was returned, then the vehicle stopped and the men spilled out and started to run down the slope in a wide arc – presenting a dispersed target.

One minute … 20 metres out. We braced ourselves. Meenu called out a warning just as the car shuddered to a halt. I opened the door, and keeping Meenu to my right, started to run for the trees. I braced for the bullets, flinching in the expectation of the hot burn of a bullet hitting home, but there was no firing, only shouts and gesticulations as the pursuit raced to cut me off. I felt a gush of relief. As Hassan had predicted, Dharma was aiming to take me alive. The slope had us panting and Meenu was stumbling; soon I had to drag her along. We pushed deeper into the forest; the crashing behind grew louder by the minute, and then I could hear movement on all sides as they caught up and moved to hem us in. Meenu was retching now and suddenly she collapsed to the ground and lay there. I glanced quickly at the watch. We'd been going for seven or eight minutes. The first of them broke through the trees to our right and an instant later, we were surrounded.

*

The room was freezing, the AC vents blasting cold air into the confined space. Meenu and I knelt on the floor. A guard stood over us. There was a hair-trigger tension about him, weapon raised at the ready. We had been brought to this viewing deck by way of a stair that connected with the control room below. The squat two story structure had the look of a blast-proof bunker, solid concrete on three sides, the fourth entirely plate-glass from floor to ceiling, and through it – a scene straight out of a movie set.

Less than a hundred yards away, spread out before us was the shallow bowl of a valley ringed by peaks. Covering the valley floor, row upon serrated row of antenna towers stretched out like a giant windmill farm, except this was bigger, far bigger, the antenna towers so densely packed as to appear to be a veritable forest of steel. In the middle of it all, right in the centre of the bowl, a giant robot-like creature stood in a clear patch of ground. Its trunk was a massive box mounted on four spindly legs, rearing up some 30 feet. Sinewy cables sprouted out from the box, like the limbs of an octopus, and curved up to hold aloft an enormous antenna dish. A bulbous video camera swivelled to and fro like a human head surveying the surroundings.

Dharma and Vaishali stood about ten yards in front to my right. Both were wearing lab coats. A second guard stood close by them. They ignored us, keeping their eye on the wall-mounted video screen that showed up the control room beneath, with its array of computers and electronic equipment; white coated figures were seated across the consoles and we could hear voices conducting system checks over the audio feed.

Outside, the sky was a brilliant blue, a cloudless ultramarine wash from which the sun shone unhindered, bathing the field with its rays, flashing off the metal dishes in a million pinpoints of light. Dharma raised his radio set and said something. I saw Das come onscreen and give a thumbs-up. His tinny voice came through loud and clear, 'All systems go.' Dharma raised his hand and brought it down in a slashing arc. I saw Das grasp and push up a large, bulbous lever. Instantly, Dharma and Vaishali raised their field glasses to their eyes and started to gaze fixedly southwards.

Where just a moment ago had been stillness, I now saw the pine trees on the hillsides sway from side to side and then bend over at an acute angle – as if a powerful wind was sweeping through them. And then I heard it: a low hum, muffled by the glass, but increasing in intensity by the second. Soon it was howling down the field. Dharma exclaimed and said something to Vaishali, pointing, glasses still held to his eyes. I could see it now, a grey mass in the far horizon. It advanced with unbelievable rapidity, a boiling mass of cloud, moving like a living beast. It blotted out the sun and the field and mountains went dark and twilight fell over us. The wind was a perfect storm now, buffeting the glass with stones and debris from the antenna field. It was as if all the forces of nature were gathered and ready for whatever would come next. Dharma turned and looked at us, face distorted. Then he threw back his head and laughed loud and long. It was a horrible sound, the maniacal shriek of a man in the grip of some superhuman exaltation outside of himself. He shouted something into his transmission set and a high whining sound started to emanate from the robot. It turned a quarter circle and the cable arms stretched straight out holding the antenna bowl up as if to receive a gift from the heavens. A beam of light shot out from the dish and hit the first of the antenna towers which fired up like a sparkler and threw its bolt at others around it. The light was a living thing. It darted from tower to tower, linking each to the others till before us we beheld an incredible glowing lattice, a throbbing, interlinked forest of light as far as the eye could see.

Lightning flashed from the sky followed by rolls of thunder so deep that even the mountains seemed to shudder. The pulsing of the field grew more pronounced, dimming and brightening with ever-increasing rapidity as if gathering power. Then an ear-splitting *CRACK* shuddered the room. For an instant, I felt the world fading away, but was pulled back by a searing, incandescent light that filled the earth and sky. For a moment we were all but forgotten; I pushed myself to my feet, and beheld a writhing rope of light, thick as a tree trunk, snaking skyward from the centre of the field. It cleaved through the boiling clouds and burst there into a shower that lit up the heavens. Meenu too had raised herself and in her face I saw the crazed wonder that possessed me. All sense of space and time were gone: the past, present and future no longer existed, only this primordial moment of terror. This was Pralaya, the dissolution, the very earth turning on itself in an act of cosmic destruction.

Dharma had advanced and was standing with his feet apart, hands outstretched – a haloed god directing the world to do his bidding.

A burst of automatic fire erupted, jerking me back into the room. I turned towards the sound and saw Hassan on the screen. He was in the control room, shooting. I heard the *ping-ping-ping* of bullets on metal. The techs were collapsing in their seats. I saw Das cowering behind a chair before he was cut down.

For a moment, Dharma did not register what had happened, caught up as he was in the immensity of the vision outside; then it dawned on him. With an inarticulate cry, he grabbed the weapon of the guard next to him and darted for the staircase, Vaishali close behind. But I too was moving. I lunged for the guard near me, grabbed him by the shoulder and butted him with all my strength in the head. He collapsed. I tore the weapon from his grasp, and turned to see Meenu struggling with the other guard. Raising the weapon, I brought the butt down on his skull, knocking him unconscious.

I took the stairs three at a time, and burst into the control room just in time to see Hassan grasping the lever and pulling it down. Dharma fired, dropping Hassan to the floor, and then ran for the console.

I cried out in shock and Dharma swung round raising the gun, a murderous look in his eyes. Before I could even process what was happening, a shadow had thrust itself between us and I heard an inarticulate cry cut off by the chatter of the weapon. Dharma screamed, 'No!' but Vaishali was already shuddering as she fell towards me. I stepped back reflexively and squeezed the trigger. Small holes appeared on the front of Dharma's coat, instantly seeping red. Another long burst smashed him back and he collapsed on the floor in a heap.

I dropped the carbine and ran to Hassan when an explosion shook the room. The glass shattered. An acrid, chemical odour filled the air. My body tingled and bucked as though I had put my hand into a live socket. The hair on my head and body stood straight up. I heard Meenu cry out, tried to reach out to her, but the agony was spiking.

A high screaming sounded from the skies. Fighter jets were flashing down toward us through the clouds, appearing out of nowhere. More explosions sounded, throwing earth and metal into the air. I had barely time to notice that a giant crater was all that was left of the antenna field, when a deafening blast lifted us off our feet and flung us sideways. The roof cracked into two and I had the briefest sensation of the floor heaving beneath my feet and then I knew no more.

How long I lay there, I have no means of knowing. I awoke to a shrill ringing in my ears. My head felt swollen, as if some object had entered my skull and filled it to bursting. And then someone was shaking me by my shoulders. It was Meenu, wrapped in a white coat. Her face was streaked with soot and the cut lip had opened up again. Her eyes were wide open, shock and pain still roiling in their depths. We fell into each other's arms. I felt her shake, then soundless sobs wracked her frame. As she slowly quietened and lay still against me, it seemed that I had crawled into a warp and emerged into another time, on another planet. A world where the sun shone dimly from an ochre-coloured sky, where a breeze swept along the mountaintop, bringing with it not the scent of the pines, but the reek of burnt plastic, melted metal and chemicals.

I turned over and gently disentangled myself from Meenu. Great slabs of concrete lay everywhere, mangled iron rods jutting from their exposed sides; and beneath them, shattered electronic consoles and mangled white coats. Blood had leached out, forming dark stains everywhere. Every movement brought a fresh bout of retching and heaving, but, finally, I managed to bring myself to a crawling position, and crept over in the direction where I had last seen Hassan. He was still there, unconscious and bleeding from the shoulder, but to my soaring relief, he was alive. The falling roof had just missed him. Right beside him was Dharma, who lay as he had fallen, his face fixed in a final snarl of rage. I gave him a wide berth. I could not bear to cast my eyes upon him, even in death. Instead, I looked down at Vaishali. A slab of concrete had fallen on her, covering her from waist below, but her face was unmarked and achingly beautiful, with no trace of the pain she must surely have felt in those last moments as the bullets smashed into her body. I saw instead the calm half-smile of a woman at peace with herself at last.

AFTERMATH

Sharana, New Delhi. 30th June. 7 p.m.

THE CLASS QUIZ IS IN SESSION. MEENU IS INSPIRED TODAY. THE children laugh and shout the answers to the questions that she throws at them. I sit slouched on my bench right at the rear of the classroom, hands linked behind my head. My thoughts are elsewhere, as they have often been these past few weeks.

It has been just over three weeks since our return from Bhutan, but my body still throbs, and now and then my pulse spikes and I tend to break out in a shiver and sweat for no apparent reason. Horror has scarred my soul so deep, and death my companion for so long that I can scarcely bring myself to believe that I am rid of them now – that we have well and truly overcome the greatest enemy this nation has ever faced in its long and turbulent history.

Unfortunately, as in the case of the Shadow Throne affair, it has become necessary to withhold from the public, the true events behind the Pralaya conspiracy. The reader may naturally be sceptical, indeed incredulous. For how can something of this magnitude be covered up from the world at large?

However, I say this deliberately and authoritatively, for like in previous case, this decision rested with a select few at the very apex of the Indian state. The media obsessed for weeks on the missing Dharma. Speculation piled on speculation till it descended into pure fantasy. None of the stories even got close to the truth. The utter secrecy with which Pralaya operated, the misdirection and the hiding of the weather weapon under the cloak of climate change, all of which were the hallmarks of that evil genius, meant that the country lived in blind ignorance of the catastrophe that had almost fallen upon it.

Fate intervened in other ways as well. Nalini Pant had reached out in those final desperate hours to his bête noir in Pakistani intelligence, Gul Mohammed. When Gul had categorically ruled out China, Pant had instantly grasped the truth about Dharma. It had taken all his persuasive power to convince Gul of the danger that both countries faced. But once convinced, as Pant wryly acknowledged to us later, the Pakistani had been able to bring into the play his government much faster than the Indian could ever have done.

Within hours, unmarked Pakistani jets had been dispatched to Bhutan. But Gul Mohammed had extracted his price, this time in ordering the complete obliteration of the entire command and control centre of Pralaya – along with its central brain in the person of Dr Pramod Das, a man of amoral evil who will carry his secrets to the grave with his master.

Of the geopolitical consequences of a Pakistani strike over neutral Bhutan, I knew little; only that Pant went into overdrive, using all the power and influence he had to get the Indian government to work with the Pakistanis in assuaging the Bhutanese and bringing them into the circle of secrecy.

It may be, now that Pakistan is aware of the possibilities of weather manipulation, that a race for this weapon of mass destruction may commence, but something tells me that Gul Mohammed and Nalini Pant are men of uncommon wisdom and may well doctor their accounts of the Pralaya affair to their bosses. For both realize that some things are altogether too wicked to be left to the whims of politicians.

It remains only to relate the fate of those unfortunates that I had come across in that horrific chamber in the monastery. The gompa itself had been bombed to rubble, the scientific staff, the horror chambers and their unfortunate occupants – all buried under mountains of rock and stone. Perhaps that was a blessing to those who surely craved release from the terrible living death to which they had been sentenced. In Dharma's system of command and control, information on their infections and its cures was held so tightly that with the building's destruction, very little could be recovered.

But deep below, in the dungeons beneath of the gompa, protected from the bombs, we found another hundred men, women and children waiting to be transported to the experimentation chambers. There to our joy, we came across Gopal – wasted and malnourished, but unharmed.

Looking at him now on the bench to my left, fiddling with a laptop memory card, I can scarcely believe that it was this little urchin that had left a trail that truly set us on the track to Pralaya, and that the survival of the nation is owed in no small part to this child, an orphan from the bustees of Delhi.

Meenu has put on her glasses and is reading out something to the class. She is very much the Meenu I have known and loved, yet she has changed in subtle ways. She wears a pink churidar matched with a white and mauve dupatta; it is a new outfit to fit a figure made considerably slimmer by the stress of this last month. She's also grown out her hair so that it hangs loosely on her shoulders. Where it had been a jet blue-back just a few months ago, it is now shot with strands of white. But when she looks up, her face is exactly as I have always remembered it – a creamy oval with its cleft chin and the quizzical, inquisitive expression. I soak all of her in once more, marvelling at this woman who time and again pierced the fog that had surrounded us at every step of our dark and desperate journey; whose love ultimately saved me from myself and now makes me complete.

Despite myself, my mind also goes back, as it has so many times these past weeks, to that other woman who had exploded into my life, turning it inside-out. For the umpteenth time, I try to recall that heart-stopping moment: Dharma cradling the gun, pointing straight at me, then the chatter of gunfire and Vaishali falling into my arms. Was it an accident? She had been standing to my right and well out of the range of fire. I was focused on Dharma and out of the corner of my eye, it seemed to me that she threw out her arms as if in protest, and then she was between us, jerking and twisting as the bullets slammed into her back. Bullets meant for me. *Was it an accident?* I ask myself yet again. Each time my instinct says no, but perhaps that is because I do not wish to believe any different of that beautiful, cruel, but ultimately enigmatic woman who died so I might live.

With a start, I become aware that all around is silence. I look around to find the children gone. The class has ended without my being aware of it. Meenu is standing at her desk and beside her is Hassan and they are both smiling at me. But in Meenu's eyes, I see it: an awareness of what has caused my intense absorption. She has seen it happen more than a few times these last few weeks. She reaches out to me; I get up and slowly walk to her. Outside, the red ball of the sun is sinking into the western sky.

AUTHOR'S NOTE

WHILE *SKYFIRE* IS A WORK OF FICTION, ITS CENTRAL THEME – weather modification – and the HAARP programme mentioned in the book has a fair bit of grounding in reality. The Environmental Modification Convention (ENMOD) held under the auspices of the United Nations in 1977 is testimony to the fact that the world implicitly recognized the dangers of applying weather-altering techniques to warfare as far back as forty years ago.

Events have moved rapidly since then. In a de-classified paper prepared for the US Air Force in 1996, chillingly entitled 'Weather as a Force Multiplier: Owning the Weather in 2025', the authors – all defence personnel – described weather modifications as a high-risk, high-reward endeavour that would employ wide-spectrum technology platforms 'to degrade the enemy' by way of precipitation enhancement, storm enhancement, precipitation denial, fog and cloud removal etc., and concluded that the appropriate application of weather modification could 'provide battle space dominance to a degree never before imagined'. The paper further states that 'by 2025 the military could influence the weather on a mesoscale (<200 km^2)'.

Other than the proposed military applications, weather modification technology has already been used to facilitate civilian activities. In a paper published by the Institute of Defence Studies and Analysis, New Delhi, Ajey Lele describes China's weather modification techniques at work at the 2008 Olympics:

> '… on August 8, 2008, the day of the Olympics opening ceremony, it was reported that the Chinese Weather Modification office had fired a total of 1,104 rain dispersal rockets. These rockets were

> fired to stop rain clouds approaching the Olympics arena ... It is probably because of such an "attack" that these rain-bearing clouds precipitated at those locations where they were hovering at the time the rockets were fired at them ... The success achieved by Chinese meteorologists during the Olympics and now during the 60th National Day Parade underlines the importance the Chinese state is paying to artificial weather manipulation.'

In other words, weather modification is here to stay and will become an increasingly dominant technological endeavour with civilian and military applications. We are indeed entering a brave new world, in more ways than one.

ACKNOWLEDGEMENTS

IN THE WRITING OF *SKYFIRE*, I ACKNOWLEDGE MY DEBT FIRST of all to my wife Afried for critically evaluating the early versions of the manuscript and offering me several suggestions for its improvement. My agent Priya Doraswamy at Lotus Lane made a number of important comments and suggestions as did the following people: Lakshmi Venu, Manu Raman, Srilata Emmerich, Amita Bala, Naresh Bala, Arvind and Ahalya Raman, Peter Smith and Ronaldo Jimenez.

Diya Kar Hazra and her team at Pan Macmillan India brought terrific enthusiasm to the *Skyfire* project and were the prime movers in the production of the book that now sits in your hands. I would like to particularly thank Sushmita Chatterjee for her superb edits that have led to a much tauter and exciting story.

I would also like to express my appreciation to Deepa Kamath and Preeti Kumar of Amplify who contributed enormously to the digital marketing strategy for the book.

The Nammalvar quote at the beginning of the book is from *Hymns for the Drowning by Nammalvar*, translated from Tamil and introduced by A. K. Ramanujan (Penguin, 1993).

Despite the inputs and labour of so many people, all errors that remain in the book are solely my responsibility.

NO. 1 BESTSELLER!

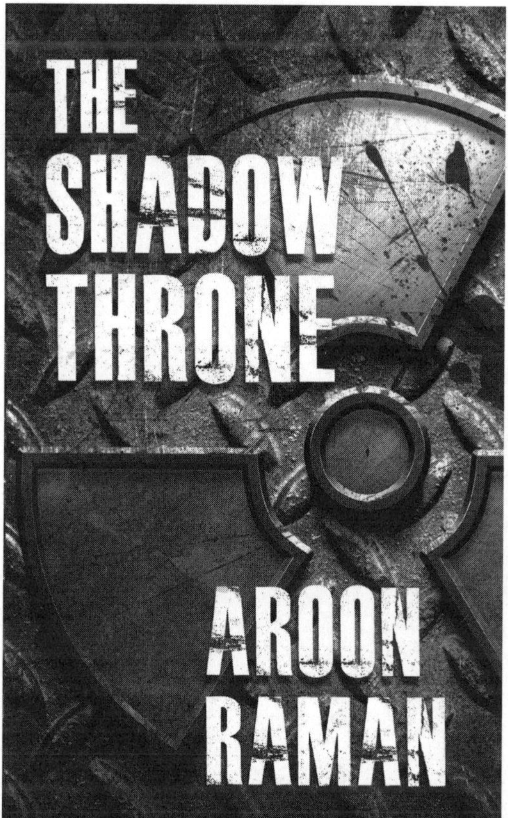

'Aroon Raman's debut novel takes off from the crowded bazaars of old Delhi and races through the barren landscape of mountainous Afghanistan to a pulsating finish that keeps the reader glued till the last page' *Telegraph*

'A political thriller that makes for a racy read' *Hindu*

NO. 1 BESTSELLER!

'This book stands out with the sheer strength of some incredible characters that Raman creates' *Millennium Post*

'Packed with intrigue, mystery and a healthy dose of history' *Hindu*